way up way out

A SATIRICAL NOVEL BY
HAROLD STRACHAN

David Philip Publishers
Cape Town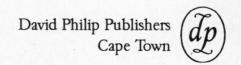

chapter one

Never put money in your mouth, my Auntie Aggie would say;
Indians pick it up with their toes.

But really impossible to imagine now was how Indians go about
picking up a penny with the toes? Could they have by nature some
sticky substance under there, as do flies, which can walk upside
down on the ceiling; stuff that they could sort of glop on to a coin
and transfer it to the pocket? Perhaps they had suction pads under
the toes, as do geckoes, which can run up walls. But very weak,
otherwise Indians too would be seen to run up walls.

Clearly the answer was that they had evolved opposable big
toes, as early anthropoids had developed the opposable thumb,
thus gaining supremacy over other primates who were handy
enough with bananas and things, but forget about hand axes and
the instruments of power. They had some trick with money. Get
the nail of the first toe under the coin, and that of the second or
third over, pick it up and ... and which pocket can you put it into?
Why, clearly, you take it from the toes with the fingers and transfer it to any pocket you choose. Yes, but then why not just pick it
up with the fingers in the first place?

Five years' worth of life provided few answers to such quan-
daries. Wait and watch. I watched like anything the feet of Mr
Perumal who came weekly to my ouma's house with a cartful of
greengroceries and a horse with a nosebag. What a vehicle! What
a horse! On the side of this cart was painted in fancy curly writing the motto of Mr Perumal: Fruits for Vitamins, Vegetable for
Longevity. He and my ouma would huddle over a watermelon,
knocking on it as on a closed door, the head cocked as they lis-
tened to what?, with the eyes rolled slightly upwards in this comradely investigation of the fruit. They would put ears and noses to
it, and go over it between extended thumb and middle finger as

over the pregnant belly of a beloved woman. Then the great moment would come, and Mr Perumal would take from his pocket his clasp knife and ceremoniously open the thin sharp blade. He would cut a steep little pyramid from the melon and give it to Ouma. She would bite off the red part and slowly chomp it up, nodding and breathing through the shnoz to savour the aroma of it. Mr P would nod and breathe through his shnoz also, sympathetically. This was the really the clinching of the deal, of course, for how could Mr Perumal ever show his next customer a watermelon with a hole in it?

The horse would drop a mound of dung on the road and sigh. Flies would buzz around its bum. The horse would whirl its tail about. Mr Perumal would reach into the square of hessian, full of hay, hung under the cart by its corners, and haul out an armful for the mealie sack which served as a nosebag for the horse. Everything was idyllic and leisurely under the jacarandas of Koch Street. Would Mr Perumal never take off his pointy black shoes? Would he never get a small stone in there as other people did? No, he wouldn't and he didn't.

The truth emerged only much later, in Natal, where the old Sammy who came door to door with vegetables was so goddam poor he had no shoes. He had no horse nor cart either, nor watermelons, because they were too heavy for his old shoulders, nor any English – he spoke only an Indian language and wore only a dhoti and huge turban, both of white cotton. I thought of asking my ma, when she paid him for her greens, to fumble and drop a coin or two on the ground so we could see him dart at them with extended toes, but she would have thought me daft.

What he seemed to have plenty of was betel, which he would mix up with white stuff and munch at. I thought it was medicine for his oral condition, for his teeth were all dissolved and his mouth always full of bloody fluid, which he would spit out in long squirts all over the garden. Later I learned it was for pleasure.

You could hear him coming way up the street, his split-bamboo leaf spring over his shoulder with a big double-bellied basket at each end, and as his skinny legs yielded to the weight at each pace the whole apparatus went squeeky-heeky – squeeky-heeky. When we kids decided who was to start a game of marbles or rounders or something, we would point round the circle chanting Sammy, Sammy, what you got, Missus, Missus, apricot.

His sons when they grew up had motor vehicles for their veggie trade, and his grandson was a pilot in the RAF in 1940 and flying Hurricanes in Malaya in 1941. How's that for Protestant virtue? He should have been mayor of Maritzburg.

But, though Indians were as grass upon the ground in Natal, I never saw a single Indian from any generation pick up anything at all with the toes, ever. I concluded the habit must have gone out of fashion.

My Auntie Aggie was of the First Church of Christ, Scientist, Sunnyside Branch, Pretoria, and wouldn't have known where to start telling a lie if she'd wanted to, and she didn't want to.

If you Play with your Person, my Auntie Aggie said to me, Your eyes will cross and your brain will turn to water.

Armed with such science, I was soon off to the big wardrobe mirror for basic research. Being as I was an a little tiny boy, I played first with the elbow, then the inner malleolus of the ankle, the medial collateral ligament of the knee and interesting skeletal bits of the person, watching the while for convergence of the irises and sounds of sloshing within when I shook my head.

Experiment failed, and it at this point occurred to me that there may be other, alternative, forms of truth, arising perhaps in my aunt's ancient ancestral memory; she, Agnes, the Lamb of God, could not pronounce an un-truth. When I again raised the matter with her, the downcast eyes and the pursed-up lips, like a mouse's earhole, confirmed without speech something that was new to me. There was indeed ancestral truth, and it was inside the broeks.

Off to the wardrobe again. This time I rubbed my bottom. Nothing. Ah, I was being too personal, too furtive. It was a social malaise that I was dealing with here. In public, I would now go out and publicly massage my right-hand buttock through that small back pocket where one is supposed to keep the hanky. No place more public than Kerkplein; I did it there, in that very place, while Paul Kruger himself, my ouma's old compatriot whom she had forsaken, all covered in pigeon-shit top hat down, cast his stern eye upon me. I was prepared to fall a madman upon the grass. Nothing.

My venture into truth and sin was of no meaning without some guidance, some greater insight. Cosmic perhaps. Okkie Gouws next door was every bit of eight, maybe even nine years old: khaki shirt and shorts, his head was shorn and he went kaalvoet, these being depression days. I had seen him ride a donkey. His school lunch was bread and dripping, food of the rough and the wise.

3

Mine had butter and Marmite. Okkie was my man.

Hel nou! said Okkie, joe jus greb joe piel laaik this, men, en rab iet laaik!, demonstrating the while that gesture which later, in North American culture, became known as Polishing the Rocket.

Okkie's boet was called Boet. Boet was every bit of thirteen, maybe even fourteen years old. Did you learn it from Boet? I enquired, your brother? Hel nou! quod Okkie, aai doe iet maaiself, man, humping himself up in a parody of copulation; iet get sou bieg, man! he announced, measuring off with his left hand about the length of a fair-sized shad on his extended right arm, as shad anglers do. The sheer malehood of it knocked me flat. But it must hurt, said I. Nou iet's lekker! said he.

It was established. Now to find the manifestations. Okkie refused to show me, because it was impolite, but already at that age I'd been around in the working world long enough to guess that Okkie was hedging; Boet was the source of the wisdom, and Okkie couldn't do this thing at all.

Never mind, I'd work it out myself. Hauling out this wee pointy thing like a living carpet tack, I worked at it every which way until it looked like an abraded chillie.

Nothing. If anything it got smaller from the sheer pain of the experience.

But art. Art. Sculpture! Ars omnia vincit.

* * *

Marthe Guldenpfennig was a woman of the flesh. Auntie Aggie told me about this with bated breath and righteous nodding of the head. Marthe Guldenpfennig had desired Oupa Langeberg. I don't mean spiritually, as her innocent smile might suggest. Concupiscently.

Marthe Guldenpfennig made her way past my ouma's house at 80 Koch Street like the Queen Mary slipping along Merseyside outward bound for the New World and the wild, free swell of the North Atlantic, without yet the bone in her teeth, the modest hiss of her discreet eight-knot wash suggesting the rustle of Marthe's tussore silk and taffeta clothing.

Marthe's style was pre-war. She had about her the murmur and pulse of a great ocean liner. Even as she stood motionless, hove to, you could sense the low-frequency resonance of her throbbing generators. 1930 held but little new challenge for someone, some foreign one, an uitlander, who had ridden the conscience crisis of 1899 and come out yet a lady. As she glided down Koch St Marthe

4

Guldenpfennig would nod as graciously to the hensoppers as she would to Professor Gerrit Bon who lived opposite and played the Poet and Peasant Overture on the honderd perdekrag cinema organ in the City Hall on Tuesday, lunchtime. The right beads, the right tilt of the hat, the right carriage of the head and the Gustav Klimt glance: Marthe Guldenpfennig was an exceeding elegant woman of sixty.

My family were hensoppers. Hands-uppers.

In her garden Marthe had this gnome of the sort which became pretty commonplace soon enough but was as yet a novelty. This gnome was made of cement and painted with enamel. His hat was red and his coat was green, as gnomes' coats are. Clasped in his hands was a fishing-rod which seemed to arise from somewhere around where one would expect to find his Person, under the coat, and his face was bright pink and shiny, as if from some awesome exertion. This gnome, *this gnome*, was doing in cement that which could not be demonstrated to me in the flesh.

Marthe knew!

What had now to be done, however, was to build on either side of this gnome an ornamental fishpond inset with seashells, into which two jets of water should squirt from his pointed gnome ears, thus denoting the turning to water of his brain. It should also be made clear by skilful painting of the eyeballs that the pupils were crossed, and perhaps in the ponds could be pretty goldfish. Alas, before such fantasia could become reality my ma moved to Maritzburg with us kids.

I thought if she knew of such profound and dangerous sensual pleasures Marthe Guldenpfennig must have baked beans in her head to lust after Oupa Langeberg.

Oupa Langeberg was but a pallid replacement for Oupa Van Tonder, who had diamonds in his head, and would get the bit in his teeth and slip off to the wild, free swell of the Northern Cape plains at the flap of a butterfly's wing. Some small random event would by chaotic system blow up a tornado in his soul which would whisk him off to Kimberley se kontrei, leaving behind neither finger- nor footprint, neither tool nor artefact as evidence of his existence in the City of Pretoria. He certainly never left any money, and I believe he never once had a diamond. Come to think of it, I don't remember his ever having a tool or an artefact either. The prospectors I have read of always had shovels and things strapped on to mules: Oupa Van had only his bare hands stuck in his pockets. He was equipped with Great Faith.

Ever a battler, my ouma had set up a genteel sort of lodging establishment in her back yard. Round three sides, rows of rooms with wooden verandahs and, in the sort of atrium thus made, highveld fruit trees of great delight: figs, kaalgatperskes and an apricot tree hung just solid with freckled fruit at Christmastime. You could perch in the tree and eat straight from the branch, breaking the yielding flesh with your thumbs to leave the stone dry and loose, so you could just tip it out on the ground and pop the whole fragrant apricot in your mouth.

Along the wall of Okkie's house next door grew a pomegranate hedge, the breathtaking vermilion of its blooms excelled only by the gemstone transparency of its wet carmine seeds, packed solid like a geode of rubies inside their fibrous cricket ball. Rip the ball in pieces and plunge your teeth wantonly in amongst them, they asked for it, and stain your school clothes with the dark pink flood of juice.

Neither loafer nor chancer set foot here. The high tone of the establishment was set by my uncle Julius Zschniffe, a Sudeten Czech of unbelievable sensibility. Let nobody tell you that accountants are without passion or temperament. Julius had both passions and temperaments nobody else so far had ever thought of having. He also had a very sensitive constitution, with beautiful grey hyperthyroid eyes, a moist and delicate skin and an artist's small hands, with which he would make from time to time a little decorative gesture, eine Eleganz. He had long curled-up mustachios of great softness, the brittle Kaiser Wilhelm spiky sort being much out of fashion since that imbecile had lost the war, and a great collection of ponderous but triumphal German music on shellac records which he played with a steel needle at sickening speed on a crank-up gramophone. People sounded as if they were singing underwater. Richard Strauss and Wagner.

Julius had also this Essex motor car with spare tyre on one running-board, battery on the other, brass radiator with thermometer on top, fold-back canvas roof and the aerodynamics of a parachute. By tea-time of a nice Sunday morning the women of the family were already taking aspirin in dread expectation of an afternoon joyride. Julius would appear in his paratrooper's gear, plus gloves and goggles, and fling water on the wooden spokes of the wheels, to swell them up for fast cornering. If the timing lever on the helm was in the correct position, the machine would emit a burst of acrid smoke on crank # 20 or so, the cast-iron engine stumbling into life as the massive pistons stood still and the cylinder block leapt up and down around them. We would be off under the most terrible tension, anticipating the afternoon's adventures.

My God! Julius would cry, as we hammered round the Central Prison curve and hurtled into the long straight past Zwartkops aerodrome, My Living God! A mile a minute!! A car approaching, and our minds would be near breaking. Perhaps there would be dust on the road, and some would eddy up, or worse, perhaps a small stone... But the real white-knuckle time was toward sunset, when the curs of this world would approach us with their lights on. A heave on the brass brake lever, the Essex would stagger to a stop, and Julius would be out on the running-board, brandishing his clenched fist at the receding criminal. Bugger! he would yell, *Bug! Ger! Bas! Tard!* while the Essex stood hissing and gasping like a great locomotive in a shunting-yard.

But some of Julius Zschniffe's emotional life was private. As an ardent lover and protector of animals Julius was an honorary member of the SPCA, and as such was certified to own and operate a thing called a lethal chamber in the compassionate control of stray cats and small dogs. This was a suitably humane wooden box equipped with a sort of funnel into which one poured the chloroform or Zyklon B crystals whatever after the stray had been soothed by the prospect of a nice warm shower, also a suitably humane glass top so that one could make sure that the pussy in question had properly writhed its way to the big SPCA at the right hand of God. Maybe they don't use them any more.

But always on the QV for cruelty, man. On one Sunday p m pleasure spin, whilst pounding downhill at possibly 1 mile per 59 sec, or even 58, we espied coming up the hill an old black bloke with a cart full of shack building materials, belabouring his donkey with a stick. Without further ado, quick as a flash, Julius operated the brass brake lever! In not an inch more than a hundred yards the Essex screeched to a halt, its mighty wheels and high-pressure tyres locked solid and gliding effortlessly over the loose gravel of the road verge. Like lightning Julius was out and over to the culprit. Lay a hand on that animal just once more and you will find yourself in a criminal court! cried he. Hau! exclaimed the driver. If you find yourself in the Hands of the Law it will be in consequence of your own turpitude, do you understand? yelled Julius.

7

Hmmm? said the driver. *SCHWEINEREI! BUH! GUH!* howled Julius, *BAS! TARD!*, seizing the stick from the driver's hand, smashing it in two on the gun'l of the cart, hurling the bits upon the ground and stomping his motoring boot on them. Ja my baas, said the driver.

All of a muck sweat Julius made his way back to the simmering Essex. The brass brake mechanism was released and by deft double-declutching the machine was once again set in motion. Being a skilled motorist, Julius kept his eyes upon the road ahead, otherwise he might have observed the driver descend from his seat, go to his cart, select a suitable plank from amongst its cargo and with this blunt club thump at the rump of the poor bloody bongol, cursing both donkey and J. Zschniffe the while in colourful Southern Sotho.

For every mode of transport there is a technique. Donkeys do not voluntarily haul loads uphill. Being smarter than horses, they find no pleasure in carrying burdens for other species.

Julius's compassion for all God's living creatures was boundless but sensible. Sentient mammals got most, especially fluffy ones, birds too. Cold-blooded things from damp places got a few per cent, while tsetse flies and anopheles mosquitoes got zilch, zero. Butterflies did well.

Anyway, came one of those scrotum-shrivelling winter nights in Pretoria and a report arrived at the Zschniffe outpost of a lioness stricken with cat 'flu at Pagel's Circus, the name itself an abomination in the eyes of the Lord. Armed with hot-water bottles, blankets, the duvet off his own bed and rump steak from the fridge, just in case, Julius was off to the very wheeled cage in which the poor creature lay on its crude bed of straw. With the great head cradled in his arms, he spent the long night gazing into the trusting amber eyes of the innocent beast. Love triumphed: the lioness recovered from the feline pneumonia, but Julius contracted human pneumonia and died. There were no antibiotics in those days. So gaan dit mos.

So it goes, hey?

But I digress. Into this discreet milieu suddenly reappeared, back from the dead one afternoon, Oupa Van Tonder; no shoes, toenails uncut and full of mud, his corduroy broek all shredded from the thigh down, like a Hawaiian hula dancer, and *stink* O geseënde Seun van God, Blessed Son of God, what a stink! He was kippered in the smoke of burning grass or cowshit or whatever he'd been cooking his grub on. No diamonds, no money, no tools, no mules, nothing. Nothing except enterprise, that is, and the usual Faith.

In a trice he had set up in my ouma's orchard a pickled fish business requiring neither capital nor equipment, except offcut timber and some old broken bits of varnished furniture from a demolition site, two five-gallon paraffin tins and a certain quantity of stockfish brought up from the Cape under wet sacks in unrefrigerated trucks. It was rumoured that he'd a readier and fresher local supply, known as Magaliesbergse stokvis, which was, in fact, rinkals. Cobra. Also matches.

Oupa Van would sing his diamond-field ditties and hum away as he prepared the diamond-field delights:

> Tarara boem-de-ay
> Oom Paul het 'n vark gery
> Afgeval en seergekry
> Tarara boem-de-ay.

* * *

The recipe was fairly homely: Half-fill a paraffin blik with fish, scaled and disembowelled. Fill 3/4 with water. Boil. Add 1 cup salt and 14 onions, cut up with a knife. Buy 1 lb tin of Windsor & Newton's Patent British Curry Powder (By Appointment Royal Family & Sir Isaac) and fling in with other ingredients. Serve hot, with 1/2 loaf bread & Madame Ball's Patent 98-Octane Pretoria Peach Blatjang, according to available finance.

The dispossessed of the Great Depression came from every corner of Pretoria, according to wind direction. No aboriginals, of course: they had their own quaint way of coping with famine, by ceasing to eat. Also possible was that they valued the enamel of their teeth. And the rest of the digestive tract, come to think of it. Come to think of it, I myself would rather starve than go to Jesus via the route provided by Oupa van Tonder. This was a meal of gunpowder, man.

But really, the pong was something cruel. My Auntie Aggie went into retreat to Know the Truth, as Christian Scientists do. The truth one had to know was: All evil things were untrue, unreal, they were Error. When she opened her door Oupa Van and his fish would have proved illusory, since they were evil.

Mind you, she was right about the fish.

But Oupa Van persevered in the Biblical miracle of the fish, the loaves and the multitude. The fearsome conflict between scriptural and metaphysical truth filled the aether with huge fields of crackling static energy. Great leaden grey-anvilled cumulonimbus clouds roiled up over Pretoria. Huge hailstones flailed the darkened city and lightning struck while the horrified populace smeared themselves with sheep dip and covered the mirror with brown paper to deflect the bolts. Science and faith strove for possession of the soul of personkind.

When Auntie Aggie, looking drawn, emerged a week later from knowing the truth, old man and fish were indeed gone and the air murmured with the ambient melody of the last movement of Beethoven's Pastoral Symphony. Oupa Van Tonder was last seen headed WNor'W, where Kimberlite and companionship are a man's love. It was mampoer that eventually got rid of him.

Try this recipe:

2 good tots mampoer, maroela or witblits i e white lightning, whipped up with a cup of fresh cream. Melt 2 tblspns butter with a nice big dollop of Seville orange marmalade, pour this hot over cold cold vanilla ice cream and the mampoer/maroela/witblits cream over that, with a few walnuts and blanched almonds for fun.

That's not what the police said Oupa was selling. They said his mampoer was made with Brasso, boot polish and maybe some human parts, and forget about the ice cream and all that crap. Well! I just *know* that wasn't true. I personally think the First Church of Christ Scientist, Sunnyside Branch, and the Liquor Squad between them put a goor on him, a spook, for bourgeois purposes.

Anyway. So after a couple of years my ouma was declared a widow lady or deserted and divorced or something. The poor öld sod deserved a bit of peace, to be sure, and old Meneer Langeberg was about as peaceful as you can get without actually being dead. After marriage Oupa Langeberg spent most of his time under the loquat tree, dressed in a pale grey suit, his grey beard and hair neatly combed, sampling that splendid fruit, along with the apricot and the litchi the best ever, if you can get there before the goggas. I forgot to include the loquat tree in the earlier list of orchard delights, and do so now.

As I say, this was but a pale replacement for the majestic wandervogel who was my Oupa Van. My grandmother spent the rest of the hours given her at a green-baize-covered table with nice tassels, playing Patience and dipping Vienna sausages into tomato ketchup and sighing Ja, so gaan dit mos in die ou wêreld. And so indeed it went in this old world. I don't think she was unhappy or disappointed or anything, for one doesn't expect many highjinks at seventy; just enjoying the quiet, I think.

But wherever Oupa Van's body may have lain amouldering, his genes went marching on, with certain mutations naturally, in the body of my grown-up half-cousin Foefie van Tonder. Which half was mine used to trouble me a lot when I was young. I used to hope it was the body. Anything but the mind. The body was broad and robust and clothed in a sports jacket with 22 accordion pleats across the back, as was favoured in the apparel of gangsters at the time, amongst whom Foefie numbered. He had but a single eyebrow, which extended from outer Port to outer Starboard over both eyes, and a brow which fell back steeply from there in the manner of Homo neanderthalensis.

This is not to denigrate Neanderthals, mind you. Recent anthropo-archaeo-palaeologico-carbodating all goes to show that those unfortunates, formerly perceived as mindless ice-age kickboxers, actually buried each other with flowers and ceremony, and by implication a sad tear, and must now be included amongst Peoplekind along with the sententious rest of us.

My cousin Foefie, whom I have seen with my own personal eyeballs weeping at the sound of the Mills Brothers singing Put Another Chair At The Table, had qualities which could well have made him say now a choreographer or, on the other hand, perhaps a great chef, greater even than his grandfather, had circumstance and the Ruling Class been kinder to him. Maybe a Hawker Hurricane pilot, like the old sammy's grandson, for he loved powerful vehicles.

Foefie had this Norton 600 motorcycle of stupefying speed, gastrip en gatjoen, bought from the profits of an enterprise involving the transportation and purveyance of traditional herbal antidepressants. Further supplementary cargoes of these he would thereafter convey on a regular schedule from coastal Natal to Vrededorp, his home town, known also as Fietas, compressed in the headlamp of the vehicle, to protect them from condensation and rain. Such a machine was known as a Kwaai Iron.

Tant Miems, his mother, would say to him: Asseblief, my hartjie, just go to the Greek shop for your Mammie and get some tamaties and a pint of milk. Ar shuddup you old cow, Foefie would respond. I mean, really, he was appalling. Tant Miems was a ten-

11

der and submissive Afrikaanse auntie, and she would go off to the kitchen for a quiet weep.

But Foefie was always ready to go to the butcher. First because he was an eager carnivore and enjoyed the sights of the place, great slab sides of ox and sheep and swine on steel hooks, and strangled fowls on wire hooks, whose plumpness and cuts of flesh he would be invited to judge, whilst the big ceiling fans quietly circulated the delicious aromas of bird and beast blood. Second because the butchers used to open at 5 a m in those days to avoid flies and the problems of poor refrigeration, and it was reason to get his butt out of bed and burn his iron bedonderd down empty Voortrekkerstraat and scare the shit out of its citizenry with the hellish howl of his tailpipes. Such was his antisocial nature.

Well, one morning at 5 30 or so, as Foefie came shrieking down Voortrekker Street at about a hundred knots, give or take a few, there, to his amazed gaze, was a horse, of all things, serenely clopping across the road. Now you just can't drop anchors on two wheels the way you can on four. I suppose Foefie was making fifty knots when he struck this nag amidships, the Norton with its drop-handlebars going clean underneath its belly like a deep torpedo, and Foefie being saved from instant death only by the great bundle of meat which he had balanced on the fuel tank, this taking the greater part of the impact between his rib cage and the engineroom of the luckless animal. Afrikaners are avid meat eaters, so it was a big bulbous parcel and Foefie was only briefly unconscious.

When Tant Miems rushed out she beheld her boy lying supine upon the road, his front just mincemeat. Here lay a pair of kidneys, there a liver, while a little farther off lay a fresh rack of ribs. From amongst the mincemeat, where one would expect the long intestine to arise, there lay coiled a couple of yards of boerewors. When the ambulance arrived it took Tant Miems off to Casualty, where she spent two days under sedation with a thermometer in her mouth.

Foefie arose after a bit, and salvaged from amongst the wreckage of deceased Norton and horse some foot or so of boeries and enough reasonably clean kidneys for a good tuck-in with some toast and tomato sauce.

* * *

I say my family were hensoppers, but that's not exact. My ouma was from Klein Drakenstein in the Cape, and that made her a

12

British subject, so when the Engelse Oorlog started she found herself on the wrong side in Pretoria. Thereafter, if one ever suggested to her or any of her three daughters that they were Afrikaners, which they were, plat Boere, they would adopt a stance like that of Gordon in that memorable painting The Death of Gordon, where he stands at the top of the stairs of the Palace in Khartoum, and really fiendish Dervishes seethe all over and one particularly beastly one is just going to hurl a spear through his noble navel. My ma would place her right fist over her heart and her left stiffly out behind her. Her left foot would be firmly planted forward, the knee slightly bent, while the right pointed the toes at the ground behind.

We're Brrritish! she would say.

The hensoppers were those Republican citizens and commando fighters who had lacked anger or obsession after the dreadful days of farm burning and concentration camps, and opted for peace.

Anyway, Foefie was not the cad I may inadvertently have portrayed him to be. Being half a generation older than me, when WW2 came along he was old enough and British enough to go immediately and join the Vrededorp Light Horse, an armoured outfit equipped with tanks about the size of a Volkswagen Beetle and mounting a four-pound gun in a metal turret, for shooting at Italians. Four pounds is about the mass of your average supermarket chicken. Not a great deal of killing was going on just then. I should say the war was still in its gentlemanly phase, before Stalingrad and Dresden and like horrors, so when Foefie fell from the fifth floor of a Cairo brothel, drunkenly mistaking the biggish French windows for a toilet door, he was posted Killed in Action.

Cynical humorists in his regiment said he had been awarded the DFC (Posthumous), an Air Force decoration meaning Distinguished Flying Cross, for aerobatics done on the way down.

There was a daughter, sister to Foefie, to carry the gene pool into the future, but she was not very noticeable with a boet like that around, and I can't remember her. I dare say some of the genes are out there yet.

My two Scots uncles Tom and Jim were very noticeable. Jim had his insides almost entirely devoured by mustard gas, while Tom had been shot so full of German shell splinters you could pick him up with an electro-magnet. Had they taken them all out he would have looked like a piece of Gruyère cheese, and since all was nice and aseptic, the fragments being well above the boiling point of all known germs when they went in, and military doctors being a busy lot in 1918, they just left everything where it was and sent him home from France. The description of his medical condition on his demob papers was sort of biblical: wounded shoulder, hip and thigh.

For lo! The Host of the Ammonite smote him Hip and Thigh.

Well, Tom set about some soldierly boozing when he got home, and singing dreadful Harry Lauder songs requesting somebody called Jock tae Stop his Ticklin', which caused him to clutch his shrapneled sides and fall down on the floor, whilst others present would stand with vacant eye and sullen mouth, the nuances of Scottish humour escaping them. Eventually Harry Lauder and Johnnie Walker between them got the better of him and he fell into profound delirium tremens, in which condition he set about composing his own H L songs and conversing with the rats who were just then busy consuming those bits of his former comrades that had thawed out of the mud of Flanders.

When Doctor McGregor an' his Wee Black Bag arrived he handled the crisis wi' true Scots wit, mon. Hoots, Tammy, said he, an' Ah hope ye'll pay ma bull afore Ah gang awa' hame, f'r y'r awa' tae join y'r regimental chums in Heaven, an' theers nought Ah c'n dae for ye.

A sort of Robbie Burns Fanagalo.

Well, Tom caught such a vokken spook, as they say in the gutter and Pretoria Central Prison, that he there and then gave up the booze, no bullshit, and took up bowls. Within the decade he had become a Springbok, and then captain of the international team. You can look that up in the annals of the South African Amateur Bowling Association. I wudna' lie tae ye'.

But my dear! Auntie Aggie was triumphant. Cockahoop. Christian Science had saved us all, first from the pickled fish, then from the booze. My sisters and I were instantly conscripted as volunteers into the Sunnyside Sunday School Branch of the First Church of Christ, Scientist. We had spent our Sundays building a house on the chassis of the abandoned Nash lorry at the end of our cul-de-sac. We had left one of our number as lookout while the other two went to find out what *really* happened to the children stolen by the Chinaman at the corner shop. That they did thus disappear was beyond doubt, for Guess-Who had assured us of it. We had earlier concluded that he boiled them up into some dreadful slimy dish, like Frenchmen eating snails, which cuisine also we had been apprised of by G-W. Latterly, after secretly peering through the shop's dirty windows early on Sundays before people were up, at sewn-up bags full of Something, a really sinister plough, and a bin full of questionable potatoes, we had concluded that the unfortunate innocents had in fact been converted into the violet-scented cachou sweeties which stood in a large glass bottle on the dusty counter. Proving this, proving indeed any theory of our condition upon this earth, was cut short by our introduction to the Scientific Process.

Christian Scientists used to call themselves just Scientists, for short, like. One pudgy such Scientist was Mr Shiceley, who had a solar topee and halitosis. From now on we would be suitably cleansed on our lovely Sunday mornings and placed upon the Sunnyside tramcar for scientific education by Mr Shiceley.

Mr Shiceley would place his hand upon my thigh, quite near the Person, and breathe upon me, saying: There is no Life, Truth, Intelligence nor Substance in Matter. To this day I associate such mumbo-jumbo with bad breath.

At that age I used to fall often off my tricycle, and usually had ugly scabs on my knees. Underneath was yellow gunge which my uncle Jimmy called matter. Come, lad, let's wash that matter awa' wi' a bit o' water, eh? At school my teacher was a really juicy fizzgig called Miss Vaughan, with a Prince Valiant hairdo and ideas about adventure in teaching the young. She had a microscope and would show us slides of plant juices, blood, spit and the like; I remembered especially the lively and seemingly intelligent behaviour of the small small goggas that wriggled about in there. It surprised me that they didn't exist in the matter too. As for Substance, I had thought that even Mr Shiceley himself was made of quite a bit of it..

Mr Shiceley also used to read to us from a book with strange chapters in it. One was called Animal Magnetism, Mesmerism and Necromancy Denounced. I had seen mesmerism done in that same abominable Pagel's Circus in which the grand guignol that was J Zschniffe's life had come to its tragical crisis. Here an oompie dressed like Fred Astaire, only plump, with a Clark Gable moustache, wove his fingers at the face of a real Jaap who assured us he was a wrestler by profession who played the Jew's harp for art. After more waving the spotlight went all blue and spooky, one of this gent's eyes looked up and the other looked down, and I

15

think they had a bit of UV in there too, because his hair went all luminous. Turning round with his hands stuck out in front of him like Lady Macbeth, he somnambulated over to a waiting violin and dashed off The Flight of the Bumble Bee by Rimsky-Korsakov, no less. Afterwards he couldn't remember any of it.

Mr Shicely said Mr Mesmer did it with helpless victims, but the results were the same as with musical wrestlers, surely, and seemed harmless enough.

Mr Shiceley said necromancy was when you talk to dead people, but if I were stupid enough to talk to Uncle Julius it wasn't for Mr Shiceley to denounce it. He was my uncle, however loopy, and it was family business.

So I really didn't know what the hell Mr Shiceley was talking about. But it all stood me in good stead thirty years on. As a grown man I was prepared for the mumbo-jumbo of certain other Scientists, though they weren't Christian.

Mind you, however, a skilled Marxist–Engelsist–Leninist obscurantist could obscure Mr Shiceley clean under the table and out of sight, any day, in the name of Scientific Socialism.

But it makes me depressed to write about him. Uncle Jimmy now, I get only happy about. He had been a professional football player, Dundee United, before the gas got him. The King sent him a nice letter praising him for his sacrifice of good health. Jimmy said he didn't sacrifice it, it was taken away by some bloody Kraut upwind. The King also gave him a ticket to Roberts Heights Military Hospital outside Pretoria, where the air was nice, bottles of cod liver oil and malt for his lungs, such as was left of them, and seven pounds ten shillings a month, which came in handy for supporting my ma and her three kids. We kids also got the cod oil goo, to keep us all fit and shiny in the winter, like Eskimos.

Friends and neighbours were all struggling, these, as I say, being depression days. A newspaper would be passed house to house down the street, people would make their own soap with fat and caustic soda and that sort of thrifty thing. But Jimmy always managed to save a wee bit of his seven pounds ten for that thing most important for kids' health, a sense of wonder. I think I hear something creeping in the snowdrops, he said, let's go very quietly and take a look. Which we did, and there was indeed something in the lilies when we gently parted them. What could it possibly be down there, under the leaves, like a stone? Mind now, be careful. He was watching our faces as he moved the last leaves.

A tortoise! A small speckled one, as big as a grown-up's hand. How did it get there? I think he just walked here because he likes our snowdrops. What does he eat? Cabbage. Bring him inside to the kitchen and try him with some. And what's his name? I think it's Rufus. You can write it on his back with crayons, he won't mind.

Weekend breakfast was brown bread and coffee, in bed. I think I hear a distant flapping of wings in the sky outside, said Jimmy; maybe it's angels? We slipped out with mugs and bread, and there it was. A gum pole with a box on top, and two white fantail pigeons.

In the war, Uncle Jimmy had the front brim of his steel helmet sharpened so that if he were even closer than bayonet range and couldn't manoeuvre in the trench, he could grab the German or Turk by the collar and slam this thing in his face. Sewn down the back of his tunic was a sharpened motorbike spoke, which, if he had his hands in the air, he might suddenly reach for and thrust into an enemy's heart or eye, with a bit of luck. He had taken from a dead Ghurka a kukri, sharp sharp, which was handy in a trench, because if your opponent missed with his bayonet thrust, you could grab the barrel of his rifle and smartly chop off his fingers. Uncle Jimmy had been in the Kosbies, the King's Own Scottish Borderers, as unlovely a crowd of death merchants as you could possibly hope not to meet in a trench.

Tom, now, was a gunner. When he and Jimmy thought no kids were about, the conversation would often turn to the war. Often I was about, unseen. Though they were neither of them what you would call verbose men, their conversation would be so intense they wouldn't notice me. Tom would try to make up his mind which were the more horrifying for an artilleryman, the early days when German Uhlans sometimes got round the rear to find the guns and hack the gunners to death with sabres and cavalry lances, or later days when the front was solid and impenetrable, and the trick was to find the range of the opposing guns and lay down a solid unrelenting hail of shrapnel, all day. Tom had a thing about shrapnel, and I didn't blame him.

They both agreed that the worst memory was of a tank riding over a trench, and seeing the juice that squeezed out of the parapets.

For Christmas Uncle Julius gave me a little tin wind-up tank, with rubber tracks and a gun in a turret. During the afternoon of that very day, while I was still playing with it intermittently, it disappeared and was never found again. Sabotage was suspected.

* * *

My ouma got one thing right. She found good music teachers for her daughters, in amongst a lot of chancers who also cured snakebite, conducted marriages, removed assegais from people's bellies and played the stock market.

An unruly woman, after leaving home my ma couldn't possibly continue to practise as assiduously as Professor Hopkins had demanded, though I must say the soap-making and like chores didn't leave anything near the five hours daily. But she would pound out with great gusto a Beethoven sonata, singing along in a way that Brer Wolfie might have approved, but Brer Earwig definitely not. I think that was why Uncle Jimmy loved her and had run off with her. However broke, they never sold the piano.

Anyway, they had this lodger called Pieter Potgieter, who also had a Clark Gable moustache, which was so fashionable as to be almost obligatory, and would tap dance on the stoep in his patent-leather tap shoes, his great lanky legs doing all sorts of fancy American Negro steps and tricks. Yes Sir, That's My Baby, he would sing. You're The Cream In My Coffee.

But the stoep was all polished up with Sunbeam wax, and he slipped one day and broke a bone. Always a cheerful and affectionate fellow, he lay in bed with his leg all plastered up and scheming a way to pay for his keep. Since he couldn't get out to look for jobs of colouring in black-and-white photographs with water colours, as was his craft, being handy with a paint brush he decided to make for my ma a sort of professional name-plate, gold paint on a piece of tastefully varnished teak. Madam Phoebe, it said, PhD, FRCM, ACSAMT, Teacher of the Pianoforte.

My mother's name wasn't Phoebe, and she didn't have any of that alphabet after her name. She wasn't too smart at the piano, either, I suppose, but she was bloody good at the forte, which was dead right for Beethoven by her reckoning, and, when a girl called Sylvia signed on, my ma so cranked her up with the allegro movement from one of the sonatas that she went to the Eisteddfod and won first prize and a great big silver cup.

Pieter Potgieter also taught my ma to Syncopate by way of rent payment. This was as fashionable and obligatory as the Clark Gable moustache above. No matter what your instrument, if you said you were a musician, people would ask Can You Syncopate?, and if the answer was No, why, you might as well go and join the SSB, Special Services Brigade, a military outfit to which magistrates used to send the criminal unemployed during the depression, because it was cheaper for the state, and the poor buggers got a small military wage and a bit of dignity. Jan Smuts when he reviewed the SSB in Abyssinia in WW2 was in the situation of Wellington with his infantry before Waterloo. Well I don't know what they'll do to the enemy, he said, but they scare the hell out of me .

But I digress again.

So. My ma had got into the productive process. Jimmy Brown would sit on the stoep mending the family clothes while she provided a fruity alto accompaniment to a Schubert Romance played by Sylvia, or played herself to Pieter's tap dancing, Yahou're the Craheam in My Cohohofeehee, Yahou're the Sahalt in my Stahew.

Passing children would stand in the street and chant: N'ye, N'ye, N'ye-n'ye-ny'e, Look at the man darning socks!

Worse things had happened to Jimmy Brown, and he liked kids anyway, so he would smile at them with his clear blue eyes and cheeks all rosy from the mustard gas. One day he beckoned one of them up to him. O my yirra, what have I done now? Is this Anglo-Saxon male going to pursue me down the street and slam my little body to the ground? But no point in even trying to run, my legs are too short and it will only further enrage him anyway. The laaitie inched up the path to the stoep, and where he sat Jimmy sewed on to his shirt a button where one was missing.

Mooi skoot. Nice shot.

Ouma used to sit on her stoep also, between potted begonias on either side, on a bentwood armchair. Phenomena would pass by: Basil Paisley on his stilts, the funny kid. A couple of Africans in tennis gear: Swart Goed! she would exclaim, Hoe *durf* hulle! How, forsooth, dared they. George Hondekos from the Greek Shop: You didn't bring my newspaper yesterday!

But on Sundays things were otherwise. In amongst the street trivia and Vienna sausages and Patience cards and things a tremor would be felt. As people taking tea in Kent had sensed the distant rumble of the guns in Flanders, so one would pick up uneasy vibes from the direction of The Location: the Melighters were coming! Get the children off the street. Come on now, just go and play round the back; never mind *why*, just *do it*! Shut the front door.

Nostromo sucks. Jacket and bridle and saddlery with Mexican silver trim, sucks. An amaLayita leader you should have seen, on his great Bucephalus of a BSA Bicycle, the chromed spokes of its great 28-inch wheels going glit-glit-glit-glit as Alexander took it steady as a rock down Koch Street, at walking pace for his men on foot. The gear ratio, 48:14, meant strong legs at slow speed, and everybody knew it. Supplementing the function of the front forks, great arabesques of brass rods rose up from the wheel nuts, above the handlebars to finials of brazing wire a foot or two above the rider's head, where small flags flew. All shiny, shiny, shiny! Over the front mudguard a cut-out shooting star, painted. The frame also, in bands of colour, take your pick, supplemented by reflectors of yellow and red placed according to choice. Under the saddle, cunningly placed, was a bulb hooter which went ihooihooihooihooi! as the rider bounced his buttocks. Balloon tyres; on the front two dynamos drove two headlamps, at the rear two more driving an arrangement of red and yellow lamps like a fireworks display.

George Frederick Handel you need for such a thing: Mufick for the Royal Velocipede.

Over neck and shoulder of the rider hung a long fine chain with a harmonica at the hip. The jacket had a fringe along the yoke and under the arms, in the cowboy manner of the bioscope, and on the head was a genuine ten-gallon hat, white or black, in the manner of Tom Mix. The hatband, as also the broad waist belt, was done over with bicycle reflectors of red, yellow and white. The lot was set off by a special pair of gold-miners' patchwork trousers and miners' gumboots, these too adorned with patterns of bicycle reflectors.

I suppose one got to be amaLayita leader by charging at the reigning bull on an equally ornate pushbike.

The harmonica and Jew's Harp, Jimmy told me, were the instruments of the footsoldier. It's a Long Long Way to Tipperary, But My Heart's Right There.

Jimmy and Tom told me what the song was about. They were the only two of my acquaintance who'd been in the trenches of Flanders. The vast network of trench and embrasure and what in the next war was called a foxhole came together at a sort of communications nexus here and there, and these nexi were called Clapham Junction, Piccadilly Circus, Knightsbridge, Leicester Square, the like.

The young Irishman wants the hell out of Flanders and back to the lovely meadows of home:

Goodbye Picadilly, farewell Leicester Square, It's a long long way to Tipperary, but my heart's right there.

* * *

An amaLayita phalanx would be about a hundred strong, I suppose, on average. Ten abreast across Koch Street, the Centurion ahead on his BSA and massed mondfluitjies squealing out a tribal air, like the massed pipe bands at Edinburgh Castle, supported by much chanting and whistling between the teeth and waving of beaded sticks. Each man wore what he could afford, but the ten-gallon hat was prized, and decorated miner's gear standard, with a lot of the bicycle reflectors, which were cheap.

Probably they came from factories, domestic work, railways, even mines, though these were a bit far from Pretoria. What they were supposed to do of a Sunday afternoon was anybody's guess. Pretoria was a dreary enough Calvinist place for whites on a Sunday, but whites could darem go for a swim or sit in a park.

But what interested me even then was why we children shouldn't see them. It was only fifty years after Isandlwana. I suppose our elders didn't want us to witness their fear of any group of confident swartes.

Anyway, there they would go, challenging the world but happily separating to allow through the few cars that were about on a Pretoria Sunday. Jacaranda flowers showered down on them as petals and laurel leaves upon a cohort returning from Persian conquest, and the air was filled with the heady, slightly bitter, subtropical perfume of the blooms.

* * *

Physical existence itself was a struggle for Jimmy Brown. He could never get quite enough oxygen. But never to make a fuss, mon. On the morning of my sixth birthday in 1931 he called to me from the house: Hey feller! Come here! On the kitchen table stood an unrecognisable shape under the table cloth. Shut your eyes and put your ear to the table and tell me what you hear, he said. Clickety-click, clickety-click, I hear a train. Look up now. O absolute wonder! It *was* a train, a wind-up Hornby train with three trucks full of sweets, going round and round on its tin track. If you pulled out a lever in the driver's cab it went backwards. Jimmy was looking at me with his half smile and his cheeks all rosy from the mustard gas, and that's the way I remember him now. The next day he died in the Roberts Heights hospital. He was a long time

21

a-dying: fourteen years.

There's not a hell of a great number of people whose deaths I mourn. An assorted bunch: Mozart and Walt Kelly and Pogo for innocence, Salvador Allende who first ever gave socialism a face. Margot Fonteyn for being just plain bloody lovely. A few others. I mourn the death of Jimmy Brown . I mourn him yet, and I'm seventy.

Uncle Tom was not, as I say, a talkative man, and when he did talk it was rather quietly. So I was quite surprised a few days later to hear him yelling at someone in Ouma's orchard: Well if it's such a bloody wonderful country why didn't you go and fight for it?

chapter two

Would you like ay piece of cake, isn't it? Marthe Guldenpfennig would ask me when I called in at her place after school. She would wrinkle up her nose in the manner of a dog, and lay a great big canine grin on me, ear to ear, and flash her nice white teeth. At the time, I couldn't have explained why I should call there. Well, I had no problem explaining anything at the time, that is, for there was nothing to explain, except the cake. But eight or nine years later, when sexuality had become my main obsession, I came to wonder why a five- and six-year-old boy should need to establish a close friendship with a sixty-year-old woman, as indeed I had done, and I realised that Marthe had worn her sexuality with the same élan as she had her clothing and everything else about her, and that was the intrigue, the invitation, as much as the cake. She was so proud of it; she wore it with great relish, a panache, a feather in the cap, even though the enjoyment of it was probably over, according to the conventions of the time. It had been her style, and remained her style, as much as the carriage of the head and tilt of the hat, and the Gustav Klimt glance.

Even at that age I had seen that it was not in the pantherine athletic sexual mode of the Charleston-dancing, cloche-hatted Miss Vaughan, with her mid-thigh skirts and the long loops of beads about the throat and breasts. The sexuality of Marthe Guldenpfennig was the Romantic sexuality of great unrestrained love. Im wunderschönen Monat Mai, she would sing, as she washed her greying hair, the sun drying it out as she sang of delight and loneliness, while the brush pulled it over her shoulder, as in a Degas pastel. The ice-cream is in the Fritz, she would sing, or You would like to make me ay cup of tea, isn't it?

I suppose Isn't it? was the translation of Nicht war?

During the hair-washing she would wear a men's towelling

dressing-gown of incalculable age, for she would be recently bathed and sort of relaxed, as one is, and didn't give much of a damn if a glimpse of breast or bits of her ageing body were revealed, or whether ladies were supposed to wear negligées, and never this sort of scrubbed-out old horse blanket under any circumstance.

My Auntie Dulcie, who was but half her age, would never have been seen dead in such a garment, as they say, or perhaps only if dead. She could never have brought herself to behave like this, not if all alone on the planet Mars. She would strap and lash and bind her miserable tits down with a thing called a bust-bodice, a sort of Ur-bra, I suppose, so they appeared as a pair of fried eggs applied to her thorax, like vinegar-and-brown-paper poultices, while my Auntie Aggie had no discernible tits at all; the poor wee things had been so dismayed in their brief sixteen years or so of existence that they just gave themselves up and stuck there like a pair of envelope flaps. If you looked at her bloody hard against a bright light, sideways, you might just descry a sort of irregularity in the discreet floral blouse of her Christian Science dress.

Each of these ladies produced a daughter of such hygienic propriety as to make one wonder whether perhaps in their early hours they'd been quickly boiled and rapidly cooled, pasteurised against the hey nonny no and hoopla of it all, especially the You-Know-What. My cousin Drusophilla, when she was thirteen, would say to me in some crowded concourse, See that man over there, undressing me with his eyes? He wishes to possess me, physically.

I mean, sis! I wouldn't have wanted to possess her physically with somebody else's Person, at any age.

Now and then Marthe would give a sort of chuckle, and sometimes a real belly-laugh, and grab hold of me and give a tight squeeze and say Ach, was ist das für ein Lausbub? and I could feel all her hard and soft parts and she didn't care because she was my pal. Sometimes she called me Chaimshmerrl, along with the squeeze. Well, my ma used to squeeze me in the same way, and she wasn't all bunched up like her sisters, God knows why, otherwise she wouldn't have run off with Jimmy Brown, but somehow with her it wasn't the same. I should think not: this was my first experience of sexuality. I didn't know it; I just knew it was enclosing and dreamy, and it was intimate for Marthe too, for she had no kids of her own.

24

I have the perfume of her still in my nostrils.

Kissing my Auntie Dulcie was like kissing a sofa, whilst kissing my Auntie Aggie was like kissing a deck chair, except she wasn't so well designed. Later, I should have said it was like kissing Reichsmarschall Goering and Adolf Hitler.

Immediately after the first hug and the first ice cream at Marthe's I knew I should feel guilty. There was of course the obvious stigma of guilt attached to anything Marthe did, for was it not well known that she had desired Oupa Langeberg, concupiscently? But it wasn't just that. I mean, there's something about sex itself… I mean, it's, it's, brutal, even if manifested by the eating of ice cream, and if we've never had enough of it that's hardly surprising, it's so disgusting. It's what Men want to do with Marthe Guldenpfennig when they come back from the trenches with their minds all grilled and their bodies all filled with steel, but God bless them anyway, heroes that they are, otherwise we'd all be governed and raped by disgusting German men with their minds all boiled and their bodies all filled with lead.

But then again, Men are all the same. My Auntie Aggie would incline her head and gently pick her right nostril, sort of massaging the front part of it as she reflectively said the word Men. Rather, Men…n. She is the only person I have ever met who could make a single one-syllable non-Latinic word have such significance, in this case, of filth. Shakespeare included.

* * *

Marthe hadn't much of a voice, really, but good pitch, and she sang with much interpretation, which is the important thing, surely. I shall sing for you about the moon, she would announce: I on the Earth, you in the heavens, we both are wanderers; solemn and troubled I make my way through this life, as you make yours, blithe and bright. I wander a stranger from country to country; homeless, unknown, I find no rest; but you, Moon, wander where you will, from the cradle of the East to the grave of the West, across the face of the Earth, and wherever you find yourself, there you are at home.

Du aber wanderst auf und ab
Aus Ostens Wieb in Westens Grab,
Reisst Länder ein und Länder aus,
Und bist doch wo du bist zu Haus.

* * *

Marthe Stänger had come to the Republic as a lass in 1888.

More or less on arrival she had celebrated her eighteenth birthday, and her father's new junior colleague, Dipl. Ing. Germar Guldenpfennig had given her at the celebration a great voluminous parcel, done up in pretty paper. Stripping the wrapping from the gift had taken a full five minutes, and, with each layer of paper stripped, a further peal of laughter would erupt from family and friends, and there were many layers. Well, eventually the final wrapping was there, pretty small, as you can imagine. If he'd just wanted to be facetious, and clever, he'd have had a thimble in it at this stage, or maybe a threepenny coin, a tickey; but there was no such thing: there finally was a crown, a crown sterling, sterling silver, a big, beautiful coin with a profile on this side of Victoria with her receding German chin and a little symbolic crown on her pate and a legend telling us that she was, By the Grace of God, Queen of Britain, Defender of the Faith. On the reverse was a classical presentation of Saint George, naked except for a Roman helmet and Batman cloak, mounted bareback on a great rhinoceros of a horse whilst easily disposing of a vile dragon like a great grotesque puff-adder, and with a mere legionary's sword, too. Sterling silver, man? When one said As Sound as Sterling, it meant something.

This coin was worth a considerable amount of fun in those days, but Marthe could never bring herself to the spending of it, such were her sentiments about Germar Guldenpfennig. It was a newly minted coin, and in its entire existence it has never once got spent. I own it now, and it hangs around my neck on a chain after a hundred and five years. I wouldn't spend it either, even if it were valid currency, which it isn't, of course. For me, it is Marthe.

Herrn Professor Dieter Stänger was Dozent at the Technische Hochschule in Darmstadt when his wife died in 1886. A civil engineer not only by qualification but also of considerable experience. When advertisements appeared in German academic publications of posts in the Transvaal for engineers exactly like himself, in the year 1888, he took a snap decision, but very positive and committed, to make a clean break from the scene of recent sorrow and get out to Africa and dedicated work and adventure. It had taken his wife eighteen months to die, and he had inherited from her the pain of her body, in his heart. He would encyst this pain and contain it within himself in such a way that it did not destroy his pleasure in his two daughters.

The enterprise which needed him was, of course, the railway to

Lourenço Marques and the sea, a project of slowly increasing desperation to the Zuid-Afrikaansche Republiek, presently hemmed in by the Brits and systematically squeezed politically through the power they held in the gold-mining industry and the Uitlander community clustered around it. Romantic adventure! Not just the silly posturing of men in wide-brimmed hats on the African veld, perhaps with rifles and dead animals and sullen black bearers all around; nothing like that. This was the defiance of arrogant power, and the use of one's refined intellectual skills to do it.

The projected work was the usual railway stuff: bridges, embankments, cuttings, tunnels, that sort of thing. The line had to be taken down from the six-thousand-foot highveld escarpment to sea level in a couple of hundred miles, and over some bloody rugged terrain too. I won't even touch on the problems of malaria and the depredations of the tsetse fly; those confronting the surveyors and engineers were daunting enough.

Here was young Guldenpfennig, then, away from home, if indeed Pretoria could be so called, often for months on end. Old Dieter Stänger kept a couple of leather dispatch bags in pretty continual transit back and forth between his project office in Church Street and the front camp.

Into these bags went unprofessional letters from the two Stänger girls. Those from Ilse were perhaps the more amusing, for they were the skittish pyrotechnics of a sixteen-year-old and full of juvenile mirth about the whole adventure of life in Afrika.

Marthe in her turn wrote in English, demonstrating the skills acquired in that language at the classes of one Doctor MacNab. Germar Guldenpfennig showed no response, though; but then I suppose he got only the written explanation of it all, and anyway there was this railway…

The relationship between herself and Germar evolved by way of this letter-writing for five full years, sound friendship appearing along the way, without the advent being much noticed at any particular time, it was so gradual.

On the rare occasions of his coming to Pretoria there was a strange embarrassment; no, a sort of nonplussment, on each finding out that the other had also a corporeal existence. In conversation you couldn't take five minutes to compose a sentence, and then there was the presence of this textural, aromatic woman and this tanned, bearded man to make such composition difficult, if not indeed irrelevant. But what was to take its place, and how on earth do you go about it when your skills are in railway construction and the study of English syntax?

* * *

A lot of things came to a head for a lot of people with the Jameson Raid in 1895. The condition of un-ease consequent on the raid filtered right down from the places of power at the top to the private lives of those like G Guldenpfennig, now nearing Komatipoort over the edge and well down into the lowveld and malaria country, and experiencing his first bouts of fever. This first one was successfully countered with vast ingestion of quinine mixed with gin and lime juice, a decoction which the doctor enjoyed as much as the patient toward sundown, leaving both a bit jaundiced in complexion but much improved in general view of life and humanity, though a touch shaky from the overall encounter with Anopheles.

Second time round, though, they realised the Grim Reaper might well come and take off this lad, and bundled him into an express coach with enough gin and lime to keep passengers, crew, all except the horses, in good spirit for the two hundred miles to the railhead, plus enough quinine to dismay his personal parasites, and a mound of blankets which fellow-passengers agreed to swaddle about him in exchange for the gin, to keep him in a furious sweat.

Arrived in Pretoria he was really an interesting ochre, and about half his original mass. Professor Stänger and staff washed him down pretty well as one does a corpse, and placed him in a bed in the Stänger home, with white sheets, some flowers in a vase and figs, apricots and taaipit peaches in a little basket next to his bed. What he was supposed to do with these latter is anybody's guess, since he was only just able to breathe and sip a little water, with salt and sugar, to counter dehydration, forget about perfumes and the savourings of the taste buds.

Marthe found the relationship easier to handle when he was more or less unconscious, for there wasn't any sort of social embarrassment at all. There being no call, nor indeed any possibility, for conversation, she could hum for him small tunes as she placed the thermometer in his mouth and combed his hair whilst waiting for a reading. She would wipe his face. Insofar as he knew what on earth was happening, he seemed to enjoy it, and would smile feebly. Big strong men would come and lift him up and take off the long cotton night shirt and wash him down like a horse, and shove a bed pan under him, while she waited outside.

Time sped, and soon enough he regained enough health and composure to demand his pyjamas, as were coming into fashion, instead of this great calico bell-tent that enclosed him. This made management of his condition that much easier, for he wasn't so floppy all the time, and Marthe could sit him up in bed and take off the pyjama top and wipe him down herself without the aid of the big strong men, and he didn't seem to mind that any more than he had minded having his hair combed. He didn't mind the admiration that went with it either, nor the occasional small spontaneous caress over pectorals and neck, though to take such advantage of a sick man is questionable, to say the least.

But came the day when she sat him up in bed and took off his pyjama top and there was sign neither of sweat nor of fever, and since he looked sufficiently recovered to have possession of his faculties once again, and his body looked just fine to casual inspection, she lay him down without his top, and grasped him by the ears, and said in German, which I don't command sufficiently to put this colloquially, so I'll do it in English: Bloody fool, she said, are you such a bloody fool that you don't know what's been going on here for five years? The answer to this was an affirmative if pretty blushful nod, as is the way with shy people, but then that meant he was a bloody fool and didn't know this thing, so he then shook his head, but that negative meant also that he didn't know it. Speech was inevitable, perhaps a croak: yes, he had known it, but for seven years, and he'd always wanted it.

Matters having now moved beyond innuendo and the combing of hair, she went to the door and locked it against her father and sister, and came back and took off the other half of his pyjamas, and all of her clothing too, and got into bed with him, and never looked back.

The Transvaal Burgher was a match for the Tommy any day, and driven by anger, too, which makes for a dangerous soldier. The Brits had not learned from Isandlwana the perils of underestimating the violent will of a minor nation under threat of destruction.

This pair under the eiderdown needed no great verbal analysis to understand all this, for they were part of it. If there's anything you want to make of your life, make it now, for the time left for fulfilment may be brief. Sharing each other's warmth, breath, fluids and love under there they established a team of two, which might be enlarged later, who knows?, but as of now established in its affection, forever. Formal avowals and archival documentation as demanded by civic decency could come when and as they might;

> Love, all alike, no season knows, nor clime,
> Nor days, months, years, which are the rags of time.

* * *

Old man Stänger had always been eager that his daughters should have proper employment, having seen the effects of depressed economies in Europe over the years, and realising the evanescence of family fortunes. The jobs for women he had in mind were not selling buttons and ribbons at a haberdashery counter and that sort of thing, however.

Young Ilse had been lucky with languages. She was a natural for the post of interpreter at the German consulate in Pretoria when that came up coincidentally with her leaving school, and had good prospects for the same job at the Embassy in Cape Town when that fell vacant in a couple of years, though for a woman to be thus appointed was a bit shocking at the time, you know, and such a young woman too… But perhaps it was seen as good advertisement for German enlightenment, who knows?

Marthe's case was even more unconventional, by universal standards, I dare say, but certainly by standards in the Transvaal. GG was in no condition for coach trips to the East, and certainly none to survive there with the meagre medical care available. He was installed in the drawing office of Papa Stänger, in charge of an ever-increasing number of draftsmen handling the data pouring in from the Moçambique border. Personnel of sufficient calibre were scarce, and there were plenty of chancers around. Why not train one's own? If it failed, well, rather the Devil you know… Marthe was given a green celluloid eye-shade and placed at a drawing-board with the night shift, pressures of the time being such that the office was in use twenty-four hours a day. Germar was her boss. Perhaps that's why she excelled at the job; since their hours coincided, they could awake all smiling and curled up together of an afternoon, the late sun slanting in upon them.

> Busy old fool, unruly Sun, why dost thou thus
> Through windows, and through curtains call on us?

* * *

All this febrile activity and midnight oil-burning on Papa Stänger's premises had a sudden and unexpected political product. Ah, if but history were allowed to run according to such common-sense imperatives.

The colonial government of Natal awoke one morning, pretty late, almost afternoon, for they were heavy sleepers, to the fact that if the Republic gave priority to this Lourenço Marques thing, Durban would become a prawn-fishing dump and LM would become the biggest, busiest and best port in Africa, servicing the gold-mining Witwatersrand, the honey-pot of the world.

What a quandary! Maybe we'll get an even better deal in Natal, and avoid the war too. So who's off to Durban in 1897 then? Oom Paul for a start, with his droopy old eyes and top hat and the thumb missing from a snakebite in Voortrekker days, and a squad of high-pressure politicians.

And who besides, but his feasibility team with the top Germans and the wife of one of them, as secretary?

Marthe and GG felt a great lifting of the spirits as they took the air along the Victoria Embankment and the Point dock area. Such a long time since we've seen the sea! We've forgotten the aura of romance it carries.

Catch a sniff of seaweed over towards the Back Beach, and just look at the Esplanade, will you, with its coconut palms, the truest symbol of tropical romance for any European.

And what have we here? A German ship, the *Atlas*, out of Bremen. On the bridge stands a figure in a white-topped cap. Marthe calls a greeting and gives a big two-arm wave and one of her ear-to-ear smiles. Grüss Gott! he calls back; a Stuttgarter. He beckons them aboard, pointing to the gangway. Captain Henn, says he, lightly clicking his heels. Coffee? Good coffee, filtered, and the blend makes them nostalgic for old days, old places and old friends.

Conversation inevitably turns to the threat of war. When he learns that they are Transvaal residents Captain Henn is perturbed for their safety, and offers to take them there and then to Bremen. But he realises he sounds absurd, and looks sheepish and grins and says Well, keep in touch, I mean it, here is my address. If there's anything I can do, *ever*, you be sure to make contact here; and he writes his name on a sheet of company paper.

* * *

Well, there wasn't going to be peace, and war came soon enough.

When old Kruger could concede no more to demands from

31

the Brits, when in fact he had nothing left to concede, and realised that he'd been less caught in a trap than driven into a boma, he did the defiant thing, and had the pleasure of declaring war on the British Empire.

There being no railway work from now on, except of course blowing them up, GG was put to new employment: refurbishing damaged artillery, Boer guns mainly, naturally, but also some British pieces captured in early fighting, when the Republican forces still had the means, and the crazy idea, of taking on the Brits in formal warfare. This wasn't really in his field, to be sure, but he was an engineer's engineer, a man who thought in that special way, a man to make a plan and an invention for every occasion.

However, the Burgher kommandos realised pretty soon they had a couple of things which made artillery largely redundant, one was mobility and the other the Mauser magazine rifle firing smokeless ammunition. At Colenso they laid down such a hail of fire from invisible sources that the Brits abandoned a battery of their best guns. Why go to the bother of trying to turn them against their previous owners? Easier to blow them up.

So GG found himself pretty well out of a job, though kept occupied here and there, certainly, where he could lay his busy hands as a supposed neutral, for that's what he was, would you believe it? Marthe had found work for her unemployed hands where most women did, in nursing, not the crisp romantic sentimental thing portrayed in Sweet Polly Oliver, but a matter of puddling about in meat and gangrene. Orthodox work for a neutral, this.

Thus it was when one morning an emissary approached Germar, clothed in threadbare corduroys and leather leggings and sweaty hat, and straight from Oom Paul himself. Kruger had not even invited him to sit down and have a koppie koffie when he heard this man's request, but turned him around where he stood, there and then, and sent him to find GG, who was frustratedly fiddling about with the breech of a defunct Creusot gun at the time, down at the railway repair shops. He was a Nataller, from Louis Botha's area, Greytown, and he'd come in his fighting clothes, straight from the General, such was the urgency of this request.

The Brits had predicted a three-month talking war, and even budgeted for that, since Your Boer is always a fellow of poor morale and not a natural soldier. But things had taken a nasty unnatural turn soon enough, with the kommandos raiding deep deep into Natal, halfway to Durban and, as you know, eventually laying siege to Ladysmith.

* * *

Towards the end of the war the British scouts, specials, were men of the veld every bit as good as De Wet's. They could live without shelter or warmth. They could slaughter and eat an injured horse at night, by moonlight, by starlight, so the circling vultures wouldn't give them away, and be twenty miles distant by daybreak. They could read the veld as their own back yard, and they used weapons and clothing pretty-well of their own choice. The Boer had no uniform, but God help any one of them captured in any part of British uniform, perhaps a greatcoat, however bitter the weather, or however wracked he might be with fever.

These Brits no longer used big pampered cavalry horses either, but ugly, small, zebra-hooved salt horses, which could live on grass and had immunity to horse-sickness, as do zebras. Furthermore, their sharpshooters had become as deft as the boereseuns who were the backbone of the kommandos. They could shoot a man through the temple at a quarter mile, given no wind, and likely as not with a Mauser, too. Eventually they were able to corner the ghostly De Wet, and hound him to earth, and starve him into submission, and end the war there and then.

Mind you, they had the numbers, and the supplies, and the finance too, and behind them two railways and two harbours, Cape Town and Durban. They were not going to let Kruger become the Washington of South Africa by strewing all this crap about the country and just exhausting the patience of Britannia [so just let them have the bloody place, we'll get on with ruling the bloody waves]. Anyway, if they had pulled out, the French or the Germans would have been in like a shot.

We don't want to go to war
But, by Jingo, if we do,
We've got the ships,
We've got the men,
We've got the money too.

At the time of this messenger's coming to GG, though, the British were bringing by train to the front great sixteen-hand horses, farriers, veterinarians, saddlers, smithies' tools, pharmaceuticals, fodder, the lot, not to mention infantrymen. The best way to keep them out of action, of course, was to derail the train; but it was easy to shove the damaged rolling stock aside, and since each train carried spare rails for the purpose, to haul away the dynamited section and re-lay the track and, voilà!, all ship-shape and Bristol fashion in but two days, and ready for more horses and more foot soldiers as the local mounted infantry fanned out to hunt the marauders.

What was needed was a railway engineer, to show them where to place their entire baggage of gold-mine dynamite in one shot, and blast an entire cutting or tunnel in a professional way, or really to weaken the structure of a bridge so as to make entire rebuilding necessary. That sort of thing.

So short a marriage! No leisure, nor peace either, to think about it and make a baby or two. The very next day he was off, with a pair of mean Malay/Basuto ponies, grass-eaters with shoebox heads and sloping hindquarters and steel hooves and immunity to every disease under God's sun, a personal farewell gift from the President himself, to the better sort of Uitlander. He was no longer neutral; he had become a combatant.

Marthe bade him farewell with one of those energetic big two-arm waves, with a dog-smile he could see two hundred metres away. Even her nice white teeth he could see.

* * *

The free-ranging special demolition group consisted of four men and six horses, two of them loaded only with explosives and demolition equipment. The plan was to use the total load for one attack, and the trick was not to be detected, for this, remember, was Natal, and hostile. Cut no telegraph lines, for this would make the Brits suspicious. Stay clear of all farmsteads. They split up; a single horseman is not a noticeable thing, and no suspicion would be attached to him so far from the front. Except GG, they were all Natal men, with Natal accents when speaking English. Weapons were hidden; they carried no rifles anyway, since their purpose was furtive. GG took the two pack animals; with his German accent he could give a good imitation of a Jewish smous, a hawker, speaking English. He would leave first in the morning and the others would find him down the line.

Well, they found the right place, none better, along the track at Chievely, on the Durban side of Estcourt. Here the grassy hills of the midlands give way to great loose boulder-strewn slopes, with the farmlands more or less in the valleys.

They took out an entire hillside, burying the line twenty feet deep in huge rocks, and filling a cutting there too, to its brim.

They started for home riding together, pretty directly, and fast, simply relying on their speed to outstrip all pursuit. The whole countryside would be alive with search parties. What dismay, then, when on the very first day GG felt the old symptoms coming on. He took a vast dose of quinine, and told his mates to find a place to dump him where he'd soon be found, and to find it fast, while he was still able to ride hard. They took all identification off him, bundled him up in a blanket and laid him under a tree by a track leading to a farm house quite nearby. Labourers in the distant fields watched them, and that was a good thing for him because it meant he would soon get help, but a very bad thing for his comrades, who would soon get bullets if they didn't ride like bloody hell.

The troopers didn't really have to ask his name. At his first words with that accent they knew it, such was the system of espionage operating in Pretoria. They even knew the day of his leaving home.

* * *

After the first grim shock she settled down well enough to the life of waiting, as so many others were doing. At least there was the consolation that he would remain alive, and get care for the malaria, and be fed, which was more than could be said for the men in the field. So: resignation, and expectation of happier times eventually; it was a bit like knowing there was a Christmas-box coming, and she learned quite to enjoy the feeling of expectation. Later she realised that with just a little bit of different luck, had he not been captured, but still out there on kommando, she could well have been with the farm families in a concentration camp. They did have their secondary function of holding families hostage.

After six months a man with one arm and one leg appeared at Marthe's place. There had been an exchange of crippled and sick prisoners, but GG's malaria had been in remission on St Helena, and he hadn't appeared sick enough, and in any case there hadn't been enough crippled and sick British prisoners to do the deal. But this was his message: he had plans. He was an engineer's engineer, a man who thought in that special way, and there was a plan for every occasion. He had considerable freedom of movement on the island as chief of a maintenance squad, had found the means of restoring and restructuring something which floated and was navigable, and by much corruption had found a way to get a message to Captain Henn to meet him in Luanda, neutral Portuguese territory. The details weren't clear, but the message was: he was going to do what Napoleon couldn't do, and get off St Helena, and come back to her.

But he needn't have bothered, the silly romantic unrealistic bloody fool, and in love too, of all things, because the malaria parasites got him before he could teach himself marine navigation with that special talent that engineers have, and they buried him there on St Helena. He'd have done better to sit around and make scrimshaw engravings on whales' teeth, saying Souvenir of Saint Helena, and cigarette-boxes from the timber of wrecked ships; then at least she'd have had something to remember him by.

* * *

All this is pretty sombre talk, but when I knew Marthe in 1931 she was anything but that. I have known few people smile so heartily, or have such an unrestrained laugh, almost a cackle, and a bit vulgar, perhaps. But looking back after nine or so years, one thing came to my attention: Marthe must have had many men about her over the years, with a personality and a body like that, but I never ever once heard her talk of any but GG. She had a repertoire of his jokes and many tales of his bushveld adventures such as delight the imagination of a six-year-old. I was an eager audience; she learned to spin the tales out to an hour or so in her funny accent. She showed me how to take a rubbing from her crown piece, putting a piece of thinnish white paper over the coin and lightly going over it with a soft pencil.

One Friday afternoon she said to me Would you like to see ay bridge which GG has built, isn't it? Go ask your mama when it's all right if we go tomorrow. Straight after breakfast I was ready. I had never seen a woman wearing trousers. Hers were not fashion creations, but ordinary farmers' khaki broek. She hadn't a very big bum, so large-size men's were okay, and needed but shortening of the legs, she told me. People looked at her in the street, but she seemed not to give a damn, and after a bit I didn't either. She had a big shady straw hat. We had a basket of sandwiches, cakes, a thermos of coffee and a bottle of lemonade. Chocolate too. We took the tram from Church Square to the station, and an electric train not far out of Pretoria, to some halt the other side of Irene, but I forget the name. We walked a mile or so along the railway line, and there it was: a pretty commonplace girder railway bridge, painted grey, over an almost dry stream, with a few willows down there below, and some grass a bit greener than that of the surrounding yellow veld.

She put down the basket and spread her hands as if to say See? There it all is. It was still in everyday use. An electric train would come clattering over it every hour or so. She took me over to one of the angled girders, and there underneath, in yellow enamel, not much faded for it was out of the sun, was painted a golden penny with a head on it, with above, in Latin, GG FECIT, and below, 1898. Germar Guldenpfennig had made it in 1898. We stood and smiled about this. We were the sort of friends who don't have to talk all the time. I looked about and down the line; all boys like to see a train coming along.

When I looked back at her I realised she was on her own. Her eyes were focused somewhere over the yellow grass, under her big cool hat, and she was softly patting the steel girder as if it were somebody's shoulder. Her lips were still, in a faint smile, but I knew she was talking to him. I knew also that she was showing him her child, though I thought of myself as her pal, or sweetheart.

So we sat down there under the willows below the bridge and had our picnic, and she taught me how to yodel and I taught her how to play boontjies, a game of little black kids, played with small stones on the front and back of one's hand. We had a few games of that and a laugh because she couldn't balance the stones there. All right, home time! We walked off to the station and she gave not a single backward glance at the bridge. Kids are very perceptive. I knew she'd been there often enough. We held hands where the footpath next to the rails was wide enough for two to walk abreast.

* * *

When old Dieter Stänger had died in 1910 Marthe had had the notion of going back to Darmstadt. Since Ilse was married and engrossed in her family it wouldn't really have made an unbearable difference if her forty-year-old sister had gone back to the lovely green sloping plain beneath the Odenwald, and the gentle, sentimental people of Hessen in their fine old sixteenth-century capital. A friendship by letter would have kept them together. Maybe it was the bridge which kept her here.

In 1914, though, there was no quandary. She'd have spent the war in an internment camp if she'd stayed, what with her origins and background. She wasn't even sure that her old Republican citizenship made her a citizen of the Union. But something made her come back after the war, and straight away, in 1919, and maybe that was the bridge too. His monument in the place of their happiness, and amongst old friends, was perhaps more to her than a miserable grave on St Helena. Otherwise she'd have gone and lived and moped away her life there, I suppose.

* * *

Well, as I was saying, before I could get round to rebuilding Marthe Guldenpfennig's ornamental fishpond and repainting her gnome, my ma took us kids off to a new life in Maritzburg. Marthe and I had our last cake, and she told me a last Bushveld story lasting well over an hour, full of encounters with dangerous beasts and eventual narrow escape. Today, I believe she made it up. She came to the gate with me and we had a last squeeze and chuckle, and I was off to new, beckoning experience. At the corner I turned for a last wave, and she returned one of her specials, with both arms extended, and a wide grin, showing her incisors, canines, and a glimpse of her molars too.

I wrote as soon as we got to Natal, and we kept in touch in an irregular way over the years. But there were no visits, for Maritzburg was four hundred miles away, these were depression days, not many people had cars and the train was expensive. I sent a few photographs, a bit embarrassed to let her see what a freak I was developing into as I grew up. Also, of course, people didn't all have cameras in those days, and photography was pricey too.

After about a year she sent a picture of herself standing at the GG bridge in her khaki broek, with one hand on her hip, still lean as ever, and a row of small boontjie stones balanced on the back of the other. The horizon was slightly slanted, and her figure leaned a few degrees off plumb, because she had asked a passing railway labourer to take the snap, which she spelt snep, and he wasn't all that handy with a camera. It was an enlarged picture, and she had taken it to Pieter Potgieter to have it coloured. He had made the shadow under her hat brim a cool blue, as Vermeer would have done, but he had made her teeth blue too, which disturbed me a bit at first, though I soon got used to it. On the back she had written: See I have been practising!, the s scratched out and changed to practicing!, then the whole word scratched out to make it once again practising!

I got the feeling she, too, didn't want me to see her getting all freaky, and finally falling into frailty, because that was the only photograph she ever sent of herself. We had a regular exchange of drawings, though; caricatures and cartoons. These were usually the main substance of my letters, because I was good at them, and because school days were usually pretty repetitive one of the other and there wasn't a great deal of news. She picked up the habit and would send me sketches, not very good, of interesting places and people with notes written all round. It was our personal art form. So it went for six or seven years.

Then in 1938, at the time of poor stupid old Neville Chamberlain, a small parcel arrived for me. What on earth could it be? Curiously I unwrapped it; part of the wrapping was a letter, and inside the letter was Marthe's crown. I was to keep it, and never lose it, and always think of her when I looked at it, for she was going off now, back to Darmstadt, because war was coming, alas, as a grown lad of twelve understood of course. This time she would not be able to come back, because as a lad of twelve also would understand, she had become an old lady, and had to settle in some safe place. After the war, when I was grown up, I could come and visit her in Darmstadt, and I could tell *her* stories this time, and we would eat cakes and play boontjies, if I still had a mind for it as a grown man, but for now whenever I looked at this crown so big and silver I should remember her songs about the moon, isn't it?

> Der Himmel endlos ausgespannt
> Ist dein geliebtest Heimatland;
> Glücklich wär, wohin er geht,
> Doch auf der Heimatboden steht!

Blessed was she who could find hearth and home upon this earth.

We continued our illustrated correspondence, now often with picture postcards from Darmstadt and its old town, with small arrows drawn with a fountain pen saying Here I had lunch, Here is where my friend Grete lives, and so on. The outbreak of war didn't interrupt the correspondence as one might have expected, for she would put her post cards in envelopes and send them to Zürich for posting. But in late 1942 the last one came, and I knew the war had intervened.

It has always been my view that visiting friends is the best reason for travelling. It was always my intention to visit her in Darmstadt one day, but I never did. A friend of mine called on her one evening, however, and gave her greetings, though they were not the greetings I should have liked conveyed to her.

chapter three

So, then, here I was in 1932, all new and amazed and expectant in the capital of Natal. My sister Lola was really ancient. She was twenty and already a teacher, I mean a real Teacher, man, like Miss Vaughan, only not so pretty because nobody at all in the whole blue-eyed black-haired beautiful slinky wide world was pretty like Miss Vaughan.

But for cuddly you couldn't beat Miss MacAllan, here in Maritzburg. Miss MacAllan should have been covered in feathers. Under Miss MacAllan you could hatch eggs, I bet. While the girls in the class were doing Sewing, we boys would do Cardboard Modelling, and Miss MacAllan would say Come I'll show you how to make a drawer from a matchbox for your Jewel Case, and I would go and stand next to her at her desk, and while she was demonstrating her dexterity she would hum The Oak and the Ash, and I would feel the warmth and snoef the aromas coming off her nice plump arm next to me there, and want to lick it and kiss her and put my head down on her lap and fall into deep narcosis and sleep. If this is Mesmerism, gimme it.

Oh the Oak and the Ash and the Bonny Ivy Tree, They flourish at home in my ane North Country: which was where she came from. She didn't dab little dabs of perfume on wrist and throat like Miss Vaughan, but man, was she cosy, and when eventually she was done and would put her head back and look at me with her sliiiiightly squint eyes and quizzical eyebrows and a slight smile, and say Okay?, I would really really wish she were my mother so I could give her a good cuddle and maybe sit on her lap a bit.

So I really really felt I'd been deported to some spiritual tundra when shortly thereafter I was enrolled, according to Education Policy, in an all-boy school, clothed in blazer, tie, straw basher and long pulled-up socks with school colours around the calf, and reclassified as Trainee Man.

A huge boy, I mean really a huge boy, as big as a grown-up, came up to me and said Hay yer, what house yer in? My Life, what could he possibly mean? 196 Boshoff Street, I said. He pulled tight the knot on my tie until I was strangling. When I reached to loosen it he ripped open the fly of my pants. Yer got a face like a pig's arse, he said, gutter oxnams gemme tickey piner tickey pop, and dropped a coin in the dust of the schoolyard. Please, somebody, preferably Okkie Gouws, you tough little bastard, just appear here and tell me what this great monster means and wants, and how to save my life.

Well, Okkie didn't appear, and I realised there and then that as of now I was on my own. One word I recognised: Oxenham's, the bakery. The rest was just sound, but I have parrot's ears, and to ask this minotaur to explain himself was clearly more than my life was worth. I mean, even then I was a real weed.

So off to Oxenham's. Gemme tickey piner tickey pop, said I. The lady at the counter gave me a threepenny meat pie, a three-penny bottle of ginger beer and a smile and I gave her sixpence. I returned to Grendel hoping perhaps now he would give me a smile too. Fuck yer, he said.

I realised that this event in itself was only symptomatic of general life before me, and in any case I levelled the score later, if that's important. Twelve years later, in point of fact, I was too terribly in love with his fiancée, and we would lie abed of a weekend and smoke post-orgasmic cigars and sing Rosamunda to a gramophone record and drink effesoet wyn, O delicious. The most wondrous thing in the world to do with someone you love. And this pampoen whose name was Rex, like a Rottweiler, used to send me messages about the terrible injuries I might expect in the near future. Not personally delivered messages, you understand. Rather like those from Uncle Jim in Mr Polly: I'll show yer fightin' wiv bolls! I'll do 'orrible things to yer!

Well, at the same time as the cigars and semi-sweet wine and the fightin' wiv bolls bit, I came steaming into Maritzburg amongst the front runners of the Comrades' Marathon, swift of limb and sleek like a snake, and there stood this dude watching the race. Hey, you running bedonderd! he said with an unctuous smile. Fuck yer, I said.

Not that it made a difference in the long run, mind you. Her fortune and future were as Mrs Tickeypinertickeypop.

41

*   *   *

Anyway, so there I was at this new school, trying to keep in the shadows as much as possible, and silent, so as not to be noticed, when up comes this two-shaves-a-day man teacher – oops, master – wearing a grimace of disapproval and a pair of fashionable grey flannels with 22-inch bottoms so wide they hide his shoes entirely.

I learned only too soon that everything in male places like this had to do with the genitalia and anus. When pondering the best way to present the Unification of Italy, say now, Ol' Dingaan Fellowes the History Man would place his hands in his pockets, cast his eyes ceilingward and complacently fondle his goolies, much as Keats, say now, would gaze heav'nward and put the end of his quill to his lips whilst pondering a suitable nightingale image. I thought the 22-inch broeks with all the pleats round the waist were designed to facilitate this activity, which was known as Pocket Billiards.

So up comes this man teacher, of all things. Hell, how can a teacher be a *man*? Your teacher is supposed to be your sweetheart or your mum. Anyway, he comes up and stands there with a pipe in his pie-hole and playing at pocket billiards, and this look on his so-called face which suggests I am a lump of Dobe under his shoe, and says to me: Have you got an exeat?

What on earth could an exeat actually *be*? Well, whatsoever it was I felt sure I didn't have one. No, says I. No what? says he. No exi–er–one of those things, says I. No *sir*, says he. No *sir*, say I. Well, says Sir, interrupting all proceedings to go puff-puff-puff pop-pop-pop on this stink thing, in the irritating way that pipe smokers have, You'd better get one from your house master, hadn't youp? He said Youp because he had this repellent Tory way of talking, as if the rest of him wasn't repellent enough.

What on earth could a House Master actually *be*? Back at 196 Boshoff Street I was the only male, and if anybody was mistress of the place it was my ma, or maybe Lola. Yes *sir*, said I. Man, thought I, I'd better find out a few things around here, and smartish, otherwise I'm going to be in deep kak, that's clear.

My quest for advice took me almost directly to a form beneath a tree. The form was that of a Maribou Stork, comprising the body of a lad called Greenballs Mitchell, who turned out also to be standing silently in shadows so as not to be noticed. He had but a poor sense of camouflage, for the hair of his head was bright orange, as was that of his pink freckled legs, and his eyes were yellow. Later, when he had become my pal along with an assortment of bed-pissers, stammerers, asthmatics and masturbators, we discovered that where cats' eyes shine pink in the headlights, and dogs' white, his eyes shone yellow, like a Krantz Vulture. He'd have been better camouflaged standing in the blazing sunlight.

An Exeat, explained Greenballs, is a signed note saying that this afternoon you needn't play rugby, which you and I are supposed to be doing at this very moment, and which is the reason for my standing beneath this tree. *Rugby! Me?* With these wee skinny limbs I've got to go and tangle in a heap on the ground with Tickeypinertickeypop and others here who look like bags of cement and already shave at the age of thirteen?

What sport do you like, then? asked Greenballs. Cardboard Modelling, said I.

No, man, you don't understand. You've got to watch the noticeboard to see what House you're in and who your Housemaster is and when you have to play rugby and do Cadets and .... *What are cadets, man?* in true alarm, envisaging a game even more violent, played perhaps with a steel ball on a paved surface. Cadets? That's when you train for the army, man, and you march up and down on the rugby field with a sergeant and go on route marches and things ...

Oh come on! The Great War's over, isn't it, or is there a greater one coming up that this place is preparing me for, and am I going to get killed on behalf of that short-back-and-sides pipe-smoking poens with the 22-inch broeks, and get buried in the side of a trench and frozen in winter, so in summer when I get all soft a tank will run over the mud and all my juices will squeeze out?

How do you know all this? I asked. My brother's in standard four and he's a corporal and thinks I'm a real sissy, said Greenballs. I'll join you, said I.

Greenballs was an unprepossessing boy. He was tall and walked with his knees bent, like a maribou's as I say, only bending the other way. He was skinny and round-shouldered and had a great big Adam's apple, his lower jaw was longer than the upper and his lower teeth were longer than the top ones, so that he looked as if his bite might be poisonous. The bright ginger eyebrows and sunken staring yellow eyes gave him a generally toxic appearance, like some fungi and toadstools, or perhaps Van Gogh. You might get a temperature if you touched him, or bust out in warts. He

43

became my first boyhood pal, now that I was out of infancy.

But. But. After a year's vilification and menace, for failing to do obligatory manly things, and standing behind trees and lavatory doors, and riding my small size-24 bicycle bent double behind a hedge, and artistic lies about religious obligation to ailing family which if true would have left only one sister and myself surviving on God's entire Earth, I realised that I would never in my whole lekker life ever need an exeat, or for that matter a housemaster, again. I was blessedly saved by chronic asthma, my entire sternum collapsing in the struggle for breath, to within five inches of the spinal column, leaving insufficient room for the heart, which developed a murmur.

What a bargain! From toptoptop of the class I went straight down to the gatkant, the bottom, among the natural imbeciles and a boy called Bartle, after Frere, who had been hit on the head by a half-pound highveld hailstone in Naboomspruit. But with the asthma came a great doctor called David Blau, who had been driven out of Nazi Germany and knew about tyranny as he knew about exeats. He wrote one out for me in perpetuity, from anything I chose, including cricket, which, though not strenuous, seemed a hell of a way to spend a nice afternoon, by his reckoning, for divers cultural reasons.

David Blau had great regard, quite rightly, for German medicine and science, excluding of course the phantasmagorical genetics of Dr Mengele and National Socialist witchdoctors.

He had this new Medizin which required many small scratches on the thigh and rubbing muti into them with a little glass rod, which took time and gave us a good long weekly tête-à-tête. At the end of two months I had the ultimate prescription: stay in bed whenever feeling poorly, according to choice, and play the harmonica, especially blues harp, which is good for the lungs.

I found out shortly thereafter that Sonny Terry kept his harp in gin, when not in use, because it is played mainly inside the mouth and gets full of spit, which causes oxidation, i e rust, so that a good harp should rightly be kept in gin. My ma, ever solicitous of my medical condition, thereafter always kept on hand a bottle or two of that excellent anti-oxidant, and when I became tired of playing mondfluitjie in a bed full of Marie biscuit crumbs, would stand me up, shake them all out, prop me up with pillows and play at the piano songs from The Merry Widow, with a fruity if ragged alto accompaniment.

44

Oh I aint rough
and I don't fight
and the woman who get me
got to treat me right
'cos I'm crazy 'bout my lovin'
an' I'm unhappy all the time.
It take a high-born woman
to satisfy my min', gawa-wa-wa-wa
Wawawa.

Well that's not The Merry Widow of course, nor, come to think of it, is it Sonny Terry, but it's good stuff to sing when your mouth is all raw from trying to ingest this tin thing and you've put it to rest for the night in its bath of booze. The gawa-wa-wa-wa is how phrases end in Blues, and are really lekker on the harp because you've got it right inside your bek, and the wa's are made with the hands.

* * *

Our next pal was a boy called Andrew Kreis, renamed Cheese, whose family had come up to Natal from Stutterheim in the Cape, and who also seemed unable to comprehend what in God's name was going on hereabouts. Not that they don't have equally daft places in the Cape, of course.

Well, he had a different personality from Greenballs and myself. He was about the size of a small jockey, and, though marginally bigger than a banded mongoose, had the character of that beast, manifested particularly when menaced by a big animal, as is the way of mongooses. One day he attached himself to the throat of the head prefect, causing him to cry because he thought he was going to die presently. Mr Glissop, the Headmaster, gave Cheese what he had asked for: Six Of The Best and notice that if ever he did anything like that again he could depart for Stutterheim in the Cape toot sweet and not be missed around here.

Me myself, if it had been my decision, I'd have made him head prefect now, as he'd beaten the last one in straight male combat on this Serengeti Plain we presently occupied. Its genetic laws made better sport than the rules of rugby.

I had further mazal, luck of another sort, though, in realising quite suddenly that I was immune from the cane, indeed the remonstrances, of Mr Glissop or any of his staff, evermore. Indeed, my pals would be too, evermore. Indeed this good luck got me to realising why I hadn't been much caned thus far. It came about by

45

a process of pure chance, my happening to loll about on my couch of pain one evening half-listening to my ma talking on the phone of some scandalous event of another time and another place, in Afrikaans. The language excels in scandal; words like *skande*! and *sies tog*! come hissing, crackling, spitting off the tongue to match the unspeakable nature of the behaviour being spoken of.

Well, my Dear! you could have knocked me down with a feather, *soos die spreekwoord sê*. The subject of the skande was Himself. In some remote corner of the space-time continuum Mr Glissop had humped my Auntie Dulcie. The sister of my ma and Auntie Aggie had been furtively screwed by Mr Glissop at some hidden time in some secret place. And ... And... And he would *never know* how much I knew about his extramarital capers.

So you see, when Cheese Kreis in his desperate quest for peace attached himself to Greenballs and myself as the shadowy couple we were, he effectively removed himself entirely from the bombing range, where before he had occupied the bull's eye, waiting for the Stukas.

There was neither cad nor bounder on the staff. All were authentic conspirators of the Universal Male Club. None would ever expose Mr Glissop's veneries. I was the wild card in the pack.

I could get Cheese installed as head prefect if I wanted to. Come to think of it, I could probably get myself installed as head master.

Well, we were the object of some curiosity, naturally, to those decently adjusted boys who were being got ready for High School,where they would be got ready for The Empire on which the Sun had Not Yet Set, which process God forfend. I suppose you could say I was a wet, because I was sickly, and Greenballs looked fairly damp, what with his gangrenous appearance, but Cheese Kreis was a fierce little fiend by anybody's reckoning, and a credit to any rugger team, though only about the size of a rugby ball himself. So there was a ripple of surprise, a catching of the breath and a hush of dread expectation when Kreis the terrier who darts in amongst the big people's ankles and comes out with the rugby ball, announced that he was giving it up entirely and forever, because he was ailing in some ill-explained way with some tropical malaise. A growth in his leg, I seem to remember, though of course a bone is a growth. To prove it, he had a medical certificate ...

Dammit, we didn't even go and watch our team in action against other young imperialists on a weekend, as was compulsory.

So one Saturday morning this boy called Loony Bin Bettleham was on his way from Mountain Rise, where he lived, to the Woodburn Rugby Ground, where our first fifteen was to engage another pack of pubescent hominids in a no-prisoners game, as they say, the honours of which were to be not so much the trophy but the right to claim ascendancy over the younger brothers and cousins of the Knusen Gang, an agglomeration of unpleasant railway apprentices and artisans, who did filthy things with Wykeham schoolgirls in the Excelsior Bioscope of a Saturday morning. These younger boeties were known to be the most brutal thing around town.

Now the day was hot, Maritzburg hot so the road gets molten and sticks to your bicycle tyres, and bits of gravel and small crappy things stick to that; also the ten-mile journey there and back was arduous, let us say, for one dressed in blazer and tie. But Maritzburg boys are by tradition good tough cyclists and don't complain.

As he came to turn down the long sweep into town, however, a sound of great romance and breathtaking thrill to dilate the nostrils came to the ears of Loony Bin.

The sound Loony Bin heard was of double-banked GMA Garratt Locomotives leaving the Victoria Yard on the haul up Mountain Rise to Claridge. Two of them, each with a double set of driving wheels; two of them with eight cylinders driving four sets of 8-coupled wheels. The sound was monumental. The tension of ten minutes' wait for these menacing metalosaurs to appear round the last curve was about as much as the nerves could stand. Mobile studio sculpture be buggered. For mobility and form and sound and smell and aftertaste in the mouth and the sight and textures of steel, steam, smoke and grease and hissing hot water where the driver is boiling an egg for his lunch: for such a thrill there is only a big steam locomotive, only the great Garratts. The thumping and rumbling under his feet gave Loony Bin the chicken skin, man.

Over the top and around to the left they come blasting at walking speed, for these locos are hauling eighteen hundred tons up a one-in-twenty-four gradient. The front engine emits a hoarse, low-pitch steamy howl from its whistle. Loony Bin's hair stands erect under his straw basher. He observes three figures emerge from the long grass next to the track and fling packets of sandwiches, fishing tackle and bait into a truck full of bagged mealie meal. They clamber up the rungs near the emergency brake and disappear into the same truck. On the Monday Loony Bin has a medical certificate explaining that his feet pronate so badly when running that he is fit only for the game of bowls.

As it turned out, our precaution of taking the train always on the outside curve was unnecessary. Towards the end of summer, when the avocadoes were ripe, the train, all two thousand five hundred tons of it, including the two GMAs, ground to a halt one morning on a very sharp bend near Claridge. Hay Lady! we heard the driver call to a woman hanging out her washing, What about a couple of avoes from your nice tree here, hay? Incomprehensible shouts and waves of the arms bade him help himself. This was no great gesture of generosity; when an avo tree is in fruit you can't find enough friends to give them to. This woman had several trees.

Klim uit julle klein boggers, gaan pluk vir my pere! yells the driver. Can he be yelling at us? We peep over the edge of the truck. Yes you! Get out man and pick me pears! Best ones from the top, hay! Cheese being lightest climbs to the upper branches, for they are very brittle, while we below do our best to see none hit the ground and burst; but they're hard and come down like bullets, man, so Loony Bin gets most because he was crackerjack at boundary catches on the cricket field.

When we came to divvy up the avoes, some hundred or so of them, we found the driver's name was Knusen. So was the fireman's. Between them and another brother they had sired the entire Knusen Gang, foul apprentices and filthy schoolboys alike, all twelve of them. Avocadoes are rich food, full of vitamins, iron and trace minerals, and plenty of healthy polyunsaturated fats. We had collaborated in building the bodies of these brutes. We had probably got their fathers into condition to produce more of them. We were not only cowards, but traitors.

* * *

Well, these sub-standard factory-reject men would stand there in their school and blather away my valuable childhood with information and attitudes which had nothing to do with my being upon this earth. I couldn't care a hoot how many sheep got born in a year in New Zealand, and I knew that Manchukuo wasn't really a province of Japan, but that the nasty little bastards had moved in there and massacred the Manchurians and seized the place for themselves, because I had read it in a newspaper while sick in bed. And so on.

But Loony Bin and I were in the choir, which had an occasional small reward. We would lead the morning hymn:

God bless our Native Land.*
May His protecting hand
Long guard our shore.
May peace her power extend,
Foe be transformed to friend,
And Britain's Rights depend
On war no more.

* Why, England, of course [nothing to do with natives, you know what I mean].

A great song, this, for a lad from the Transvaal. Oupa Langeberg was as fond of aphorisms as he was of loquats: Others may have gold or Mausers, only the British have Rights. A pretty crude one, but true at the time. Not bad, actually, since he'd made it up himself.

When the Brits quit the country with the economy in their pocket, they left the rights of the Natives [nothing to do with England, you know what I mean] in the tender care of the defeated enemy, who were in some haste to demonstrate that they were now the only Ones with Rights, en vok die res.

So gaan dit in die bitter ou wêreld, né?

Anyway, the small reward was now and again to get a good Anglican hymn about Hobgoblins and Foul Fiends daunting our Spirits, that sort of thing, and also, since we were placed on a sort of verandah to one side, the Indian Mynahs didn't defecate all over us from the Jacaranda tree beneath which your usual run-of-the-mill education fodder stood huddled. Choral singing had its few points. We couldn't see anything else that did.

But you can't stop kids getting educated, you know; they're so bloody inquisitive.

* * *

My ma was a woman of little schooling. About zero after reading and writing and doing sums. People like these bubble and battle their way to the top. The whole family had been living on Lola's salary as a teacher, and that wasn't much. So one morning when the weather was nice my ma put on her snappy red hat and paid a visit to the manager of a local Building Society, on whom

49

she laid a narrative of such profound tragedy and motherly self-denial, filling his wastepaper basket with snotty tissues, that he arranged for her there and then a bond on the old house we occupied; without deposit, collateral or anything. Try something like that today and see what happens to you. The advertising jingle says Come on in and Get Your Slice. The slice you get will be Fourth Dan, down the centre of your cranium.

Next she approached an old biddy down the road who had started a pre-primary school, known in those days as a kindergarten, in her back yard, and failed. The assets of this miserable enterprise she got also on the Pay You Later, Hey? system, the original Lend-Lease. These comprised a board saying Principia Kindergarten, in green, six or seven green-painted tables, chairs to match, some back numbers of a periodical called Child Psychology and a jumbled assortment of kids' percussion instruments – cymbals, triangles, tambourines, drums, that sort of stuff.

Starting with the percussion band, she reckoned her pupils would have a pretty comprehensive overview of society by the age of six, when they went to a Government School. Well, they got an overview all right, but whether the best is debated to this day in Pietermaritzburg. Many turned out to be architects, for some reason, which may account for the strange architectural character of this and some other Natal towns today. One still comes across these alumni occasionally in the streets of Empangeni, Ladysmith, Port Shepstone and the rest. Easily recognised, they don't swing their arms when they walk, and their eyes are focused at infinity. Now that I think of it, I have seen my uncle Tom in that condition.

Well, she gave them all she had, but maybe there was too much of it all for the wee tads' developing brains: reading, of course, and writing, but then also Afrikaans and endless singing to an old whore-house piano my ma had picked up cheap, and such a lot of dancing that some parents feared their children might catch the Saint Vitus' Dance, of which there was an epidemic at the time, and which it was believed could develop in children from too much fidgeting. The din from the percussion band was shattering, but the neighbours were mostly employed, and during the day their servants would close up all windows and doors. The Rev Reeves next door got full decibels, and took to prayer. So many kids joined that my ma decided it would be good advertisement, and fun, to rent the City Hall and present a free public concert, which she did that year and many following.

I saw George VI with Frau and Princess Margaret Rose and sister Queeny Windsor herself in that same City Hall, in 1947, and it wasn't nearly as full as it would get for my ma's concerts. The din of these, too,was appalling.

Thirty years later my ma went to the municipal traffic office to apply for a driver's licence. When the Chief Traffic Officer, Billy Beckett, saw her name on the list he insisted on taking her himself for the test. Came the day, and they spent an hour driving about the streets of Maritzburg giggling and remembering the 1939 City Hall Concert, in which he had been Prince Charming all dressed up in satin with make-up on his face, and had sung Stay in my Arms, Cinderella, to the whistling and stomping of half the population. He forgot to test her reverse parking and I suppose all else except stopping at red lights and the like. In fact she couldn't reverse at all, since she had become plump with age and her head couldn't swivel about much any more. Well, with the rearview mirror a little bit, perhaps.

So shortly thereafter when my ma went to live in Richmond, a sort of grapevine was set up amongst the residents for telephonic warning when my ma was seen to leave her gates in the Morris Minor. I mean it got to be like Dodge City when Billy the Kid came to town: folks took their children off the streets, women took to the hills with them while the menfolk crouched behind store counters.

For example, a little Indian lad who wasn't nimble enough found himself one morning on his bicycle in front of the approaching Morris. Knowing that there was no escape once this missile had locked on to you, he baled out and made for a handy jacaranda. At this point my ma was examining all the levers and pedals available to her for crisis conditions, as one does, so that she could choose one and avoid an accident, and she didn't see him duck, so when she ran over his push-bike she thought they were his poor little bones getting crunched up so, and went into considerable shock. But the Greek from the Tea Room took her in and gave her a can of tomato juice and said it was okay, he would arrange it so that they needn't call the police, the old girl could just pay for damage done. A sort of facilitator, like.

Well of course, the laaitie who had started the morning with a real beat-up one-speed grid arrived home with a shiny new fifteen-speed racer, bought from his uncle's shop. Come to think of it, he probably knew how to pick up coins with his toes. The Greek too.

But the big denouement of the melodrama that was my ma's driving history came one Friday afternoon, just as everyone was shutting up shop in the village and refuelling at the filling station for a happy week-end's family motoring. It was then my ma hove into view, coming to get her whack of petrol for her visit next day to the folks in Durban. As she turned into the filling station she missed the brake and thrust her foot upon the loud pedal, skilfully dodging all waiting customers and merely wiping out a petrol pump that was busy tanking up the Mercedes of Mr MacLaren, the richest man in town by far. Everybody ran like crazy, including Mr MacLaren and his pump attendant, for all had enough intuitive understanding of Heisenberg's Uncertainty Principle, Probability Mathematics and the general systems of physics, particularly perhaps Newton's Third about equal and opposites, to realise that when you get such a mass of steel striking a similar mass, you must expect a spark or two. Hoses were left in customers' cars, pumping, so that twenty thousand gallons of high octane was getting sloshed all over the apron and down the gutters of the village. Also the demolished pump was squirting all over.

Don't switch on your ignition! No cigarettes! No sparks! folk were crying as they made once again for the hills. My ma was too plump for the athletics, and her door was bust shut anyway, so when the Richmond Fire Brigade arrived in their red Land Rover with the fire extinguisher in the back, they donned their fireproof overalls and removed her to safety whilst calling on their radio the Pietermaritzburg Fire Dept, who covered the thirty miles to Richmond in twenty minutes flat and buried everything at the filling station, cars the lot, in a metre of foam, for we were now in the metric era and there were eighty thousand litres of petrol sluicing down the gutters.

Thereafter a petition was put out in Richmond, requesting my ma nevermore to use its streets, and in case this civilised appeal failed, a threat was made to the Town Board by property owners nevermore to pay rates if she were not curbed from doing so. But she was a civically-minded old soul, and confined her driving thenceforth toward Durban along the N3, a major motorway carrying four thousand vehicles to the hour. One morning at about eight a m, a busy time on any arterial road, she was found by a traffic officer to be travelling up the down lane of Field's Hill. As I write these words my eyes close and my every instinct tells me not even to think about it, for it does not bear thinking about. But there for sure she was on this steeply curved down-hill, along with Town Hill the deadliest anywhere, with the mighty diesel rigs pulsing and bellowing round the bends in first gear. Rely on your rig's brakes on a gradient like this and you'll end up at a hundred and eighty with your wheels on fire in a gravel ramp, if not jack-knifed and rolled over with your cargo of oranges spilled a hundred metres down the road or the air filled with chicken feathers and fleeing fowls, something like that.

But my ma was making her uphill way carefully and slowly, as ever, and keeping well to the left for safety, i e in the fast oncoming lane.

I dare say the cop risked his life by parking his bike there with its blue lights flashing, and a yellow strobe, too, while he called up his mate and got the Morris right up against the dividing wall, there being no verge along that stretch. My God, sobbed my ma, I'm a Woman Alone, I've brought up Three Children without Help [she didn't say they were on average 45 years old], and my ankles pain so, and, and … At this point the cop took out his hanky for her to blow her nose. Keep it, he said. Bad mistake; what could he do now but turn the Morris around with the help of his mate and point it at Durbs and tell her to be more alert? You try that and you'll really get your head stove in with a Kung Fu chop.

All this I tell you to demonstrate the truth of the saying Yes, My Dear, One Thing Leads To Another. Alone I should never have conceived this piece of wisdom . Luckily I had my Auntie Aggie on hand from an early age.

* * *

As I was saying, you can't stop kids getting educated, man. My ma employed a wee tiny San man called Bellum to work in the house while she was making with the junior architects. He had been brought to Natal from the Cape by the ffinchham ffamily, good ffarming stock, to whom he belonged. It seemed that Down There people like Bellum didn't sommer go here or there; they had to be taken wherever by people like the ffinchhams. Shades of the old Apprenticeships. Take your reclassified slaves with you on the Great Trek. Well here he was, uncomprehending, also asthmatic, and anxious: the ffinchhams could release him on contract, sort of, and my ma had him on contract, sort of, and paid him wages, sort of, but not so's you'd notice it.

Bellum was a dinkum Bushman, with small, delicate limbs, a small, wrinkled, triangular face with Nelson Mandela eyes and peperkorrel hair. He spoke Afrikaans, Namaqua style, with some of the consonants pronounced as clicks. His name must have been Willem originally; Down There, as in many languages, Vs get changed to Bs.

For all his diminutive size, Bellum was favoured by women. He told me they believed him to have magical love-making powers; a sort of sexual imp, or tokoloshe, he said. I personally think it had something to do with his sensitive nature. I don't mean he was any sort of wilting aesthete, any sort of ponderous Van der Post with his laboured shamanist aesthetic and the vacuous Charles Windsor nodding sagely at his elbow. Bellum didn't know about the Mantis mating with the Eland and giving birth to the Moon.

Bellum's circumstances didn't leave a hell of a lot of room for mysticism. But in his coarse, stultifying, urban world he had some strange how kept his intimacy with nature, which I purposely do not spell with a capital. Bellum taught me aerodynamics. Siet djy jirrie vollok? he asked, showing me a long-expired dove. Ei kan nog vlieg! Ekke sadjou wys. Taking this old biltong bird and loosening up its anatomical hinges with small drippings of boiling water so they would soon harden up again, he produced there and then a Lilienthal glider, which flew. Furthermore, he explained a problem which had caused the Wright brothers near-total despair and near-abandonment of the Kittyhawk project: how to use a rudder to cancel unwanted drag on the outside wing in a turn when extra lift was needed there to bank the aircraft into the turn. This had bloody nigh cost Wilbur his life when he side-slipped into the ground.

In fact, Bellum had explained to me why a bird has a Parson's Nose. Kom kyk jesso! he would exclaim in the midst of the dreadful drudgery of housekeeping, siedjy darrie vollok, kynet sy stêt, pointing to a yellow-billed kite hunting over the back yards of Maritzburg, where folk still kept chickens. There was the tail working as both rudder and elevator.

Also, he knew about the aerofoil, the low-pressure area above and the high below, which is the centre section of a bird's wing; how the wing-tip feathers work, because the spar of those feathers is toward the leading edge and the whole feather tips up to provide thrust on the downward stroke of the wing. How's that for theory? I haven't come across many licensed pilots who know how a vollok gets it right.

* * *

So here we all are, in school, and the lovely long hours of our childhood slip away from the future into the past, as directed by the arrow of time, with hardly any of their loveliness impinging in any way on this our miserable present.

We sat three to a desk. The two lads sharing with me were twins named Barkle and Torpid. Barkle was a strange name, it seemed to me, but Torpid was ridiculous, man. It turned out that their names were in fact Michael and Norman and they both suffered from adenoids. Well, inevitably woody noody, these two found fairly soon that aviation was as important in their lives, every bit, as the mutton industry in N Z and the fate of the Manchurian populace. We took to building balsa models of a weekend. A crappy lot; the rubber wind-up prop would shake the thing half to pieces, and after a ten, or fifteen, second flight it would hit a tree. Bellum's biltong dove had flown better. The answer was a glider, a high-performance glider, a sailplane.

Even in those remote pre-electronic days there was so much information around that you had to be bloody stupid if you couldn't find out the basics of any subject, with a good librarian as a pal. Mrs Nel, known as Eskimo, at the Municipal Library, loved us. I still have a blueprint she got for me, all unasked, from the Royal Aircraft Establishment at Farnborough, labelled General Arrangement of SE 5A with Hispano Suiza Direct Drive Engine. This, she knew, was my favourite Scout of WW I, along with the Fokker D VII. She just thought I might like it. But ag, man, general Theory of Flight, as aerodynamics was called then? She got us heaps.

So we designed our sailplane. Even small boys have easy access to the technological and rational part of the culture, the stronghold and seat of men's power, from which they contrive with much cunning to exclude women, leaving for them hysteria, which is supposed to arise in the uterus, as the name suggests. Well, Eskimo had dodged this device. She showed me the algebra for spacing the ribs along the spar of a tapered mainplane.

This was a real beaut. A six-foot, narrow, long, high-aspect ratio wing, like an albatross's, for optimum low-speed lift, with the tips turned up, like a vulture's, for good rolling stability. Narrow oval section fuselage, and a T-tail, the tailplane at the top of the fin and out of the wash of the wing, for good pitching stability. Rather than cut the ribs from balsa sheet, standard practice, we built them up on a jig with thin strips, so the wings weighed nothing.

All this was skeletal stuff. None of our families owned a car; we couldn't fly this ballerina in town, and she would have to be taken to Loony Bin's house at Mountain Rise by bicycle in cardboard boxes. I mean, really, it was like bits of an Airbus being built all over Europe and stuck together in Toulouse. Assembly and final covering of the skeletal airframe were to happen at Mountain Rise.

Bellum could see the general form developing, but it didn't mean much in its separate parts, without covering. The poor fellow didn't get much chance of enjoying the enterprise himself: at the end of his day's work all he had energy for was a crash into bed with a zol.

All was ready on a Sunday morning. The met conditions were right: a steady small wind from the south, but not so much as to make turbulence up the hillside. Rising temps for good thermals. We had the sailplane on a table in the Bettleham dining-room, finished, final, complete. We had stolen every white toothbrush in sight to make her cellulose dope with acetone. Beautiful.

As it was a Sunday, we got Bellum off duty. He borrowed my sister's pushbike and we rode out to Mountain Rise. We had the ballerina ready for him, white, slim. Silence. More silence. Absolutely stunned silence. I have seen that reaction at first view of a P51 Mustang or a DH Mosquito: a slick ship, a pilot's aeroplane!

Hiiiiiiiiiiiiiiiw! said Bellum.

So across Royston Road to the southern slope of Mountain Rise, where the grass is waist-high and yellow, good safety for launching so light a lady. Okay Bellum, vat jy hom. Moet hom nou nie gooi nie. Hou hom net so saggies in jou hand, dan loop jy net mooi voor'ntoe en bimeby sal sy van self uit jou hand uit vlieg. Bellum looked sideways at me with his small grin: *I've got to tell him about dainty light things and the flight of birds, angels, whatever.* Hell, if you put feathers on his fingers and elbows, he could fly himself.

Like his own being he held the Lady in his little fingers. The waist-high grass was up to his shoulders. He walked slowly forward and let slip her jesses and she rose from his hand, gently, easily. She wasn't flying much faster than walking, groundspeed, the wind was about three knots, and so she continued for a minute or two: a good stable aircraft, no wild pitching, rolling and yawing, for she was built with skill and love.

So, then, steadily, gracefully, riding the orographic lift, ridge soaring like a yellow-billed kite, she found her way over to the acre or two of black wattles where now the filthy factories stand, and picked up a thermal there at a hundred feet or so. There's always turbulence in a thermal, of course, so she dipped a wing, then another, this way and that as she rose, until at five? six? hundred feet she was spat out on a reciprocal course and headed for Bishopstowe.

With the wind under her tail she was making six knots I reckon, and still climbing, white and pretty and a piece of good sound European technology. Hell, how are we going to get her back? Go jump on your bike and ask people back there if they've seen …

Los hom! said Bellum, softly, taking my elbow, Los hom! Hy's vry!

We called her She, he called him He.

He was free!

chapter four

Bellum was called back to service by the ffinchhams, to look after their cows or bloody goats or something. My ma was obliged to find alternative labour, which she did in the person of Evelina; a short, squat, silent, pockmarked Zulu woman of complete despair, and submission to whatever dreadfulness this dreadful world might lay upon her. The defeat of her nation was embodied in her personal defeat. The fate of depressed people is to be bullied, they invite it, and bullied she was, by my ma, who nagged her mercilessly in Fanagalo, a pidgin lingo of insult to the recipient and debasement to the user. In two years I heard Evelina utter but two words.

My ma had the notion that the Zulu word sula, to dust, meant to sweep. Even that she got wrong, saying suza instead. Evelina! she nagged, Mina tshelili wena suza lapa lo verandah; yini wena henzili? wena suzili half. Hamba manje, suza stellek lapa lo verandah, suza lapa lo kitchen, suza lapa lo bedroom, suza lapa lo bavloom, suza Zonkezindawo!

I told you to fart on the verandah, and what did you do? A half a fart. Go now, fart strongly on the verandah, fart in the kitchen, fart in the bedroom, fart in the bathroom, fart Everywhere!

Hau Missis! said Evelina, looking with due formal Zulu embarrassment down and over her left shoulder, while her whole frame was gripped by disciplined internal convulsions. Since the response my ma got was clenched teeth and a lot of spit blowing between them and heaving shoulders, she delivered Evelina a smart thump round the earhole, which quickly brought her to her senses and sent her about her domestic duties.

Evelina, as I say, was squat and silent, and not a demonstrative person. She must have thought very carefully about things, though, because it took us all by surprise when a couple of weeks later, on pay day, for absolutely no reason at all, she came out of her corner like Muhammad Ali, floating like a butterfly and stinging like a bee, and delivered the Old Girl an overarm left to the forehead like a tennis service, dropping her where she stood. Like a stone. She then went to her room and put on her funny floral hat and shoved off before Sergeant Kok could come on his combination Harley-Davidson with sidecar containing a black konstabel called a Government Snake, and take her off, and fling her in a police cell.

She was last seen near Anchorage, still going strongly and headed for the Aleutians and thereafter the Sakhalin Peninsula, stark, remote, icy, underpopulated and known for nothing except that Yul Brynner came from there. It was of course part of the Soviet Union and she would be safe there from Sgt Kok and the Government Snake.

At this point my ma tried to get Bellum back. My mates and I had tried to keep in touch, but how with an illiterate, and how if you have no transport? The farm was a bit remote, but the old lady made contact all right, since she was driven by something more compelling than our silly sentimentality. Eventually a letter came back: the ingrate had disappeared, just like that, my dear, about a year ago. After all we had done for him, giving him a chance in life, a chance to break away from the dreadful life he had in the Cape …

I had worried about him for quite a long while, so skinny and cold in the winter, and unable to work on the roads or wherever like a muscular Zulu. But the pressures of new life and experience are great upon the young, and after a few years I came to picture him as a small desiccated mauve Laughing Dove, light and dead, but still able to fly.

* * *

Barkle and Torpid were not slackers in school, as I was. I mean, except in the matter of the adenoids, they were normal healthy boys who wanted to get on in the world and please their parents and not become convicts and things like that. They had respect, even esteem, for teachers; but then they didn't have a dozen of them prancing around the piano at home of a Friday night singing

> When the day is nice and hot,
> And you can't get ice cream cones,
> It aint no sin
> To take off your skin

And dance around in your bones.

The only time their school work ever touched on the real world was when we were given a problem in arithmetic about some twit who tried to fill his bath with both taps running when he'd left the plug out. Arithmetic? Barkle and Torpid had seen an algebraically designed aircraft in full flight, man, and they had made it happen. Allegiance to the school was strained, and came to crisis when we discovered who old Mrs Household over the road really was. At this point they joined the subversive Blaue Kapelle, one having contracted a dreadful chronic ailment from the other, and both becoming absolutely unavailable for cultural activities after 2 30 p m on any day whatsoever.

Here we go, into the wide blue yonder!

I dare say we would have subverted the entire school eventually, but the next year would be our last. After that Wolseley College, and Isandlwana.

Who Mrs Household really was, was the wife of the very same Goodman Household of Karkloof, reputed to have been flying a self-conceived and -built glider there decades before Lilienthal in Germany, before the Zulu war, as far as we could ascertain. Mrs Household was old, old, ninety something, with sharp eyes and mind. I think people would chat with her about the old rumours from time to time, but by way of light conversation, sort of; nothing really to challenge the old brain, to dust off the cobwebbed memories. So she soon warmed to our curiosity, and really pushed herself to recall the actual place of the launches, and what the glider looked like: Like this?, showing her an antique photograph of Lilienthal hanging in his riding britches amongst the rigging of his weight-shift kite, and how did he control it? By warping the wings like this, or moving his body like that?

But she couldn't do much. Family had forced him to stop flying because it was unnatural. They had feared his death, too, which was fair enough. He had given it up before they had met, and she wasn't sure how much of what she told us was hearsay, or how much had actually been told her by her husband after marriage.

But the natives at Karkloof know about it, she said. Oral history is sometimes better, she explained. You would think written history would be safer from twisting because one goes to work in a disciplined way, researching documented facts and archeological evidence, but it's too easy to hide behind these respectabilities and produce a system of pure myth, she said, convenient to the sensibilities of the historian and whatever regime or class he comes from. Look at Hitler with the Jews.

Look at us with the Great Trek, said Cheese.

Bravely spoken, sir, said Mrs Household with a wrinkled grin, Look at Schliemann of Troy, using legends older than Homer. There's a legend about my husband, and the old Zulus have it unaltered from the first.

Written history falls into the trap of trying to record only demonstrable evidence, so the greater part is left to the imagination and distortion of the reader, who later perceives all that as true because everybody hereabouts believes it. Spoken history doesn't allow that; since it is improper to reinterpret history to suit your personal need, all the apparently irrelevant nuances of the circumstance are included in it, all the feelings, all the colour, all the unrelated stage décor, and in that mix the main events are embedded. Oral historians establish all this early on, because these things are important to the community, sometimes even for its survival. Legends are as important as evidence, said Mrs Household.

You go and ask the Zulus at Karkloof, she said. Get the oldest, like me. A small smile. The flaccid old flesh and skin hung draped on her osteoporotic bones like a discarded dressing gown, but her brain: plenty athletic, man.

So here we were, impatient and inquisitive, neither team nor gang, for rugby players and Knusens belong there, but a band, a Kapelle, a subversive orchestra of frontiersmen. Something like that. With Barkle and Torpid we were a formidable force. On, on, to Karkloof!

This was going to be a true expedition, no packet-of-sammies-and-raincoat-in-the-bicycle-bag trip. We would get a pack animal and full camping gear, warm clothes, cooking things, bags of dry rations and an air rifle for birds. We would go on foot like Livingstone and Burton, and write things in note books. We had six months until the winter holiday. The doubtful factor in all calculations was the pack animal: a donkey was too small, and an ox too slow, so we decided on a horse. A horse was more intelligent too. We didn't know there was a difference between intelligence and cunning. The only horse we had ever touched in the flesh was the one in the shafts of the ice cream cart at the Grand Theatre on Saturday morning; you could tickle its nose whilst eating your

Eskimo Pie during the interval before the Ronald Reagan film.

We saw a horse drinking from the umSunduzi River. We asked at the nearest house How much for the horse there? Five pounds. Less than a quid each. We could do it in a few months, tidying up at the Municipal Library, cutting Mrs Household's hedge, fixing kids' punctures. Chuck in a bridle and saddle and you're on, said Cheese. You saucy little sod, said the owner, Okay. Right, deal, said Cheese. Can we keep him in the field here? No you can't, not unless you pay me. But he only eats weeds, said Cheese, and you get those for nothing. I'll get you the back of my hand for nothing! said the owner. Okay. Where's my fiver? We'll fetch him in a couple of months, said Cheese. A him has got a great big prick underneath, said the man. This him's a her. And if I can sell her in a couple of months to somebody who isn't full of bullshit, I will.

Anxiously, anxiously we watched our horse, day by day. The money accumulated so slowly, tickey by tickey, bob by bob.... Would somebody move in and snatch her away from us at the last moment? Four pounds ten, four pounds seventeen and six.... Five! We had made it! Lucky! No crafty horse dealer had noticed her in that out-of-the-way field. The owner gave us a saddle made of some sort of cardboard and an old split bit of vulcanised rubber, the best sort, though it was bloody old, with a big-ring snaffle and single old rein.

This horse we called Mary because she was full of grass. She was also full of such malice as to make it likely she would be with us at the hour of our imminent death, amen. She knew every shit's trick in the horses' book, plus a few that no horse had ever thought of putting in the book. A basically inactive horse, when she saw a barbed-wire fence she would perk up, as if from joie de vivre, whilst sidling over there to lacerate one's leg. We weren't caught once, but if one lifted up the long hairs which covered her body like that of a mastodon, one would there see dense scar tissue from stem to stern, evidence of her use of this device over the years. Maybe she had in the past caught someone slower of wit and reflex, and lived in blind belief that this would happen again, for horses are great believers in inductive reasoning, and cured of this only with great perseverance.

Of course there was run-of-the-mill malice: scraping one off on trees and biting one's arse as one went to open a gate and then covering the entire ten miles home keeping the reins juuust out of reach after one had dropped them to clutch the arse. That sort of thing.

She was a tapered sort of horse, from the zebra belly forward to the ears, and she had no withers to speak of, so that everything you put on her back, self included, would end up around her neck after a sudden stop, unless you hooked your toes in behind her elbows. This was pronounced when she was sweating and slippery. Not that she did a great deal of sweating, that is, unless from standing in the sun, or from fear of exercise; nor was there much sudden stopping, for that matter; this was a walking type horse, a walking, yawning, gasping, groaning, sighing type horse.

We thought it might be a problem of diet, for in that field she had eaten what she could find – though I must say it puzzles me that zebras look so perky on such a diet – and we started collecting nice little nuggins from all friends for her to eat: you know, carrot tops, potato peels, bread crusts, left-overs from dinner, anything, really. She developed a taste for sausages, also cigarettes, which smoke we dissuaded the catalytic puffer from inhaling first, otherwise she would get terribly irritable.

We gave her brewers' grain, left over from making beer, and free at the Castle Brewery in Longmarket Street, and cubes on feast days, and built a shelter in the paddock, permission for which Cheese had got, with his usual charm, from the owner. He thought we were barmy laying all that love on this piece of pet food. What twelve-year-olds can do with pocket money we did. We brushed her daily and pulled the ticks off her anus. We examined her hooves and picked out everything, even thorns, with a special blade on Torpid's scout knife. We examined her teeth, what for? She must have been a hundred years old. Life was darem lekker for this animal.

Well, we concluded that that was the way she was. I mean, relationships work both ways, you know. I mean, Silver Spear of the July Handicap was worth five thousand pounds, a thousand more than a Spitfire, and we had paid only five for this horse. We had wanted a pack animal, and we had bought one. Now we should all love one another, and if there was a bit of riding also, well, that was a bonus.

Having established this in my moral system, I set out one jaunty Autumn afternoon briefly to take the air with Mary; you know, just to excite the old appetite before supper, more or less strolling along Alexandra Road and whistling a catch from William Tell. Suddenly there appears before me a middle-aged duck with a small fluff-dog on a string, both out for a waddle. My God! she exclaims, in the name of Compassion could you not give that poor animal a rest? Get off and walk a little, for Mercy's Sake! like I am Chairman Mao driving this creature on the Long March or something. I mean I hadn't been going five minutes, really.

It was thus I came to realise that Mary was going her way with her eyes shut. Logically speaking, I could make no case against this, since I was on board and at the tiller to steer her around trees and things and there weren't any antbear holes around here to break her legs; but hell, man, why didn't I just let her walk into a lamp-post or something and become the laughing stock of Scottsville, in the name of Spite?

But problems were past. First day of the July holiday and we were off. Dress yourself in khaki bushwear in South Africa today and try to make your way across any farmer's land with a horse laden with backpacks also in khaki, as they were in those days, and my guess is you will be met by a hail of assault rifle fire if you haven't arranged your visit beforehand.

The only stipulation we had was that we should shut gates behind us, and we didn't have to be told that, all kids had a bit of the boerekind in them in those days.

We were able to navigate pretty directly by compass during the day, using a 1:50,000 survey chart that Eskimo had got for us as a farewell gift, picking out beacons as waypoints. But the mapreading was only boys' adventure, man, because at night we could see the reflected lights of Maritzburg, and taking five fist-widths down from the long axis of the Southern Cross, we had the Astronomical South Pole, and could make a fair guess that we were on track, since we were heading for a district, and not a pinpoint.

In any case, the farmers told us where to go, so we didn't really need the astro-nav either. All were envious. Messengers would come loping across fields to tell us to pull in for lunch. Soon enough, news of our presence in the district spread so that the messengers would come to say that the scones would be coming out of the oven in half an hour, and if we got there soon we would have them hot with whipped Jersey cream and umsobo jam. It got so, eventually, that we were covering no more than five or six miles a day, the distance between farm houses and vast farm-style dinners.

Families sat discussing the Household Legend with us after supper, for there was no question of our not sleeping over. All were intrigued, and the closer we got to Karkloof the more intense the intrigue became. Enthusiasm! Wild theories of flight! The entire agriculture industry of the district would have stumbled to a standstill if every father and son had come with us who wanted to. We didn't need the air gun for birds, because we were so loaded with chickens, cooked, and mealie bread, and coffee cake, and biltong and individually wax-wrapped little dainty packs of sandwiches and things, that we found ourselves at our destination with our rations intact.

One evening Mary was put into a stable with a string of polo ponies. She thought it was an abbatoir or something, this being her first time, and went berserk. I had never seen such a display of energy from any horse, never mind this old hayburner; rearing and prancing about, like a Delacroix Mare Frightened by Lightning, nostrils flared so, you could see what was going on inside her brain, bloodshot eyes rolling and teeth champing at the air. I stood aghast. Eventually they had to do as when getting a race horse into a starting gate: a strap beneath the stern with two big Zulu grooms on either side, pulling, and another at the bow, pulling there at the halter. When they got her in, the polo ponies all went berserk, thinking this was some mammoth or dread flesh-render from their ancient collective equine memory. I mean, she didn't even smell like a horse. Maybe it was the sausages.

When we woke for second breakfast on the morrow – first breakfast was for dad and sons, pre-dawn – we found that Mary had been shod. You can't take her on a trip like this barefoot, said the eldest son, she'll smash her hooves to pieces on rocks and things. We were much too embarrassed, and proud, to tell him we had never seen this horse do more than walk on nice soft surfaces, like fire-breaks. Her feet were like carpet slippers.

But things were not going right; we had set out for a life under the stars and had so far not slept a single night out of a bed, and overslept at that. Mary was so full of high-protein polo pony nosh, and groomed so often, that her long winter coat had all been brushed out and her barbed-wire scars were showing. She looked like an old cargo ship shoved around harbour by the tugs, with scrape-marks along her hull. We had to make a plan. We did that on the next day's march.

On arrival at the next farm we explained: We had come on this sentimental backwoodsmen's journey, and so far we had not had a single night out of doors. Their kids were fourteen-year-old twins, boy and girl. They were enchanted. In their whole long lives as country kids they had never slept in the outers, and it took a sextet of Townies to suggest it. The incongruity of it! We had a great old laugh. They were coming with us for a night in the plantation.

Where would you like to sleep? asked Dad. Oh, over there where the gums have been felled, so we can make a fire without setting the plantation alight. Sound thinking, lads! So into the bakkie; groundsheets, blankets, thermos flasks, a big pot full of curried chicken, rice all cooked, matches for the fire – this is winter, hey? and even in Natal bloody cold, man, sub-zero. Mary was stuffed once more into a stuffy stable with a lot of poensy dressage horses. See you in the morning, then, Mom called after us.

In the Southern Hemisphere you look into the galaxy. The Milky Way is just all matter and radiation. Who the hell ever saw space as empty? The seething white light of the black hole at the centre, red giants, white dwarves, blue close stars, orange distant ones, novae, supernovae, nebulae, neutron stars, globular clusters, pulsars, cosmic strings, superstrings, everything imaginable and unimaginable blasting its energy down upon us as we lie here in the vast field of stripped gum logs, all contorted, like a Paul Nash painting of downed Heinkel bombers in the Battle of Britain. You can hear the frost forming on a night like this: small cracklings in the bits of bark and stuff lying on the ground. Cold, cold, cold, but we're snug, snug, snug, and every now and then one of us gets out of the blankets and flings a big branch of eucalyptus leaves on the fire and it flares up woof! and the lovely perfume of it mixes with the cool, moist aromas coming from the stripped gum bark; and there is this girl with tits like they've been turned on a lathe, and I love her totally, totally, both of her, for eternity.

Man, I'm a sucker for romance and blue eyes, though I admit on further thought that the metaphor is inappropriate in the last instance.

Permit me yet again to digress, and explain why. Some years later, I find myself in a night club in Joburg in the dark dangerous days with this lovely blue-eyed lass called Cookie, doing oyster kisses around mouth and elsewhere, as is the custom of the time, and which, according to the morals of the time and the lighting in this club, includes most of the human body. Quite suddenly I realise I have something gritty in my teeth, and equally suddenly Cookie says to me Oh my God! I've lost my contact lens! Never to worry, quoth I, taking it from the tip of my tongue.

I think we must go and sit down, says Cookie. We do. My God, she says, I feel so embarrassed I must go home. Oh balls, I say, for she is my buddy and I can use this coarse male language with here. Balls, Cookie, put it back or take them both out and put them in your bag and we'll go on dancing, we're just getting nice and friendly, you know what I mean. No, she says, it's like going to laugh and your false teeth fall out. Oh come *on*, I know you haven't got false teeth, for crying aloud! What the hell are you talking about? No, we must go home, says Cookie. We do.

Anyway, so here we all are, and here I am 103% in love, with this awesome erection under the blankets on this really snoeky night amongst the gum logs. I haul out of my pocket my mond-fluitjie, for I'm sleeping in my clothes, Reagan Style, and I play, for her, for her only:

> Well the first time I went a-hoboin'
> I took a freight train to see my frien'

She looks long at me and after a bit she says; Do you only play native music? and I say No, anything, really; because I'm still quite a lot in love with her, though the erection is not what it was. What would you like me to play then, eh? The Blue Danube, she says, and I realise it's her mother who is the admirable woman in this family on account of the date loaf all wrapped up in wax paper for tomorrow's journey, and the crunchies which we're going to have just now with the coffee from the thermos flasks.

Life invites, don't hang about. I could get through a complete relationship in an hour. Last time I did it, it took me thirty-two years.

So from then on we slept wild, for the idiosyncrasies of the flying circus were known way ahead of our arrival. Far, far away the electric locos would send their desolate cries across the white frozen grass where the ill-assorted populace slept in beehive hut, rondavel, igogogo shack and pricey electrified house; hauling their trains through Lions' River and Mooirivier and Ladysmith and Colenso, places of romance and death, places all where since Australopithecus prometheus the fire-ape first had a bit of leisure and took to killing for power not the pot, Death has been the main industry.

But we are all cosed up here, with our heads wrapped in jerseys, just a gap for breathing, and frost on our blankets, and as the great headlights sweep their accusatory white fingers across the wattle and gum plantations and the locos' keening bewails the dead, we are able to say Don't point at me, matey, I'm innocent! And we are.

* * *

We are now ten days into this trip and neither a Household nor a wise Zulu historian in sight. Where to start? There were Household granddaughters in the area, married to locals; let's try to find one and perhaps start there. We load our gear into the backpacks and rope them across the saddle, two to each side, two in the middle. Off down the fire-break to the strains of Cock o' the North. I play the music, the rest sing the words, dirty version:

> And if a lady
> Wants a baby
> Give her the Cock o' the North

The break continues across a dirt road, with two gates. We open the first to go through, and there standing astride his bicycle, smiling at us, is an old man in the long calico robes of one of the religious sects. I see you, boys. We see you, father, we reply. I am here to tell you it is a beautiful day, and to ask tobacco. Alas, we are but boys who do not yet smoke, says Greenballs; he is the one who speaks the sort of Zulu the old rural gentleman understands. That is as it should be, he replies, for ugwayi causes one to stink, and only old persons such as myself should be permitted to stink a little from taking such comfort in their frail years. But it is yet a beautiful day. He reminds me of a North American Indian: It is a Good Day to Die is not morbid, it means one should die with the mind at peace and the eyes full of beauty.

We introduce ourselves. He is Wisdom Mandla Mdlalose, Bishop in the Seventh Day Adventist Church of Christ in Africa. What is your destination? he asks, and where are you from? We are from Town, and this is our destination. He looks perplexed, for we stand in the middle of a road. Greenballs explains that we do not seek a place, but information, about a man in this place in years before any of us present were born, who was able to fly as a bird flies, without the aid of a motor, in a machine of his own construction. The conversation is halting, because Greenballs isn't all that fluent. We wished Bellum were there: he could even speak Bird.

Yes, I have heard of this, since people talk of it yet, though it was long ago, but you will find nothing if you wander about asking old izikhehle like myself, for we do not know. Our hearts sank a little, but we determined to push on and cast about, and what the hell, it was the quest that was the adventure anyway. We made to move off. Stay well, father.

If you wish to know about this flying, you should ask one who saw it. We thought he was being philosophical, and looked at him silently. He lives where I live. You may speak to him if you give him ugwayi, but you do not smoke.

No, *surely*?

But we're off to the Kwa Tanda Bantu Store, Prop. M. Ismail, the Bishop leading with his long-shafted white-painted bentwood cross tied to the bar of his bike with a piece of string, and his blue white-trimmed robes hitched up with another piece of string, and his calico mitre pulled down firmly to his ears in riding position.

> Stand up, stand up for Jesus
> Ye soldiers of The Cross!

He has Zulu words. We have English. He loves it. People loafing around the store hail him as he approaches with his new platoon of choral crusaders.

* * *

Gum trees suck up every last bit of water from the ground, so around store and cathedral and manse and community houses the ground is dry and bare and compacted by a million bare feet. But the gums are not the pit-prop sort, they're spreading and shady and there's a whole grove of them, and the cathedral is quite pretty in there and cool, because it has a thatched roof, and it looks quite English inside with its creosote gumpole beams. It's got pointy windows, too, though it is difficult to build these with concrete blocks. Above the single-storey nave a bell-tower stands, with an iron bell and a rope. The manse is behind: two separate rooms also of amabhulokisi, with the space between roofed over, all under galvanised iron. There is room for small assemblies in this space between.

We dump our stuff there, and unload our unused rations, because we realise we are going to be guests here. No, Bishop Wisdom says, these we may take to the old man who has seen the flying. We go down to where he lives amongst a lot of incipient dongas and feral-looking livestock, fowls, dogs, goats and the only skinny pig I've ever seen in my whole life. There he sits on a mat, sunk in decrepitude, ancient, immobile. We are presented by the Bishop, and the old man turns his rheumy eyes on us and smiles with his gumless teeth. A grandiose but shaky gesture with outstretched arm assures us that his home is ours. The Bishop says we will come back later with food and, if he feels like it, he can tell us about the flying. We go back to the Manse, where kind souls have collected perhaps the only five mattresses in the community to supplement the one on the Guest's Bed. We can't refuse, it would be ungracious.

Things move slowly in the country, and Zulu conversation is leisurely, so the evening chill is already slightly in the air when we take Mary down to the kraal and cover her with an army blanket held down with big safety pins, because all of her nice warm winter coat has been brushed out by the polo pony grooms. Local hairy horses and Zulus look upon her with disgust. A poodle in a park.

So down to the old bloke in the evening then, and we unload half our total rations there, dry beans and sugar and oatmeal and mealie rice and salt and half a pound of bacon, which was in case we got no birds with the air gun. Also two tins of Walfish Bay pilchards in chillie tomato sauce because we couldn't afford bully beef at the Kwa Tanda store since we're travelling on pocket money. Two tins of baked beans and two bags of Horseshoe Tobacco, straight leaf and nothing else in cotton bags, so dry you can rub it down and use it as snuff, which is why the old Zulus favoured it.

The old man's name is Mthethwa, one of the clans loyal to King Cetshwayo right to the end, however bitter the punishment, he tells us. He asks where our fathers are from, and I tell him mine is from Scotland. He asks if Scotland has a king and I tell him there was one, but the English defeated him and drove him out. It is as it was with us, he says; the English are very savage. He apologises when he finds the others have English names, but they all smile and we all put each other at ease, and so on; one does not not just barge into the subject of one's conversation, it is thought abrupt.

So we get round to the matter of the flying. He remembers it. We glance at each other expectantly; how is he going to describe it all? Like some old sangoma or witchdoctor or something, all in sort of magical terms? He tells his great-great-granddaughter to fetch some stalks of grass. In front of him where he sits on the ground he places the stalks, broken off to the right length, in two symmetrical fan shapes. One to the left, one to the right; they are the wings of a dove. All in silence, he spreads three out behind,

70

and points to Torpid's scout knife. He opens the spike thing and pokes three holes in the ground. Into each he sticks a short length of grass; one is clearly the position of a rudder, and pointing to the other two he says Many wires came from here. Of course they did, they were flying wires and landing wires, and those were two king-posts. There was no way the old fellow could have imagined this; it was a diagram of Lilienthal's glider. Household and he had started with the same hunches. It is a diagram of a dove.

That is the machine which this young man made. He put thin thin cloth on it and rubbed on oil and stood it in the sun, over there, pointing with skeletal finger to a hill a couple of miles off. Tomorrow I shall take you there and you will see where he flew as a bird flies. We ate a big potful of samp and beans with chillie pilchards and drank the sort of tea made by mixing together the leaves, sugar and condensed milk and boiling them for a good long time, to waste no flavour.

We lay on our mattresses wondering if it could really be so easy or lucky, but we were soon off to get some more of our innocent sleep.

* * *

We start the march with the great-great-granddaughter in a condition of cefezela, she is blushing all over, though it doesn't show because she isn't pink, she's chocolate, Milk Chocolate with Whole Fruit. But the hung head and slight smile reveal this blush-ing. And why is she blushing? Why, because she is going to lead us to the sacred wooded hill where the young man flew as a bird, and this being a nice hot day she is travelling bare breasted and...

Oh fer Gooooood's Sake, here we go again, six erections all hid-den behind handy jerseys and things, which just happen to be hanging over the arm in front of the pants.

White boys are strange, they take such care not to look at the nipples.

Well, she's off, playing a soft little melody on her umakhweyana, a delicate thing of a strung bow with a gourd as sound-box. Sometimes she strokes it, sometimes she taps it with a stout stalk of grass, whilst varying the timbre of the instrument by pressing the gourd against the softness of her left breast, quite the most beautiful musical technique we have ever seen. She sings a soft lit-tle melody, for herself, like a vukuthu, a rock pigeon, gurgling and cooing. And we're strung out there Indian file and pretty breath-less behind this sprite, this sylph, this maenad, but not from the exercise.

Who let his fancy run upon nymph of Helicon? Lord Pan, or Lord Apollo, or the Mountain Lord by the Bacchantes adored? Old Sophocles himself, mounted on Mary, brings up the rear, working on the drama he is going to unfold on the magic mountain.

Mary was not only freight carrier, but also ambulance in this outfit. We had our stuff in the backpacks so that if there were an injury or an attack of asthma five bags could be carried while the victim rode with the sixth. She is acting ambulance now: five of us had lifted the old man up on board, and now he sort of falls off into our arms. We pour him upon the ground and arrange him like an ancient Welwitschia under the old wattles on top of the hill, and he remarks that all these trees are new up here. In the days of the flying all was long yellow grass, and they had all helped to move stones to one side to make a path for the young man to run along, for to trip when thus starting to fly would be dangerous, the young man had said. He shows us the place, and indeed there are dumps of stone to either side of a clearing.

He tells the girl to go down the hill to a place he will show, and she trips off making her pigeon music. He sits on the ground and smokes some of the Horseshoe, and the prevailing wind coming up the hill takes the smoke off at about four knots. The hill falls away at an angle of one in five or so. A bit less than half a mile off in the valley is a big spongy wetland, a good place for a soft landing, perhaps, also a grove of crusty old eucalypts. The girl is down there now, moving about as the old man directs with his skinny arm. She digs a heel into the marshy ground to show the spot; that is where the flying ceased, he says. He moves her this way and that, and four times she digs in her heel. Four such flights, at a gliding angle of about one in ten or twelve, we reckon, not bad for such an unlikely wing plan, and the best he could do with that wire bracing, and that's a fact.

Then a last one right over the gums there, which were small at the time, he says. How high was he over the gums? The old man puffs and cocks his head. Four times as high as those trees today, he says. Hell, man, that's two hundred feet! Are you sure, father? He nods.

Never mind the altitude, he must have flown three-quarters of a mile.

One time he came down right here, pointing directly in front of us. What? Did he fall? No, he flew about and came down here, pointing. Hell, there must have been some wind coming up the hill, to match his airspeed, maybe to exceed it. He can't have been ridge soaring in a kite like that. We reckon he must have put it down in real panic, hanging there between the kingposts, desperately trying to shift his weight to avoid going back over the crest of the hill, where he'd be dead, perhaps, in the turbulence, where the air is like water when it's broken over rocks.

Maybe that's when they stopped his flying, eh?

We eat date loaf and drink condensed milk tea from the water bottle. We make pencil sketches of the place in the manner of Livingstone, also a couple of the old smoking Welwitschia and the girl, nipples and all. Indeed, the nipples are drawn with the finest scientific enquiry, in scrupulous detail with a sharp pencil.

Mary should have been a camel, so she could fold up her legs for people to get aboard, but we load the old man up from atop a stone, and off.

We felt like staying, but hospitality is an expensive thing for poor people, and we decided to be away next day. Old Mthethwa asked for the drawings, and got them. The Bishop asked me to make him a picture of Jesus in the cathedral, and came from the store with a dribble of enamel in a tin and a brush with no hairs worth talking of.

The cathedral was but a single big room, with no furniture whatever in it barring a chair and a table, which was the altar. I made a lovely picture of Jesus on the wall there, with his hand raised in blessing, as I'd seen in my sister's art books at a place called Ravenna, and a nice big halo, painted in pink with this paint Mr Ismail had left over from his baby's cot, and a decorative edge to it in black coal-stove polish.

As we left in the morning the drums were already going, incessant, unceasing, non-stop, dominating, and the old women were hayiza-ing, ululating about the circle where the community of Seventh Day Adventists in its calico robes was shuffling around in a circle, endlessly, endlessly, under the gum trees. I don't know what they used the cathedral for. Maybe when it was raining. But this was Saturday, and this was Africa.

Well, we didn't feel lucky that we'd come so directly to what we'd sought; somehow it was seemly that, if a thing is true, you should come straight to it. We all six knew, as I know to this day, that Goodman Household was the first ever, in the whole world, to fly a controlled aerodynamic machine as an aviator, and not as cargo. Balloons are aerostats, and people fly in them as did the ducks and sheep of Montgolfier.

So now we are away home, three days ahead of schedule. We decide to head off west towards Howick and Cedara, and to cover territory, man, and not stuff about gloomping at breasts and things. We decide to push it by road this time, stopping only for water, Reagan style. No more hot baths in tiled bathrooms with toilet soap. We would wipe our faces at rivers, and sleep all stink and dirty.

We do it. We start the days late so Mary can stoke up with grass, and stop early so we can rub her down and bundle her up in the army blanket with the safety pins and let her graze near some stream or dam, while we make tea and doss down there too. Such water in those days was not so bloody toxic your face would fall off if you washed in it.

We are near Cedara, and we wake up of a morning to a landscape white, white, white with frost. And on the horizon over there is the Drakensberg, the Dragon Mountain, uKahlamba, the Barrier of Spears, white and arctic in its snow, brittle in the clean cold air, and we see where Langalibalele, poor stupid sod, thought he could get away from colonial malevolence by taking his people and beasts over a ten-thousand-foot pass to safety on the lunar landscape of the plateau.

And there we see where Durnford, another poor stupid sod, went to head him off, and broke his body trying to ride a horse up the Drakensberg, of all absurdities, but broke Langalibalele too, because he did this thing, even though it cost him this broken body. A poor stupid sod who went on to become the ultimate absurdity: a Liberal Soldier. A Liberal Soldier of Queen Victoria, nogal, qualified to die a brave gentleman at Isandlwana and get vilified as the culprit in the disaster because he was (a) a liberal soldier, and (b) conveniently dead.

But all this is still way over our heads, man. We are still with Buck Jones and Hopalong Cassidy and those blokes, though we do find Gene Autrey, the Singing Cowboy, ridiculous. While we're eating our breakfast porridge a bakkie pulls up, with a logo on the door, saying Cedara Agricultural College, and the driver climbs out and shouts You lads all right? He hauls over to Mary and asks This horse inoculated against horse sickness? O my Here! Problems. We look at him blankly and he pushes off. Great!

But he's back, with a hypodermic the size of a bicycle pump, and says Look here, curls it up in his fist, and goes bang, bang, bang, *bang* on Mary's rump; the first three bangs being with the fist and the last with the needle inside the fist, and she doesn't notice it. If you just stick the needle in first shot she'll kick you, he says. He doesn't know this horse. You could saw her in half and she'd just yawn. He squirts her full of juice. How's that? he asks, smiles, gives us a piece of paper with a prescription on it, says Do it every year, and disappears. Everybody is so nice.

And so we make our way, a day later, to Hilton, where we tank Mary up with water and fill our bottles, and buy her some mealies with our remaining money, because that, our last night, will be at World's View, the big bluff two thousand feet up thrusting into the belly of Maritzburg like a great prepuce, and there's not much grazing there. We park her in the cleft at the front of the bluff, cut by Piet Retief for his wagon track a hundred years ago. Tomorrow we will follow his road into the city. Now it's dark and we sit in our blankets drinking tea and looking at the light of our capital: a hundred thousand people, mostly daft.

To be a Chauvinist in Natal is considered a virtue. We qualify.

chapter five

The first thing I did at Wolseley College was to invent the orgasm.
I don't mean discover it, for there was no way such a bizarre piece
of behaviour could have evolved biologically, ready and waiting to
be discovered, and no Lamarckian process in the culture could
have brought us to it. I mean, it would take somebody as loony
and maladjusted as myself to end up doing something like this.

Of course we weren't ignorant about the gymnastics of sex.
We'd been in plenty of small boys' places where the act was dis-
cussed, mostly sotto voce, and its mechanical processes demysti-
fied with the aid of French post cards and clinical encyclopaedias.
And in quite a few big boys' places where their personal perfor-
mance of this back-breaking business was proclaimed for as many
others to hear as possible, with such brutality and braggadocio
that one could scarce believe such coarse behaviour could ever
produce something as dinky as a baby.

Loony Bin too had a much older sister, who was given to
Saturday afternoons in bed with a local farmer. Quite inadvertently he had heard them discussing the matter of contraception,
which was by way of the condom, in those days known as the
French Letter.

Crossing the old iron bridge over the umSinduzi late one afternoon, we there espied under the lovely big old gum trees a pair of
lovers, rolling and fondling in the lush grass and beautiful ambient light of an Autumn evening, as lovers do. Military style, we
dropped our bikes behind a bank and leopard-crawled over for
surveillance. Would they never have done? On and on and on... I
had once watched a python trying to swallow a duiker...

Eventually it got a bit chill and they moved off. We darted over
to the place where the grass was still all squashed down and warm,
as if a reedbuck had just slept there. Right down under the grass

on the earth, all muddied up, lay a little length of glass tube, maybe from a motor-car fuse. Loony Bin picked it up between finger and thumb. He held it aloft. There you are, said Loony Bin in triumph, a French Letter!

What I'm trying to say is, we had the theory of sex all buttoned up.

But how could anyone describe an orgasm? It goes eeeeeeeeeyuf, o-yissis, ererer, Phew! Or something.

I've known some girls burst into tears at that point, and one went into such hysterics of laughter that I thought I might have to phone Lifeline. Maybe boys show these extremes of behaviour too. One or two ladies never got it right at all, and didn't know they were supposed to, and would look at one with blank amaze as one said Well, it goes yowwwwww, glug glug glug, OmyGodekvrek! and wonder if they should really struggle to achieve something as risible as that.

Well, I hadn't known about orgasms. So it came as some surprise when one day, whilst soaping the Person in a nice hot bath, an ablution which took longer than it used to, these days, on account of seeing in the mind's eye the Nymph of the Sacred Mount Helicon, my eyeballs started to protrude to such an extent, and to cross so extremely, that I was looking straight from one pupil into the other, whilst every neuron in my head short-circuited and I fell into deep cataplexy as the tides sloshed about inside my skull. She was right! Why had I doubted in my arrogance? All pleasure of the moment was lost at the prospect of life in the Asylum, locked up alone in a sound-proof place so other lunatics wouldn't hear my screams.

Later on in the afternoon I took control of my mind and looked rationally at my fate. If I was going to spend my days in the squirrel cage, I might as well go in there totally insane so I wouldn't sit and fret about liberty with the half a mind I had left. I would limit myself to twice a day, though, just in case. I mean, it was a useful thing for a lad to have, man. I mean, you know... I mean, it was *handy*... As long as nobody knew you were doing it...

It took a couple of months to find that most of the people I knew were doing it most of the time.

* * *

The second thing at Wolseley College was not an invention but a discovery. Political guile. Knowing that one's headmaster knows one knows he has humped one's aunt would no longer be available. As of now I would have to engage in the manipulation of circumstance and power.

Here I am in this really adult place, then, and in the first week I'm there I get the arse beaten off me by a prefect because I have left a sandwich in my desk overnight, and get stood on top of a library ladder in the Prefects' Common Room and obliged to sing geography notes. All said prefects think it is just the most comical aspect of getting one prepared for Manhood in the Empire, and fondle their goolies inside their 22 1/2 inch broeks, for these blokes are the same size as the masters, and they wear 22 1/2 inch broeks too, and their goolies are just as dangly and fondly, maybe danglier and fondlier.

And there is this 22 1/2 carat poep called Poepie Pope, who wears cricket boots to school for teaching Latin, and his Proconsul mind is so obsessed with Having a Knock that he notices no beauty in Ovid, and his standard salutation to anyone in God's Wide World, except maybe his wife and his kitchen girl is What about a Knock this Afternoon? And he beats the arse off me because I don't ever Have a Knock with him or anybody else, and when he's all breathless from bum-beating he tells me I will come to no good unless.

Poepie Pope's favourite expression, when people have been Having Knocks with him or when anything else in the world is going well, is Everything's Sir Garnet, then!, and this is really terribly subtle, because it alludes to Sir Garnet Wolseley, and that's who the school is named after, and whenever Sir Garnet had beat the arse off some more Ashantis or Zoolahs or Boors, all Back Home had said Everything's Sir Garnet, then! And when he had remodelled the whole military system Back Home and Gilbert and Sullivan had written a terribly subtle aria about him which went I am the Very Model of a Modern Major General, everybody thought this was too terribly subtle and said Everything's Sir Garnet, then!

And Oliver Ratherham the headmaster puts on Gilbert and Sullivan operas and sings this aria and he *is* the *head*master of the school named after the major-general after whom the aria was written, and I don't know, it was all so humorous, and terribly subtle, honestly.

Next I'm off to a dude called Dog MacDougal, the rugby man, who also teaches Science, but he's only got as far as Boyle's Law in his brain, about as far as the dude who wrote the syllabus. He babbles on about physics, by which he really means the history of physics, useful stuff, to be sure, except he's like a person hard of hearing studying the history of music. He can't hear the crashing of the cymbals and the braying of the trumpets as the brass band down at the slipway there goes berserk while the irreverent heathens of the quantum generation kick the props out from under the ship with their bare feet, and instead of slipping sweetly into the water she rolls over on top of the shipbuilders.

The greatest adventure ever, in the whole history of this inquisitive species, is happening before his scientific face , and he looks right through it with blank eyes, like a piece of Lord Leighton sculpture, while these delinquents invite him to have an opinion. But he knows, you see, because they don't play rugger with him, nor Have a Knock with Poepie Pope, that intelligent as they undoubtedly may be, they undoubtedly are not talking about the real world, otherwise they would cut their hair and iron their clothes and make themselves comprehensible to Me, Dog MacDougal, a scientist.

The ineffable equations of Quantum Mechanics have left dear old Albert where he sits muttering God does not play at dice. I know this because Eskimo at the Public Library tells me. She hasn't the mathematics to explain their work, but she knows where the lads are working. It is a great thrill. But Dog MacDougal thinks old Albert too is stupid, a central European weirdo who believes a rugby ball must be square because it isn't round. I'll bet he's never even seen one, never mind held one in his male hands.

Have you got an Exeat? asks Dog MacDougal, playfully wrenching a few hairs from my left temple. Rugger, boy, rugger! I don't play rugby, sir, I'm asthmatic. Yes you do, says Ol' Dog, and as for asthmatic, we had a boy here last year who was cured of asthma by a few good games of rugger. A fine bit of inductive reasoning this, such as I've been trying to cure my horse of.

You've got two legs to run on and two hands to catch a ball, and if you can't run fast, run slowly; go to the Prefects' Common Room and ask someone to cane you, says Ol' Dog. Off to the prefects, laddy!, giving hairs on the other temple a farewell tweak.

Well I don't go to the prefects, and I don't go to rugger, and I don't go the next week, and I don't go ever after, but I do have some really fancy asthma as a right old face-off develops. Ol' Dog doesn't even look at me these days, and I know what is going on in his candid manly brain. I remember Jasper. He ran into his lot last month.

Jasper had a father who was an attorney. Dog MacDougal beat Jasper for rugby reasons. Jasper told his father. The prefects arranged us all in two long rows away from their Common Room as the staff took tea way over there. Jasper ran the gauntlet, and all thrust fingers at him. *Out! Out! Out! Out! Out!*

The poor sod went stumbling over to his push bike, and pushed off. All thrilled to the sheer catharsis of it: a trembling comradeship engulfed us, for we were pumped full of moral adrenalin for the rest of the day. There was companionable smiling, for all but one were right. It was my first experience of Fascism at work, in the round, in the flesh.

How could he come back after that? He was irresistibly expelled, forever, if informally. But he *did* come back, the swine, and the very next day too, and, what's more, he'd even phoned his mate and found what homework was due, and came to school with it all neatly done, and intelligently. Rumour was his pa did it.

That was also my first adult experience of cowards and heroes, if a bit early. A hardegat, hard-arsed bastard. The only way. Well, maybe a bit of guile would help too. As I say, this was the next important discipline in my education.

* * *

So I was lying on the same old couch of pain, as usual, wondering what I could do about this planet, when what do I hear, but Useful Information. My sister Polly, one up from me, is having it off with a prefect from another Maritzburg school, and in between copulations they are having a nice chat about this and that, very relaxed, you know. And this prefect is saying *Skande! Sies tog!*, only in English this time; And You Know What They Did Then?, that sort of really heavy breathing stuff. And whom is he saying it about? Aha, the Head Prefect of Wolseley College, no less. And what is he doing? Aha, he's skroefing the headmaster's daughter, that's what.

I mean he's really into artistical acrobatical steeking with this daughter, not just sort of innocent incidental mating consequent on love. In fact I make a point of remembering some of these yoga exercises so I can try them out myself when I'm head prefect, which may indeed be soon if the scheme in my head comes to fruition. So after an hour or so I climb out of the window and make my way silently to the kitchen, where I try not to wheeze asthmatically as I switch on the kettle, because I want to pretend

I've been there a long time. I make this cup of tea and walk towards my bed through the lounge where they're sitting. Oh hullo Bonzo! I say; that's his nickname because he looks like one of those pink bull terriers; howzit, Bonzo, I didn't know you were here, how you doing, man?

He also thinks I'm a wet, but there's nothing he can do about that on account of my sussie. He plays Combat Rugby against Godefroy Raleigh who is head prefect at my school, if it is mine. Godefroy is known as Walter in his close circle, because of, you know, Sir Walter Raleigh. In fact Dog MacDougal calls him Sir, and all the other prefects and the First Fifteen nudge each other and have a great old manly sort of guffaw, because of a master calling a boy Sir, and it's quite naughty really but we all take the allusion and it's really very subtle and in any case we're all established in our manhood and we'll all soon be out of here and members of the Old Collegians together.

So I sit down and drink this tea and I say after a suitable interval, like: Hay Bonzo, man, do you know our Head Prefect and Captain of our First Fifteen, Ol' Walter Raleigh? Hell, do I know him, says Bonzo; man, remember I'm the Captain of the First Fifteen of Saint Bollocks' College. Ja, I forgot, I say. Man I admire this man, I say. You know, I saw him skroefing Ol' Fiona over at Miss Stalker's paddock on Sunday, I really admire a bloke who can skroef like that. Wish I could. Ja! he says, and his eyes light up, because he has only about 250 brain cells and his memory banks take him back only about five or six minutes and he's forgotten he's told all these details to my sus but an hour ago. And I give him all the minutiae of this Gothic Wrestling, just as he had given them to her, plus some lurid details of my own perfervid imagination, such as to cause Ol' Bonzo the hot flushes, and I know that the next day Godefroy Raleigh will know that I know all about that bundle in the hay, but then also perhaps about other bundles. He will *never know* what I do and don't *know* via Bonzo and my sus. Or elsewhere. I am the Wild Card in his Pack.

And so I kick the props out from under any plan Ol' Dog' may have in the prefecture as surely as Paul Dirac kicked them out from under his physics, because I am now getting smart in this matter of trench survival, and I wear a sharpened bikespoke down my collar, so if any fucker has got my hands in the air and looks away for a moment, I'll stick this bloody thing in his eye.

It isn't surprising, then, when a day or two later later Godefroy

Raleigh suddenly appears round a corner as I leave for home. Oh, er, You, he says. Er, if you're not busy will you help me carry some team photos to the prefects' room? Okay, I say, but I don't return the small smile he bestows on me. Not sullen, you understand, nor cocky, just forthright and confident, for it is important to get the demeanour right, from the beginning. He has framed rugby pictures purposely placed on a desk. Between us we carry them to the common room and place them on a table. Thanks, er, he says. Hay, look, it's teatime! he says, which indeed it is, if cups and saucers and a jug of milk and pot of tea and small dish of assorted biscuits mean what they used to. I know what the next question is going to be, and when it comes I put the ice on him straight; honestly, politely, but no fraternisation, thanks. No, no tea thanks, I've got a lot of Latin to do. I have him by the danglies and fondlies. What house you in? he asks. Chelmsford. Hay, that's my house! he says, genuinely pleased because he has something I need. Any time you have problems, you come to me, hay? We got to help the new blokes along. Okay, I say. You can call me Wally, he says. Okay Wally, I say.

I had come a long way from the top of the library ladder in a month. The others of the Blaue Kapelle had been less lucky. Cheese had no chance at all. Hell, one look at him was enough. He was diligently in and out of the ankles of the big lads, pumping up the score, because he didn't know what else to do on a rugby field. They took off Loony Bin's shoes, had one look at his feet and put the poor miserable sinner in about the 24th Team. But it was Greenballs who was the truly piteous sight, running about all six feet of him there in amongst the tiny little new-farts with his great big knobbly knees, all pink and ginger, and his orange and yellow hair and eyes; with all that inside a multicoloured rugby jersey he looked like a mobile totem pole amongst the others, all running rings around him, nogal.

I rode my bicycle past this tragic scene one afternoon. There was Greenballs, a ten-storey Hindu temple, leaning against a goal post and casting an imploring gaze on me. What was I supposed to do? I shrugged my shoulders and he looked for a stone to throw at me.

* * *

Barkle and Torpid moved to Durbs, where there were pocket billiard schools equivalent to this tribal place. They said they would keep in touch, but of course they didn't. In fact the Blaue

Kapelle fell apart over the next few years, as these things do; later Greenballs and Loony Bin left, so at the end it was just Cheese and me. But Fate arranged it, for who else can do things thus appropriately, so that we all arrived on the same flying course together in the Air Force.

So then, with Wally out of the way I was safe, for the year anyway, because Ol' Dog, Poepie and the rest couldn't get at me through The Spirit of the School; they would have to do it administratively, and that was hopeless. Of course they had patience, I knew. But I had patience too, as well as this motorbike spoke, and a lot of survival instinct.

Well what about next year, then, when Wally would have left? Why should Ol' Dog not be working at this very moment with Wally's successor to power in the Ashanti Ring next year? And why should Poepie not be? And man, I'd now been only a couple of months in this Florentine place and already I could see the political structure of it all and more or less identify the categories in the power struggle. I was sure there were many more Poepies and Dogs on the staff to run into in the next few years. They ran the Ashanti Ring with successful senior pupils, and set the whole culture of the place. The Headmaster, colourfully called The Sheriff by the boys, was indeed just that. It was he who brought the formal authority of the Education Department to bear on aspirants in the Ashanti Ring, but it was merely formal; in no way could it affect this culture established by the Ring. He had himself risen from such a ring, somewhere, and knew the workings. He was the Prince.

I had, thus, more or less a whole year to devise my survival. But in the event it took a lot less than that.

Owen Ratherham was a pompous and narcissistic little twat who had been handsome when young and gained a degree in something. Along with his ascent of the rungs in Education he had learned certain profiles and postures which went with his increasing status therein. He had paid no heed to chancers who had climbed up the fire escapes to overtake him and get to Universities and places. He was solid. Solid in his community of captive malehood, crushing and competitive, the currency of the competition being the character of the men produced for dominance in the ascendant culture. We-ell all right then, for leadership in the ruling class. Claim credit for production of such character, and you were up and away. No chancers here.

A neat belly under his thorax seemed to have detracted not a jot from O Ratherham's self-image. Nor did the fact that his hair was grey and most had fallen out: this he supposed gave him an aura of wisdom. Nor did his studied mode of elocution.

O Ratherham paused in the middle of his mathematics and elegantly took the glasses from his nose. In a studied sort of way he placed upon his lower lip one of the earpieces, and upon his brow an expression of disgust. God bless My Soul, said O Ratherham, you look as if you have amoebic dysentery. Fuck, thought I. No, Sir, asthma, I said. O Ratherham turned silently to look out of the window with that expression on his face which one wears when someone on the London Underground has sneezed on the sleeve of one's shirt.

I've got to find a way to swaai this ou, and I go to Polly's art books to see what might be useful there, because I'm handy with a pencil as old Mthethwa noticed. There I find a lot of very sarcastic drawings by blokes called Daumier and Hogarth and others, in fact I have a lovely time going through one hundred years of sarcasm next time I'm ill in bed, and come up with the absolute best, who is called Rowlandson, and who places in my hand a motorbike spoke of such sharpness as to frighten even myself.

I sit for a week in bed with Polly's pen and Indian ink, getting the technique right, and at the end it comes up smashing! A lovely drawing of O Ratherham with his big hooter and receding hair, all exaggerated and truly satirical, and his belly like a great big pumpkin, but I don't dress him in the academic gown he wears to morning assembly, I put him in the uniform of Sir Garnet Wolseley, and out of his mouth comes a Rowlandson-type balloon, and in this balloon I write About Binomial Theorem I am Teeming with a Lot o' News, With Interesting Facts about the Square on the Hypotenuse. And this is really terribly witty, because Ol' O R takes us for maths and at the same time these are the words from his favourite aria by Ol' G and S about Ol' Garnet W after whom our school was named.

So now comes the tricky bit; planting the device without prematurely triggering it and blowing myself to bits. This thing is on good cartridge paper, man, all ready for mounting and framing, and I have made it to fit inside my maths exercise book, and I'm off to school with a bottle of Polly's ink and a pen. I sit during maths as if I'm drawing, and I see O Ratherham slowly sidle round behind me as he's talking about the binomial theorem, so he can catch me for doing something illicit. So I oblige when he is close behind, and quickly shut the book with the drawing in it, as if I've just realised he's there. A hushed silence as he stops next to me with that Got You This Time look on his face. Everybody thinks This bloke's in the dwang now! There's a gasp all round as O R slowly opens the book. He sees the drawing. All nearby see the drawing. Oh horror, it is of Himself! I look so guilty.

Will he nail me, or will his vanity prevail? He slowly takes the drawing from the book in a studied sort of way, for his every gesture is studied, and walks away. I notice his bum and shoulders bouncing a bit, and realise he is chuckling, silently. His vanity prevails. The plot thickens. He places the drawing amongst his papers and goes on sidling amongst the desks as he talks. Next time he comes past me he briefly points to the bottle of ink and says Put it away. I do.

News of this terribly witty thing spreads around the staff, and I start to notice those who teach me glancing from time to time in my direction to see if I'm drawing, which I must admit it was my intention they should do. The next one to catch me at it is Ol' Jonks, the English man, and I've spent a whole Sunday on his face, and got it dead right. He is King Duncan, because Macbeth is our set book, and I've got him with his crown tipped up and a bottle of Castle Lager in his hand and he's sniffing the top and saying This Castle hath a pleasant seat, the air nimbly and sweetly recommends itself unto our gentle senses. And it knocks everybody flat in the staff room it is such a scream, honestly. Hey Jonks, it's *just like* you, man! What a scream!

Okay, so the next is Ou Skaap, the Afrikaans man, and because everybody found Macbeth such a scream, I do him as ou Hamlet, because this is really quite a soulful ou. Only I do it in Afrikaans this time, and the balloon coming from the mouth of the Ghost says Omelette, Omelette, ek is jou Pappie se Spook. And this one is really *too* much and one can hear the billowing bellowing laughter from the teachers' common room at tea time.

So each gets a turn at this thing casually dashed off in some class, apparently, which has in fact taken me a whole day to do, at home.

Then I move to the school library, and after looking something up there one day I forget my note book as I pack up, and the prefect on library duty finds it, and inside is a side-splitting cartoon of Ol' Wally fondling his danglies inside his rugby shorts in the middle of a game, dashing along there for the try-line with the ball under his arm, and he's dongling his finglies at the same time. The drawing disappears. The library from now on is full of prefects in their gold-edged blazers, studying like anything whenever I go in there. Often over the months I forget this note book, for I have such a dreadful memory. By the end of the second term each has got a caricature, always satirical about some physical attribute, mostly genital, but always rollicking enough.

These Prefect Caricatures go also to the staff common room, of course, for these senior lads will be out of the school next year and into Old Collegians, as I say, and we can all take a jolly good joke together, even if it comes from this New Fart, who ought to be watched.

But nothing for Ol' Dog or Poepie Pope. iFokololo. I spend my entire winter holiday working on theirs, for they must be perfect. I note the way this French fellow called Daumier tips the corner of an eye to get an effect of stupidity, how a Spanish bloke called Goya draws evil hands. On the first day back at school I leave my book in the tuck shop, which in this place is called a refectory, like we're a bunch of goddam monks or something. I drop it off where any new third-former can pick it up, or maybe one of those lesser pupils who are going to be here only for two years and then off to apprenticeship in some trade and not even *try* for leadership.

In it is a scurrilous lampoon of Ol' Dog. No attributes, no balloon saying anything, no humour, certainly no affection, just standing there in his tasteless clothing, a spitting image with the mindless smile of Alfred E Neumann. What, me worry? It does the rounds before ending up in the staff room. The entire school sees it.

Poepie Pope waits a month for his. Same. Cold, bitter. I don't even give him a cricket bat, no comment, no balloon, no spice, no forgiveness. I drop it off in the Refectory. It does the rounds too. A propaganda piece; an embodiment of brutality, bigotry and ignorance, with a sullen frown and murderer's hands, and what a likeness, man; I've worked a month on it.

Nobody asked anybody to half-inch it from my note book. In any case, if it happens to look like anybody, who can say that was my intention? There may in fact be many, many more that unintentionally look like many people. And if either Poepie or Dog give even the smaaaaallest hint of resentment, or do *anything* which might in *any* way be construed as revenge, what cads they would be, since all in the Ashanti Ring had such caricatures made of them, and had taken it in true sporting spirit. I had penetrated the ring. I had also caught the eye of the Prince.

I had stuck my finger up the nostrils of Dog and Poepie as Rowlandson had stuck his finger up the nose of Napoleon.

Ars omnia vincit.

chapter six

Isandlwana is a singular piece of geomorphology. If I say it stands a solitary basalt tombstone in a landscape of rolling hills, I don't mean to suggest that these are the cosy rolling hills of Ireland or the Green Green Hills of Home, as in the weepy Welsh song of Tom Jones. This, my boy, is Africa.

Alan Paton wrote about the rolling hills of the Harding–Ixopo area, and the lovely dripping mists and the fecund earth that nourishes and nurtures us. A man of the struggle, he wore on his brow a frown of indignation, like Boris Pasternak, at the sight of purposeful human debasement about him. His anger was as potent as was his tenderness. He drew one with great artistic imagery and craft into his crusade against power without scruple or conscience, and there you are, at the start of his wondrous book, in the great cool motherly hills of southern Natal. But his meteorology was all wrong, as was his notion of agricultural practice in Natal and Zululand. The misty hills do not willingly nourish and nurture the human species any more than bongols willingly drag loads uphill for it.

Ja well no fine, so I agree that it does drizzle here too, but as I remember rain in this monsoon climate, they don't bother to put it through a sieve very often, you just get your year's ration dumped on you in a few good whacks during the summer, by the bucketful.

In this piece of prime South African agricultural real estate those farmers without capital plant mealie and pumpkin pips and pray Let it rain, but on the other hand for God's sake let's not have another Cyclone Domoina so everything, pumpkin pips, people, pigs, property and prospects all end up in the Indian Ocean.

Please, let it rain now so the cane doesn't get all brown and ugly, but then again, please let it stop raining before the stuff starts flowering and the sucrose content drops and our profit too and we all end up planting pumpkin pips and praying that it will or won't rain as the case may be and perhaps wash all our prospects and property into the Indian Ocean.

Anyway, Isandlwana stands there amongst its dry, rolling hills, a thousand-foot-high Monument to Death, triumphant after two hundred million years of waiting whilst the Drakensberg went on eroding, the valley floors turned to ravines, most of everything ended up in the Indian Ocean, Australia, India, Antarctica and South America left good old Gondwanaland, great swathes of creatures evolved and became extinct, from Species to Phyla, and the sun blazed down.

And whose arrival was it waiting for? Why, that of the 24th Regiment of Foot of course, whose else?

And arrive they did.

But really, there isn't anything that looks like it anywhere around; it looks as if it were built: built of basalt to look like the lion on the matchbox or the base of Nelson's Column. But when the Welsh lads of the 24th, the Second Warwickshires, clapped eyes on it they knew exactly what it was: it was the Sphinx on the regimental badge! The regiment had won its honours in Egypt, Egypt was its single-word motto, and the sphinx was its lucky charm. What an omen! What a place to establish themselves while their mounted men scoured the country for the Zoola Buck.

The Zulu regiments in the Nqutu gorge were waiting for their own omen, the new moon in two nights' time, since it is unlucky to start a great enterprise with a dead moon. But they didn't need their omen after all, for quite by chance Durnford's Basotho horsemen discovered them up there, and as they rose as one man and fell upon the 24th and the defence broke at the centre and the butchery started, at that very moment, five past one, the sun went into eclipse.

Isandlwana had its own omen. The searing white light of the midsummer sun, reflecting off rock and pale yellow grass to burn the eyes even under the peak of the cork helmet, was switched off.

The troops who at Waterloo had thrashed Napoleon's élite cuirassiers and infantry, who had triumphed over Old Boney's own – his guns – and armed with unrifled Brown Bess muskets at that, had been slaughtered almost to a man by a bunch of barefoot marathon runners with spears.

The two-hundred-million-year-old trap was sprung.

The sun went out briefly in the British Commons too – well, all right, the gas lamps – for something unnatural was going on. We had taken Civilization and the Word of Christ to the barbarians and the barbarians had murdered us. They had *won* !

The sun lit up again, of course, Galileo had assured us we need have no fears about that. But why would the shadow of Isandlawana not go away, nor shorten, nor *anything*? Even at night it lays its strange gloom upon us. I mean, what were we supposed to *do*? We showed the world what stuff we were made of at Rorke's Drift, where a mere handful of our exhausted boys, some of them that very day straight from the ghastly massacre, heaped the Zulu dead about the biscuit boxes and mealie bags like cockroaches after a good squirt of paraffin . We did it formally at Ulundi, with a nice tidy Waterloo-style Square of British Redcoats, and crashing volleys of rifle fire, one every six seconds, according to to the book, such as would cause the world's fiercest and bravest to quail, Frenchman, Prussian, Anybody Whatsobloody-ever. So if these silly sods were stupid enough to attack such a formation and end up like another heap of cockroaches, *they* should look silly, and not US.

* **

I knew from my Uncle Julius that the colours of Imperial Germany were Red, White and Black. Come to think of it, they were the colours of Onkel Adolf too. So when I arrived at Wolseley College and saw the bugle band on parade with their insignia of black and white for the Zulu War plus red for the blood that was spilled there, I was reminded less of that heroic conflict than the German Starvation Army:

Noch eine Seele gerettetet gerettetet
Noch eine Seele gerettetetettetet

Another soul saved, saved. Up and down endlessly they marched on a Friday afternoon, drums with leopard skins, drums with tassels, bugles with lanyards in regimental colours, uniforms with epaulettes and brass badges and a strutting bantam up front with a silver-topped mace doing clever twirly things with it and flinging it up in the air. Before the year was out they were at war with Onkel Adolf.

The Assembly Hall was hung about with battle flags from skirmish and war, colonial and international, and an ensign full of assagai holes from the stabbing of the butchering Zulus as they found crouched behind some small rocks a young subaltern making a desperate break for Rorke's Drift with the Queen's Colour wrapped around his body; that sort of sentimentalia. The school crest, indeed, was an arrangement of stabbing spears and Martini Henrys, with a simple motto Deus et Domus, God and Home, all in celebration of such cheery events.

There behind the headmaster's table a plaque declared that this hall had been used as a hospital in the Boer War, the Khakis lying in nice straight military rows on their military beds, while pretty V A D nurses in long grey skirts and starched white aprons sprinkled chlorine bleach around and washed their hands with carbolic soap and tied up wounds with boiled bandages and said prayers to God to keep out dirty germs and stave off the gangrene.

Here we were immersed in Old, unhappy, far-off things, And battles long ago. We were immersed in silly military chutzpah and male bullshit.

When the war came I briefly hoped that our teaching staff would be taken away to the army and, with a bit of luck, get shot by the Wehrmacht. One could see it coming from far, far away. Of course David Blau had told us that; but then also the news one got was highly formalised radio and newspaper stuff and newsreels at the bioscope, all tightly edited, and it was easy to accept and ingest the neat prepacks making us receptive to the declaration.

Even our comics were about it. By comics I mean funnies, British style; on Saturday morning the bundles would arrive from Durban, all redolent of new paper and printing chemicals and only three weeks old, fresh off the Union Castle mailship. My choice was Wild West Weekly, Triumph and Champion. In the Champion was a long, long serial about Basil and Bert, two British lads with baggy pants who went about the world having adventures with a sequence of no-good rapscallions and crims, one of whom was called Dick Tater, a right scoundrel he was too, a replica of Hitler. He wore an SS uniform, only instead of the two esses he had a pair of spuds on the lapels, and on the cap too, in place of the Totenkopf.

Dick Tater had this bloody big gun, and he would roll it out and point it across a great wide stretch of water, obviously the English Channel, and say: Bring up ze Gun, load it mit Tin Täcks, Toffee Äpples, a few of Mum's Rock Cakes und a Cannonball, and send zem ze Lot, wiz our Love. All the nouns were with capitals, as in Kraut.

We knew it was coming, as I say, and I'd got to hoping maybe they'd conscript our lot of militarists and put them in the trenches and maybe give me back Miss MacAllan. Or even, can you just imagine it, Miss Vaughan; I reckoned I was just about right for her now. I mean we might as well be doing cardboard modelling as most of the crap we got in this place.

Well, there was no conscription, because of the Nats and the Ossewa Brandwag, and all male teachers were declared Key Men, and the army wouldn't make up their pay if they just buggered off, something like that, so none went. Well, one did, from my old school, and he was the first man of the Natal Fusilers to die.

All our lot did was make everyone swing arms a bit higher, in the cause of the King, and from patriotic zeal. Everyone, that is, except me and a spastic or two and a couple of basket cases from traffic accidents who had to get their eyes blinked by hand every half-hour.

So I had a bit of extra time for the next important cultural phase of my life which was just coming along, for culture seems to manifest itself in these bursts, or quanta. Mind you, this next burst was of such import that Cheese Kreis himself, who, on account of his mongoose energy had been press-ganged into every conceivable activity including the playing of a gerettetetet drum in the bugle band, even he, I say, perforce just *made* time for this next phase, such was its urgency.

* * *

The Kreis family lived in Prince Alfred Street, named after the Prince Imperial, so tragically killed in the Zulu war because some bounder at Sandhurst had neglected to teach him how to bound on to a horse in an uncavalry fashion, and the horse had trodden on him when he fell trying to mount without a groom, and a gang of Zulu bounders had bounded on him when he was down, and stuck him full of holes.

The home was in a little dip in this street, like a shallow saucer. Also occupying this shallow saucer, next door to the Kreis family, was another called Grimsby. The Grimsby family comprised mother, father and two children, a boy and a girl, aged thirteen and fifteen years respectively, and named Matthew and Mavis, respectively.

The girl, Mavis, would so entirely fill this shallow saucer in Prince Alfred Street with pheromones that of a warm windless afternoon your normal heterosexual man might fall from his bicycle whilst navigating it. Harm could come to a lad in this depression. As Odysseus and his men taking passage past the Sirens, so one's comrades would have to rope one to one's cycle, whilst stopping their own noses with beeswax. To cross this dense miasma on foot, your average heterosexual youth would don gumboots. Each pace would produce a sound as of a cow pulling its foot from mud, such was the density of these vapours.

At times, from the middle of the depression, this hypothetical heterosexual lad might catch sight of the Br*ss**r* and P*nt**s of the Grimsby daughter pegged upon the Grimsby clothes line, whereupon his retinae would become so infused with blood, and the world so red to his gaze, that he might drop senseless to the ground, and awake enchanted in the presence of Circe herself, himself having been metamorphosed into a swine.

This daughter, Mavis – I having had a serious traffic accident in this dip in P A Street one afternoon, and having received emergency treatment in one of the family bedrooms and fallen into deep traumatic sleep – this daughter Mavis, I say, was confronted by one of her neighbours who sought to borrow a cup of sugar, which he thought might be stored in that same room.

Jesus, he said, why are you here? I'm not Jesus, said I, and I am here because I have had a most dangerous puncture and come to this kind family for succour and aid. Why are you here, then?

My ma needs sugar. We've run out.

Balls, man, we both happened to say more or less simultaneously.

So we push in silence through the hedge and make our way to where Mama Kreis is brewing up afternoon tea. I may have been metamorphosed into a swine but I'm not yet such a swine as to ask about her stock of sugar. Hullo boys! she cries, for she is a good family woman and very socially minded, Hullo boys, I'm just brewing up some tea here, for now, and baking a batch of scones for this evening. I've invited Matthew and Mavis over from next door for a good game of rummy this evening, they're such nice kids, aren't they Andrew, hey?

Ja, he says.

You must come! she says to me.

Ja, I say.

So I go, and here we sit, then, and play this rummy. Mama Kreis is at the head of the table, and she's keeping score with all these pads and pencils and things, and there's this nice big tray of scones and crunchies and crumpets and stuff, and a lot of jam and whipped cream and all things lekker on a tea trolley on one side there, and down the table on either side of Mama Kreis are a lot of enthusiastic family kids, both families, and at the opposite end sits Mavis, with Cheese and me on either side.

So we play this rummy, and after a bit the pheromones start to exude from Ol' Mavis, man, and they boil up through the top of her polo-neck jersey and spread out like a fair-weather cumulus atop a thermal, and I lose concentration entirely on this game of cards and carry on in a merely automatous fashion.

It's your turn! calls Mama Kreis. No, ja, I say. I'm just working this out in mathematical, that is, probability theory, gimme a minute. But I play any old card, because on my oath I don't care if I win or lose this game since my concentration is upon the knee of Mavis Grimsby, all the bone and ligament and tendon of it, and my hand is on its way to where the the contractile muscle starts, and the lymphatic overlay, and a little fat and subcutaneous things, and the skin, and the rose which is the source of all true joy in this world, and just as I feel on my knuckles the brush of some fine hairs unconfined by her broeks I feel also a set of coarse, unlovely objects there. I grip them. They are the knuckles of Cheese Kreis.

I take hold of these knuckles and we sit there like a pair of imperialists eyeballing each other across the Congo River; De Brazza and Stanley. Our game of rummy has become a mere mockery, since I am playing with only my left hand and Cheese with only his right. Mavis wins hands down, every game. So long as the delights of this world shower upon her, why not enjoy a rousing game of fortune?

We confer, and conclude that if we can be friendly partners in the management of Mary, we can be also in that of Mavis. It proves a good working arrangement, and more efficient with only two managers rather than six, more streamlined; though Mavis, I sometimes felt, might have preferred the greater Board of Directors. But Cheese and I did what was expected of us to keep her contented, propelling a steady stream of sperm over accretion disc and event horizon, and generating such vast quantities of radiant energy, including X-rays, as could be picked up by small boys with crystal sets i' th' antipodes.

We thought there might be a problem of blocking drains with expended French Letters, and for a while contemplated burying them, but very deep, for they had a half-life of a hundred years or so. The energy thus wasted, properly harnessed, might well have saved Maritzburg from the dreadful atmospheric pollution of today.

* * *

Well, now, the system we devised was a good one and all went very harmoniously for many, many months, more than a year, in fact. I soon found that pheromones were good for the asthma, if not an outright cure, and Mavis, I must say, looked the living picture of robust health, what with all the exercise and deep breathing. Cheese was criticised for the declining quality of his rugby, though, which had fallen off markedly, I must admit, and was looking a little pale because he was spending more time indoors than was his wont, but he explained both of these symptoms by his doing a lot of Latin, so there was no fuss, really.

I, then, would be Mavis's friend on even days, and Cheese on odd. On weekends and school holidays we moved to a morning/afternoon schedule, but never rigid; I mean, we would exchange credits if Cheese had to play a game on Saturday, or if it were just such a beautiful morning that I just had to take Mary out for a trot. I mean, we didn't cavil about a little extra love going to this or that side, for love is free.

The Second Law of Thermodynamics, however, states that any closed physical system must fall into increased entropy, that is, disorder, unless opened to some external source of energy; and to keep this one bouncing along, as it were, we had had to open it to an inflow of energy of another type, namely money.

This is not to suggest that Mavis was a mercenary sort of girl, Lord love you no! She didn't demand bioscopes or chocolates and things; for her birthday we got a quilted bedspread from the Girls' High School jumble sale, which made her most happy.

No, the problem was that we couldn't afford the French Letters. We got them from a slot machine at Chetty's Bazaar, top of Church Street, at half-a-crown per packet of three, and since we emptied this shop's slot machine about twice a month that obviously meant finance way beyond our means. We had ceded our shares in Mary to Greenballs and Loony Bin, who had sustained their interest in her care, and in fact had got a nice bridle and saddle for her and made a really neat shelter; they allowed us still the use of her, so all was companionable and saved us the pocket-money, but not nearly enough.

WUW — D

My ma gave me money for a pair of good, reliable school shoes from Ogilvie's; I went down to the Indian shops and bought a horrible pair of papier maché sort of things and a gross of French Letters, a hundred and forty four, wholesale. This took care of the problem for a month or two, but it never really got solved: basically the problem was that if we went out and looked for after-hour jobs we'd have no time left for Mavis.

Cheese and I were not lovely to be near. Now that we had, as social workers so daintily put it, become sexually active, all our glands were pumping their varied aromatics and juices from every pore and orifice; when Mavis was with us and adding her hormonal aromas to the mix, people would move away, even in crowded places. At the bioscope we always had empty seats around us. On rummy evenings Mama Kreis would put out one of those lavvy air-freshener things and switch on a fan to blow from her to us. Where'er We Walked, Cool Gales would Fan the Glade.

What I am trying to get across here is that I was not really a candidate for romance. Yet it was Romance which solved our solvency problem, by my falling out of Mavis's bed, as it were, and into Love.

Everybody had heard the Hallelujah Chorus from Handel's Messiah, as indeed all have to this day. I had once heard it on the wireless sung by five thousand game rangers with a fifty-ton organ in a cave in the Yosemite National Park, U S A . So I had a pretty sound idea of what to expect when I saw a poster stuck to a pole advising the folk of Maritzburg that a recital of Handel's music was to be given one evening, by people who called themselves The London Baroque, with as soloist one Amy Shuard, soprano.

A great orchestra would be there, covering the terraces at the back of the City Hall stage with big and small tympani, and xylophones and tinkly things and something called a whip, also a cannon with gunpowder, permission of the fire chief, in case the 1812 Overture were to be played. Then, packed on the stage itself, rank after rank of strings, brass and woodwinds, while in front of this lot another bloke dressed up like Fred Astaire, only without the top hat, would wave a stick about and his hair would fall all over his eyes.

Behind this community of musicians would be the City Hall organ itself, the height of a three-storey building, at least, and in mass fifty tons, if not sixty. This layout I understood well from reading an encyclopaedia in bed on my days off school.

The City Hall I knew end to end and top to bottom, from going to the art gallery upstairs, and from going on the hour to a huge ornate brass clock in a small room there to see a procession of little painted men march out and strike the hour with hammers. If you went up the back stairs to this clock, you could get into the auditorium from a door at the back of the room.

So I went through this door just before the concert started, in case the tickets were numbered, and just as the lights went dim and everyone was seated, I went down to the front of the balcony and got a nice seat there overlooking the stage, over on the side.

There on the stage sat a group of, I suppose, ten or so people in darkish clothes made of British wartime austerity cloth, which didn't take ironing too well. They sat relaxed and smiling at each other and the audience as they tuned their strings, waiting for the singer.

This pork-barrel of womanhood, a forty-four gallon oil-drum of it, would now appear and roll up to centre stage and wring her plantain digits over that flattish part of the satin covering of the great abdomen, where the great navel was.

An earsplitting cry of *Hallelujah!* would follow, with a ten-finger, two-foot, all-stops-out double-manual vibrato low-frequency earthquake blast from the three-storey sixty-ton Municipal Organ.

A pretty young woman appears in a very dainty navy blue dress, with white lace at neck and wrist. Very dainty indeed, and her hair done up away from her face, like Lana Turner's, only dark.

Is this it? I ask myself. Where's everybody? If I'd paid for my ticket I'd complain. But this must be Amy Shuard, because the audience is clapping. I clap too. She holds high her head and smiles. She parts her lips and sings Let the Bright Seraphim, and I bloody nigh fall off the balcony, true as God. I mean, how on earth can such a sound come out of a human being? How can anyone possibly throw back her head and open her mouth and hear that music come from her body? She is eine Nachtigall in voller Kehle, a Baroque nightingale in full song. Limpid, precise and passionate, the notes pour from her throat. A trumpet comes in and calls its challenge. It is the triumph of the Human Spirit! I have found song to be many artistic things, but this is more, it is Truth; listen to this, lad, and you will understand your whole life and the entire Universe. It is the fine chiselling of form until the truth is reached.

I get chicken skin on my limbs, and I want to weep.

I gape at her to catch every note. I swear that as she turns her head this way she turns it to sing to me. She has dared the U-boat infested oceans to do it. I am wholly immobilised by this woman. Paralysed. I can move only if she wants me to move. I will never do any other thing in my whole life ever but follow her wherever she goes, *wherever*, and listen to her singing.

I will forgo the crass company of oestrous women, and turn my mind away from lewd triumph of the flesh, especially the genitalia. I leave Cheese in sole possession of Mavis, a prisoner of his own prurience, unless he can co-opt a few members of his rugby team to bear some of the financial burden of French Letters necessary to keep her in good health.

Eventually he co-opts Loony Bin and Greenballs. It does Greenballs such a power of good that his knees straighten up and he puts on weight and becomes a big strong man. Mary reverts to her mastodon life, and walking about with her eyes shut.

But these changes and benefits are as nought to the huge reconstitution of my life. During this new metamorphosis I see in the Natal Witness that Miss Amy Shuard is to sing on the Durban South Beach on Sunday morning, in the tradition established by Dame Myra Hess, who would have her concert grand heaved on to the steps of Saint Paul's at lunch time during the Blitz on London, and add a little wonder to the leaden lives of the people.

We will have songs from light opera and the like; you know, Franz Lehar and that lot, including some of the melodies my ma has sung with a drop of the anti-oxidant in her. But how to get there? I have no money, none.

I tune up my ancient pushbike, cleaning the ball bearings in a tin of paraffin, sticking them back with grease and adjusting the cones fine fine so there is no wobble in the wheels, and practically no friction either. I dismantle the braking system entirely and reassemble it, nicely adjusted. Everything is cleaned, oiled, greased, efficient. The old grid has no rubber parts, except the tyres; rubber is scarce in the war. The pedals are of wood, as is half the saddle. This is a minimal bike; no mudguards, no lights, no reflectors, nothing, nothing, nothing, and but a single Amalaita gear of 48:14. This bike, ou maat, is mean.

I pack iron rations and jersey and mac in my school bag and buckle it over the bar, and I'm off to Durban fifty-four miles away at four on Saturday morning, with asthma muti in my pocket just in case and ten bob in advance on next month's pocket money. I have no asthma, but some interesting leg cramps along the way, but never to worry, for that you drink black tea with plenty of sugar and salt. People whose hearts are as full as mine don't give a hoot about small distress like cramps. On, on; Beauty beckons!

So I'm about an hour out of town at first light, and I find myself in dense, opaque mist, low cloud, with absolutely zero visibility, and just jolly lucky it wasn't back there earlier when it was dark, because I have no light on this pushie, and I'd have had to sit somewhere and wait. But I'm in full rhythm now, all the hinges working and the plumbing pumping the juices around and the ventilation system with all its fans blowing, and it's quite cosy in the mist, actually, with the hiss of the tyres on the tarmac and the sound of my own puffing uphill the only sound other than the plinking of droplets from the wattle leaves and the chirping of small frogs proclaiming their territories. All sound dampened, it's like riding through an eiderdown.

By dead reckoning I know where I am; Umlaas Road, Camperdown, Cato Ridge and Harrison Flats, for these are days before the N3, hey? and I'm riding over the crests on a single strip of tar. Khefuza! Khefuza! Khefuza! I puff inside the eiderdown, to keep the rhythm. So around eight or so I know I'm pushing up Inchanga, because she's due, but also because this two-mile pitch is so steep I'm not only walking, I'm creeping.

And as I come over the top everything coincides: behold the glorious sun darts her beams upon the world!

I come out of the mist as my glycogen stores are depleted and I'm starting to burn body fat and getting pumped full of endor-phines, and friend, there is no trip on the face of this planet like an endorphine trip. My glands are squirting out the morphine and my brain has the receptor cells for it, thank you, so I am a sort of one-person drug ring, grower, pusher and user, and I need neither needle nor smoke, for the whole thing was intravenous from the start.

I look down on the Valley of a Thousand Hills, and there are a thousand of them in the early light, disappearing way beyond the Umgeni valley on the remote horizon, into Zululand and the end-less ancient bitter beautiful landscape of Africa. Aloft the early rap-tors are getting the chicken, and the Zulu kids shout from hilltop to remote hilltop, as only they can, over valleys still stuffed full of cloud. Otherwise no sound to break the brittle silence of the clear, fecund, wondrous morning.

Wem Gott will rechte Gunst erweisen,
Den schickt er in die Weite Welt,
Dem will er seine Wunder weisen
In Berg und Wald und Strom und Feld.

I sit there with my heart full of fruitless love for the gnädige schöne Frau, and eat my breakfast of bread and South West pilchards, and a tomato and some cold tea from the water bottle with sugar and salt for the cramp. There is no sense of the sorrow of unrequited love, for I'm not so bloody stupid, man! This is an adult woman with a career. There will be no contact. She will be on her way without a personal word to me. The reward is of total dedication to something which for the first time ever I can absolutely believe in, mixed with this lovely ingredient of sexuality. To think you can really love without sexuality is silly, as silly as believing you can really have good sex without love.

I make my way with a heart full of song, Tirra Lirra, and confidence, and expectation of great joyous surprise, and for the first time in my whole brief life I am at one with the Universe, if not its master, and I laugh a great triumphant laugh as I hurtle down Field's Hill with the wind tearing at my hair, and I wave a fist in the slipstream and give the cry of the triplane pilot when he spots the Camels down there: Es geht los!

***

I arrive in Durbs with plenty of afternoon light still, because it is summer-time and a good season for being in love.

I chain the old grid up to one of the wooden piles of the Coo-ee Tea Room, which stands on the beach, and towards sundown I go off and buy fish and chips and a bottle of strawberry Sun Crush. I watch the dolphins beyond the white water as I eat my supper, then I go and kip in the sand under the Coo-ee and wait for Amy in the morning. I'm up with the beach cleaners, early, and go for a bathe in the breakers and a fresh-water shower out of doors, and let my shorts dry on me, since I don't have swimming trunks. I give my shirt a rinse too, because it has fifty-four miles of guff in it. I flap it about in the early off-shore wind, and in half an hour it's dry enough to wear.

By this time all is about ready at this wooden stage they have on the beach there for the holiday crowds. I buy some more fish and chips and some Better Kind Peanuts, and I've got through the fish course and into the monkey-nuts when she arrives on this stage, and she's standing up there so close we could have a conversation if it weren't for the din of the breakers. She kicks off with some Richard Tauber songs, and when she gets to the one about Une Chambre Separeé, she looks at me and smiles with her singing lips, and makes a gesture with her hand which tells me she is singing this for me, maybe because everybody else is there for the sun and candy floss and I'm the only one listening, maybe because she recognises mine as the pimply face from the balcony in Maritzburg, maybe because she can see I'm in love with her.

So then there's this pause while she drinks something from a glass and talks to the little ensemble there who are making the music, and she comes up front again and this time she gives me the smile straight, with a gesture of the hand and a nod which says This One is Just for You, Pal, and she sings for me the same song from Die Lustige Wittwe as my ma has sung when de-oxidised, only I've never heard it like this, and she is giving me a jewel I shall carry about with me for the rest of my life.

She sings against the crash of the sea and the gusting of the wind, but it makes her the more a part of Nature, and I realise a great truth, that I'm going to love this song forever, because I loved her when she sang it for me, and I do, to this day, though I know it is not the music of the H-moll Messe.

I was sixteen. I could see no advantage whatever in being sixteen, except this. I still see no advantage in it, except that. Whatever happened to me that I am unable to love so totally, and undemandingly? I am jealous of myself, if you can picture something so absurd. That kid over there doesn't have these areas of dead muscle all about his heart where the partial failures have left their scars.

The music you love, you love because of your feelings at the time of hearing it. If you don't believe that, you might as well go and study Dialectical Materialist Musicology in a College for the Deaf.

* * *

Well, all the adventures of body and heart here recounted, and especially the last, had not done my school career much good. I had been content in the last years to loll about with the steerage passengers, but I'd fallen down the scuppers now, and sloshed about in the bilges with a lot of dead vermin and general effluvia. The thought of any Latin examination filled me with gloom, but the final in December caused me to lie sleepless in bed, bathed in a cold quicksilver sweat. In my nightmares I was forty-five, moving into middle age and still trying to claw my way out of this macho sink, still slashing and burning my way through De Bello Gallico with this cricket-playing baboon. It was already Easter. Eight months left. Hell!

Ja, I put it pretty glibly when I said I wasn't fooled by the hopelessness of my affection for this lovely lady. There were other things beside hope; an expectation of some further condition of mind, some development perhaps, or some conclusion. But there was no conclusion, just an end. This really was coitus interruptus of the heart.

I would give one last great heave, though; I would by some superhuman exertion sublimate my passionate energy into a great physical triumph. I would get together what gear I could find and make an assault on iNtabayikonjwa, the Mountain of Thunder, the Mountain at which You Must Not Point, for it Causes Bad Weather. I would get so engrossed in physical effort, and so tough, that I would feel no pain of the heart. I would reverse the process of not feeling cramp because I was so much in love. Then I would pull up my socks, put shoulder to the wheel, acquit myself like a man, grind my way through the entire Latin syllabus and clear off out of this miserable male cemetery.

I would end the gnawing process of spiritual death. I would define my own self and my own triumphs from now on, and if there were none it would be from my own bad judgment. The perils of this dangerous place would vanish.

I would leave this place on my own terms. But on with the history.

I put this mountain plan to Cheese, who was a good confidant and could feel the hurt in me. Three things, he said: first, you do not ever climb eleven thousand feet alone; second, you don't do it without full alpine gear when winter is dropping its hints; third, he knew a better place. Well what the hell, I'd leave him to it if he wanted to nurse my body and bruised spirit. He wanted to prove his friendship? Okay, he could come and be my keeper.

Cheese being Cheese, however, I found myself soon enough so immersed in organisation that the pain was getting a bit less even before we left. All this was stolen time, let me emphasise, and stolen from Poepie Pope . I would show the sod I could make it without him.

So Cheese tells me about this better place he's been to, but not quite, because he's only been to the bottom of the last bit at seven thousand feet; though the way up from there looks a really bas-tardly proposition to eleven thou, and if it's suffering I want, well, this is my place.

And he tells me the only reason why I chose iNtabayikonjwa was because of its romantic name, and I confess, this is true. The lot he has in mind has really poxy names, like Champagne Castle, while if there's anything you need at the top there it is not cham-pagne but a mug of hot soup to save you from hypothermia. Then there's Dragon's Back like we're a bunch of Chinese, and Cathkin Peak, but you'll never know who Cathkin ever was unless you look him up in a history book. He won't even mention the name Monk's Cowl, it is so embarrassing.

But the worst, he says, is the disaster which has befallen Sterkhoring, a great strong horn, an erection, sticking up into the womb of Heaven, and which is now called Mount Memory, for the poor dumb sweethearts and husbands who died in the First WW and are busy dying in This WW. Somebody got a memorial cheap, we conclude, and I think of my Uncle Jimmy, who would rather have had a few extra quid for my ma than a free mountain, any day.

These peaks and crests form three sides of a deep, steep, nar-row amphitheatre, called most inappropriately of all Eland Grove by some, though the eland seen there must have had baboon's feet to get up this trough of rough, rounded river rocks flung down the valley, and must have learned to eat scorpions as the babs do, for the only vegetation there is on a lot of disillusioned-looking pro-teas which feel they would on balance rather have sprung from seed elsewhere on the mountain, anywhere else, or perhaps not even have sprung at all, such is their plight. Thrashed by hail, split by lightning and pounded by further rock-fall as cataclysmic flash-floods come hammering down the basin, they do not present to the eye the lush and peaceful scene associated with those gentle giants.

Some call this place Keith Bush Hut, these days. There is no hut any more, for whatever reason, but some unlucky lad lost his life hereabouts, and sorry that all he got was a few sheets of corrugat-ed aluminium. If he'd been important enough, and a soldier, he'd have had a bit of Drakensberg named after him, like the military man, Gray, who scored a whole pass.

Anyway, that, Gray's Pass, is where we're going.

The relative who had taken Cheese there was a Mountain Club

man, and had forbidden further progress because his young bones would warp, his musculature go all slack and his heart become enlarged, according to the barbarous superstitions of the day. But Cheese and I are going to show a few people a few things.

When we've got all our absolutely essential clothing and tent-age and sleeping gear and stove and fuel together, we have left six pounds of load each for food, because we aim to take twenty-four pounds apiece, including the bags. First Aid is reduced to a roll of sticky plaster for bleeding things, Dettol ointment for septic things, and a bloody big pink butazolidine pill we had got from a vet for Mary on the last trip. This was anti-traumatic treatment for racehorses, so they wouldn't go mad with the pain of injury whilst on the way to the surgery, and have to be put down. We calculat-ed on the ratio of 6:1 in body mass between Mary and us, which allowed a safety factor, and reckoned that a good bite of about a sixth of this thing would get one of us with a broken limb or the like safely off the mountain. There were no helicopters in those days.

So we load up oatmeal, lots of it, as basic grub, spaghetti, and Bisto gravy powder for flavour, dried peas, and some sticks of bil-tong, which was cheap in those days and is expensive now for rea-sons I am unable to comprehend. The only heavy item is onions, and we take one per day, plus an extra for emergency rations, mak-ing five. For our first night, before the carrying really starts, we have each a whole tin of bully beef, an avo each, and a loaf of bread between us. Plenty, plenty salt, for the cramps, and asthma muti. We're away. It goes wild! Es geht los!

There weren't many cars at all on the roads in those days, because of the petrol rationing, so we start our hitch-hiking at first light on Town Hill opposite the Show Grounds. We have made a big sign on a piece of cardboard which says Monk's Cowl via Estcourt, which we reckon is a good day's hitching, and we stand there looking so young and appealing with our rucksacks and water bottles and things on the bridge over the Dorp Spruit that almost every vehicle stops, and we get the feeling that some of the drivers would as lief chuck out their present passengers for the chance of giving us a lift. And so los does it gehen that we are at the Monk's Cowl forestry station at ten in the morning, the last lift coming from a farmer who used twenty miles' worth of rationed Diesel to get us there.

Thus, you see, we realise that we have half a day extra available to us for the climb, which otherwise we'd have spent travelling. So we don't bother about base camp. Here you can step straight out of your car and start climbing and this we do, and push on past places pretty soon with really corny names like Crystal Falls and Arthur's Seat, King Arthur that is, himself of the round table, because we're at the level where hotel folk come with sunshades and packed lunches.

By early afternoon we're up to about eight thousand feet on the contour path running Nor'-Nor'-East, right under the brow of the escarpment, and at about four we reach iNtunje, the eye of the needle, a column which has collapsed against its neighbour and eroded and fused in there to make the hole. The only good name so far.

This being a blissful balmy summer afternoon, we bivvy on the grass and lean on our elbows and tell jokes and sing a couple of Mountain Club songs which Cheese has got from his uncle. Even from here the view is great, halfway across Natal towards distant Greytown, where vast grass fires block out the horizon with smoke grubby pink from the setting sun. A secretary bird lands on its great long anti-snake legs and stares at us. We eat up all the bully and avoes and half a loaf, and sleep in the grass along with some oribi on the next hill, so distended we can't roll over. We have a laugh at that too. A happy evening.

During the night we wake for a wee and a look at the stars, but the stars, all hundred billion of them in the galaxy, we don't even notice because of the condition of the moon, which is full and has a complete double halo around it; two ice-rainbows in the middle of the night! Ice-crystals at thirty thousand feet, what can it mean? We find out, all right.

Trouble is, we arrive at the bottom of Gray's Pass at noon next day, all because our lifts were so good. Oh ja, I forgot to explain that this military man called Gray went to nip up the berg to the north of Langalibalele and come south and capture him, but he couldn't even find the pass, let alone Langalibalele. So I believe. The problem with naming airports, roads, mountains and the like after people is that within one generation nobody knows who on earth they were, nor what they did. Nor does anybody care.

So we're at the bottom of this pass, then, in that very un-Arcadian grove where the mythical plantigrade eland have their being. But are we going to be all wise because it's only midday, and have a nice loaf and loll about and brace ourselves for the pass, which is a day's haul, tomorrow? No, we are not. We are going to push on, and reck not whether we get caught half way by nightfall. This is a nasty steep bitch of a pass; not a sheer face, of course, and no rope-work, but steep enough to have no grass in parts because it gets torn off by the wind, so one has to navigate from one small stone cairn to the next, marking the route, and there's four thousand feet of it. So we're off and up. Even at nine thou the lack of oxygen is noticeable; not critical, but you notice it's not like riding a bike to Durbs. We stop and puff every ten minutes. We reach a traverse of rock and scree, over towards where the cleft of the pass starts.

At about four thirty pee em the sun disappears behind the escarpment, and we think we might just be having a problem, because we're exactly half-way up and our old animal instincts start telling us that when the sun is down you think of making a nest, and the only creature that could make a nest here is a lizard, or perhaps a dassie, because the average angle of the surface of the planet around here is about sixty degrees. And as we think this instinctual thing the wind winds up to about eighty knots in ten minutes, and we realise why vegetation has a problem in these parts.

We're on rock now, and we make off to the right where there's a little vertical bit about ten feet high, with water dribbling down it, and what you might optimistically call a flattish area beneath it, where the level is about thirty degrees. We crouch there and make a plan, and we need one soon because the temperature is zero and dropping, according to the thermometer I have stolen from Dog MacDougal. We won't get down again before nightfall, there's no way to pitch a tent here, for we're on solid rock, and for sure we can't bivvy. We have to make some sort of shelter, and right soon, in this force 8 gale, and we can't unload our tent and spread it flat and work something out, because the wind will zap it all away and over the six-hundred-foot sheer drop just twenty paces away on our left here and we'll then die of exposure, most certainly.

We sit, one on the gear while the other creeps about collecting rocks, and slowly we unpack the tent and put a rock on each part as it unpacks, and eventually we have it all out, without poles, and rocks all round with everything inside, bags, grub, sleeping stuff, clothes, everything, like a great big pie under the lee of this little face in the thrashing wind. We lay a quick row of rocks across the bottom of the pie, the biggest we can lift with our numb fingers,

106

to sort of stand on whilst trying to sleep, and not slide down the mountain as we squirm about. We crawl in there and put on every wearable thing, and make a sort of hollow space between the bags. Most insulation we put underneath, where heat drains away. There won't be a lot of sleep.

Now to get as much heat into us as we can before the long night starts. The temperature is minus twelve. I hold the torch while Cheese wriggles out and smashes some ice from the rock wall with his sheath knife. We make a little cavity inside the pie and there boil up a quart or so of porridge, and we keep the Primus going while we eat it. We curl up, lepel lê, lying like spoons, with one sleeping bag over us and all else below, and set-tle down to a hideous night. Eventually that strange torpor that comes with fear gives an hour or so of frozen sleep some time after midnight.

At very first light I'm out and smashing off more ice for tea, fast, before my fingers freeze. All we can think of is a piece of flat ground, where we will be able to handle the weather. We eat the remaining half loaf with the tea, and off! The wind soon backs through ninety degrees and comes howling down the mountain; if we hadn't made the early start we'd have lost the protection of the little rock wall. We realise our gear is inadequate, and if we continue to lose body heat at the present rate there will be a good chance of hypothermia. We eat boiled sweets for energy.

After an hour or so we reach the cleft of the pass itself, and turn left. The wind is really blasting down here, with nothing to check it, and still sub-zero, and though the sun is now up it has no heat, and though our heads are wrapped up in spare shirts and shorts and things over our long woollen scarves, we can still feel the heat draining out of us. But at least we have tumbled rocks underfoot now, and don't have to have our ankles twisted to the slope as we struggle against the wind. And half an hour or so up ahead we can see a sort of rock feature sticking up in the cleft like a clitoris, with what may be a flattish part facing us, and perhaps we can stop there and eat, and give our bodies a bit of fuel. This becomes our immediate haven. As we lean into the blast our faces are a hand's breadth or two from the basalt face, and our pace is about six inches.

We are distinctly light-headed as we arrive at this rock, but it does indeed have a vertical flat wall, seven or eight feet across, and some scrubby growth in the lee. We dump our packs to either side and flop down between them and rub our cheeks. In between a couple of tiny bushes we find some air still enough for the primus, and as we light her up the sun gives us its first meagre warmth, and the drainage is halted, though not yet reversed. We make porridge, thin, so we can drink it hot with plenty of sugar and salt, and while we're busy with this we see way down below four figures coming up the pass. Our sense of adventure has returned a little with the sun. After an hour or so these figures are close enough to be seen as face-climbers, fully equipped with true alpine gear; ropes, helmets, Eispickels, crampons, the lot, and bundles of pitons jingling at their waists. Goggles, too, and their faces masked against the freezing windlash.

By the time they reach us we have got the big pot out in this tiny cavity of quiet air behind the rock in the hissing wind, and the ice all melted and the peas all boiled with one of the onions all chopped up and plenty of Bisto and salt. They snoef it as they come up the pass. You blokes want some soup? we ask as they come abreast. Oh brother, soup! Incredulity. They have their mugs out and their mitts off and they're warming their frozen fingers on the mugs, and we're all six huddled behind the little face as the sun gives us all a really nice squirt of warmth, and it's bloody close and comradely, though nobody's talking because this isn't conversation weather. Whisky? One of them pulls out a water-bottle of it, and we all have a noggin.

You fellas are lucky you're going down, in those clothes! one of them says. We're not, we're going up. No, balls, man, we didn't see you at Keith Bush last night? No, we were half-way up. You slept half-way up, in *those clothes?* Where the hell did you put a tent? And why aren't you dead, you silly buggers? We tell them of our last camp, and they're really perturbed, like maybe they'll have the unpleasant duty of reporting corpses on the mountain pretty soon. No, man, we'll show you a cave to sleep in tonight, and tomorrow get down straight away, please, man!

So we brace ourselves after a bit, and thrust out again into the screaming wind, leaning into it as our clothes slat and batter about our bodies. Then it starts to sleet, as if we weren't wretched enough, the drops blowing parallel to the ground down the pass, and suddenly Bluppity-blup-blup, the sound of running gumboots, and we damn near collide with three Basotho men running out of the rain and down the pass.

Mountain men! A rugged lot. These are bundled in blankets

and balaclavas, with grass ropes at their waists and pangas in their hands and a pack of yellow dogs with curly tails, real izikhodoye, African pie dogs, cow- or camel-shit eaters, and this is a poaching party off to clear snares in the Natal forestry reserve. Hoarse male cries of greeting, and they're away into the mist.

The defile of the pass at last levels out, but we're still leaning into the wind. The relief of walking flattish is offset by a new misery. We're wet as well as cold; the wind squeezes the melting sleet through every chink and gap in our school raincoats. The face-climbers are off to club buddies farther south teaching abseiling, but before turning off they escort us to the iNkosazana Cave, a shelf under a low ridge, with frozen drips on the ceiling and the floor covered in frozen baboon and dassie shit and a great slab of ice in the middle of the floor. We're lucky it's all frozen, they say, because it doesn't stink.

Our bags we drop to one side, while on the other we kick a place clear of frozen faeces to make a place for the tent. It's all rock in here, of course, so there's no way to use tent pegs, and we're away to get rocks instead. We get it up, sort of, though it's all slack and twisted, but that's nothing, man, what we need just now is a home, any old home! Then we're down to a little tarn about fifty yards away for water, and as we're putting the bungs in our water bottles the cloud comes down at the snap of a finger, just like that, dense, dense, and we don't know where the cave is, exactly. We then do the only wise thing we've done on the whole trip; I'll go for the cave and you stay here, and we'll keep shouting to each other till I find it, says Cheese. Good search system. Eventually he does and he calls to me and I go to him. Inside the cave we can barely see the tent.

We creep inside while the wind slams it about, even inside the cave. The sleet is in there too, with the wind, but it's turbulent wind, which won't knock us flat, just keep us nice and wet. Cheese laces the tent up, while I stuff the ventilation holes with wet clothing, for the spray is coming in there too. But okay, man, it will clear up tomorrow and we can dry out a bit.

But it doesn't clear up tomorrow, nor thereafter; the sleet becomes snow and the temperature drops to minus seventeen, and we lie in damp bags and damp clothes and freeze while we eat up all our food and writhe about day and night trying to find some relief from the really frightful cold. We massage each other's feet and make Biblical jokes, we load damp socks on the pot while we cook. Nothing helps. We need not distinguish between night and day; we sleep when we can, in desperate snatches. We make a set of dominoes of cardboard from the dried-pea box. Nothing helps.

On night three Cheese says to me Would you like a drink, man? and I say to him ar fuck off whaddya mean a drink what the hell is happening to your sense of fucken humour man? And he says No serious, and he produces from amongst his goeters a wee one-tot bottle of Tequila and a tiny little green lemon, and says to me Pass the salt. What appeals to me about this ou is he's so *weird*, man, I mean, he must have known that amount of alcohol wasn't going to do any good; what he was telling me at this ultimate moment was that there was still a civilisation out there to which we belonged, and that with a bit of luck we might just get back to it. And how did he know to save it up to this moment?

But we are now really at the end. We have eaten all our food except one onion. We have no fuel in the primus. Tomorrow morning we leave this place, without breakfast, without warmth, without any source of energy, and if we have to try for the top of the pass by stand-and-shout in the blizzard, that's what we'll do, whatever the likelihood of getting lost and dying. We curl up in total misery and squirm about together through the night, until in the early hours we fall into desperate frozen sleep, maybe the comatose sleep forever of hypothermia.

But no sooner asleep than something terrible happens. Something's on fire! I stick my head out of the tent, half-stunned with sleeplessness and hunger. The sun is shining straight into the cave, there's not a breath of air and the baboon/dassie shit is already starting to smell.

Hey Cheese! What's wrong, man? By this time I'm already out of the tent and the cave. Come, come! We stumble blinking over to the tarn. Its surface is frozen an inch thick. We break loose a huge sheet of it, like plate glass from a shop window, and I hold it up and pull faces through it at Cheese. He takes it and has a turn, pressing his open mouth against it and blowing while he squints his eyes, and I can see right down his throat and I tell him he hasn't brushed his teeth recently. We stroll over to the edge of the escarpment, the sheer two thousand foot face before the mea-gre grass starts, and it's like walking to the edge of a table, it's so sudden, and there it all is, the whole of our entire lives at our feet, and right at the limit of our sight, though perhaps we imagine it because the air is so crisp and crystalline, is the ocean, eleven thousand feet below.

Nothing grows more than six inches above the ground here, not even a small conifer which creeps a foot or two close to the rock, and down the prevailing wind. Down there all is still frozen hard, only the tips of the short yellow grass are thawed. The wind has scoured the place, all snow has been ripped away over the edge. We get out everything from the cave, the lot, the last little bit, and spread it about in the sun and still air, and stroll over to look at a frozen waterfall like wax dribbling down a candle, and feel really cocky that we're so nice and warm with our hands in our pockets.

But hungry, oh brother, hungry! We give our gear an hour or so to dry. We've still got a day's travel to where there's even a chance of food, but we sit at the edge of the tarn and watch the ice-rats sitting up on their haunches warming their bellies in the sun. The rocks where they live around the edge are beautifully placed, as if by design, and in amongst them the dwarf red-hot pokers grow. The tarn is about uniformly a foot deep and the water invisibly pure. The bottom is of coarse quartz sand, pristine, and level as if raked, and across it scuttle small translucent crabs. God must be Japanese, says Cheese.

So we bundle everything up, tight and trim, and we're down the pass still revelling in the sun and really saucy, and about five hundred feet down we come across the frozen corpse of one of the Basuto poachers, and that of his dog, too, plus a small oribi with the noose-marks about its neck. The buck is thawed out enough for us to hack and wrench off a hind leg with the aid of the sheath knife, so we do that and leave the rest for the birds and babs. By the time we reported it, they would probably have eaten him too. As I say, there were no choppers in those days, and I don't think people were so fussy about rescuing dead bodies.

Back down at Keith Bush, we waste no time: Cheese sets about the braai with the skeletal remains of the poor desperate proteas there, while I skin this leg of oribi and stab holes all around it and shove in bits of our surviving onion. Our stomachs are rumbling something desperate, but we discipline ourselves and let the fire really burn down to a nice deep bed of coals, and meanwhile we carve a pair of nice artistic Y-pieces from local sticks to make a rotisserie for the leg of venison. We braai her up really lekker, and from time to time sprinkle her with a bit of water or rub her down

111

with the skin, for this is dry meat; but then what the hell about dry, anyway, we have plenty of saliva, and appetite to fill in the shortcomings. We feel like Henry VIII, but we don't chuck our bones to any deerhound; there's a pound or two of meat left there, so we shave it all off and keep it for padkos.

chapter seven

I don't know how these devices work. I suppose the instinct which made me do this Berg thing was that which makes a dog eat grass to get discomfort out of its digestive tract, or perhaps makes an ostrich eat stones to reduce its gizzard contents to manageable condition. And believe me, getting half frozen to death is as distasteful to me as is the consumption of cellulose to a carnivore or the swallowing of basalt to a herbivore.

My idea of a bloody good time is to loll about in bedclothes all stuck together with natural emulsions, with a bottle or two of Cape stein wine on the bedside table and Romantic music with bits that you can hum along with whilst running the fingers through somebody's hair or lightly scratching the lumbar region of the back. Actually to enjoy the agonies of fruitless love is kinky; it is to enjoy hanging by the balls. Yet I know people who fancy it. These are the slapgat dilettantes who give Romanticism a bad name.

In my gizzard I had had a great solid lump of longing, swallowed whole, with the most agonising heartburn. Now I had ground it up in there to bite-size bits with chunks of ice and fragments of oribi bone. What nourishment!

But enough of Philosophy, Romance, Love and Coitus, I say! We are in the iron grip of reality. In two months the final exam is going to hit me, and I am going to fail it, because with Poepie Pope's help I know sweet bugger-all about the Latin language, and with Poepie Pope kicking it all about with his cricket boots I'm not surprised it is a dead language.

But wait. When reason and intuition have failed, there's always crime. I am going to cheat my way through this. I do some reckoning and I calculate that if I get a hundred per cent on the Latin–English translation, and zero on the English–Latin, I will pass, and with the minuscule bit of grammar that I know I might get a percentage point or two which will help in case I don't make the hundred with the Latin–English.

Staan uitmekaar uit! Laat die ding piek en tjoes! Step aside! Let the dog see the rabbit! I get a mapping pen from my sister Betty. She does piddling girls' subjects at school, like Art, and not truly vital productive male stuff like Latin, so she has this pen, which I borrow, and I write out small, small, on tiny bits of paper, translations of virtually the whole of the Vergil, Ovid and Julius Caesar set for the exam; the Aeneid, Metamorphoses and De Bello Gallico, and I stick these scraps of paper in all available interstices in my clothing, in sleeves, turn-ups, cuffs and inside my necktie itself.

Then I set about systematising my tactics. Let's see, if I have this bit that goes like this here, and that bit which means that there... but then again, if the bit that goes like this is there, then all I have to remember is to slide out that bit that means that here..., and after a week or so of this jiggery pokery I realise that I am so familiar with it all from this criminal scrutiny that I know it all by heart anyway, and the cheating is redundant, and not only that, I find that all these stamp-size fragments which have been the instruments of intended fraud in fact have a certain appeal, and I start to read them for fun, and find that I actually *like* them, and I sit about wasting valuable crime-time whilst reading the stuff and feeling a pang for the sad fateful love of Pyramus and Thisbe, so much like Romeo and Juliet, and swallowing a small unmanly lump in the throat.

In fact, to this day I remember much of it, and I here quote without looking it up, I swear to God, a fragment from the Aeneid, which describes the winds imprisoned by Aeolus in a cave, whence he can release them at the thrust of a spear, and in fact describes also my own desperate condition in trying to escape from Wolseley College:

Ille indignante, magno cum murmure, circum claustra fremunt.

Indignantly, with a great murmur, around the bolt they fret.
How's that?

Anyway, I go and write this exam, and I really confuse the examiner, for sure, because I give her on one hand a lot of dog-Latin such as would cause an illiterate legionary mirth, and on the other

114

a lot of hypersensitive stuff about why the juice of the mulberry is as the blood of star-crossed lovers, and this, ou maat, is a really heart-wrenching translation.

So she gives me a good mark, because maybe that's how she found her way into the love of Latin, and I'm away. Los hom! Hy's vry!

For a few days I wander about really confused. They say old folk often die as soon as they retire, because they can't find anywhere to fit in, and I'm like that now, except I have no intention of dying; it's just that the world is so propvol of easeful and engaging things, and I can't yet believe I'm away from the arbitrary discipline and the sneering ugly furtive homosexual innuendo. Never again will I get the fly of my trousers ripped open and have to understand on the turn what part this is of the male ritual, dogs sniffing each others scrota. Is this a menace from a superior dog demanding submission? Is it to triumph over my sexuality, or is it perhaps the salutation of an equal, inviting me perhaps to rip open his fly too? but then again it may be a tentative invitation to romance? All these things one has to understand to be part of, to survive in, such an all-male madhouse. One has to be quick at body language, facial expression, tone of voice.

One *had* to, that is; but now no more!

Nou ja, I dwaal about Maritzburg for a bit and wonder why I'm walking on this side of the street but then again would it make any difference to the condition of the Universe if I walked on the other side? And after some days or weeks or does it matter anyway I dwaal into Shuter's book shop and buy a nice drawing book and I dwaal off to my ma's pal Auntie Jean's place in Montpelier Road in Durban, near Mitchell Park, and I spend my days drawing in the little zoo they have there: buck and birds and a bloody great elephant called Nellie who plays a harmonica with her trunk while she takes kids for rides. And while I fill this book with animal drawings and loaf about and sing a merry song because the sun is shining on me, I notice something abnormal is going on, and I give it some thought, and after a week or so, that is a month or so since I left school, I realise what this abnormal thing is, and the abnormal thing is that there is no sign of any asthma about, nor any suggestion that it might ever come about, and indeed it has not come about to this day, fifty years on, indeed more.

As I realise this I start having some really naughty ideas, there and then; and there and then I pack up pencils and pad, and I'm back to Auntie Jean and I tell her Farewell, I must be off to Maritzburg, for duty calls.

When I get off the train there I don't bother to go home, but make my way straight to the Kreis family, who are settling down to afternoon tea and another load of crumpets and stuff. Hey, Cheese, c'mere! We move outside, and he's still chomping on this big spherical doughnut with sugar all over it. What's it man? He has picked up the sense of excitement. What's it, hay? Let's go and join the Air Force, man! What about your asthma then? It's gone, but I'll take a chance. Okay, when? Now. Okay. He stuffs the remainder of the doughnut in his gob and goes inside to wash it down with a last sluk of tea. See you, Mom, he says, and we're away.

The recruiting office is a prefab in the grounds of the Supreme Court opposite the City Hall. Outside, an artistic marble angel on a monument casts upon a number of marble heroes of the Zulu War, white ones of course, with their eyeballs rolled up as in Bernini, a marble wreath in memory of the Dead, whose names are inlaid in black upon the white of the stone.

To get to this monument we pass beneath a smallish colony-sized Triumphal Arch, the inscription on which informs us that They Shall Not Grow Old As We That Are Left Grow Old, and gives us a list of those like Jimmy Brown who are in this felicitous condition of never growing old in consequence of the mustard gas. It is much longer than the list of the marble angel; in fact it is much much longer.

The Triumphal Arch has a few droopy flowers which the near-by florist has placed there because it's Friday and they're not going to make it through the weekend anyway, and I mean there is a war on and we must all do our bit you know.

Defending the marble angel is an iron cannon pointing at the pharmacy opposite, and which came from some brig or sloopan-tine or something, in Port Natal in Eighteen Oh Forty Two or something, which blew the shit out of some Zoolas or frontiers-men or some dreck hypothetically hostile to the Queen, or some-thing. Make your own colonial guess how it got here. Before the war we used to chuck thunder crackers down it on Guy Fawkes' night, but fireworks are history now; we're going to get the real thing, point five Browning machine gun ammunition and twenty mil cannon rounds with explosive heads.

So a military doctor asks us if we have ever suffered from any of the following: the Black Death, the Bloody Defluxions, the Dhobi's Itch or Asthma, and the answer to all these being No, we are now in the Air Force, he tells us, and ready to not grow old as he that is left grows old, pending a hell-out medical in Pretoria where it will be decided whether we will be with the unlucky erks who pull the chocks from under the wheels of the Spitfires, and grow old doing it, or Sailor Malan inside the said Spitfire, who is unhappily still growing old, but not for much longer, I dare say, the way he's been behaving recently.

* * *

So there we stand, the two survivors of the Blaue Kapelle, on Maritzburg station with rail warrants in our hands, and veterans of four hours' military service, waiting for the Durban/Joburg train. Barkle and Torpid we haven't seen for two years, and the parents of Greenballs and Loony Bin have been transferred six months ago, as people are in such times of war, taking their families with them. We have given our mothers no time to burst into tears as we grab toothbrushes and bid families farewell. Cheese has scored the remaining doughnuts, though, in a paper bag.

Our compartment has four experienced-looking men in it who have been fighting Rommel in North Africa. They have campaign ribbons on their breasts and stripes on their arms, but they do not condescend to us, for that is the behaviour of an inexperienced soldier, an almost-rookie. They give us Château dop en damwater from the washbasin tap, and teach us army songs of wonder where their new love is, their true love, with the hairs on her dickie di do right down to her knees. Cheese hauls out his bag of doughnuts and I a couple of sticks of beef biltong and we wash this mixture down with the brandy. The bedding man pulls down the bunks and makes up our rail warrant beds, and we cuddle up in the crisp sheets in vague alcoholic stupor, but happy. I am on the middle bunk, so later when we stop and I am woken by the clanking of milk cans down at the guard's van end, and I pull down the blind of the window at my head, I see the station sign saying Lions' River, and I remember peeping out like this as a kid, and wondering if I might see a couple of lions, with a bit of luck.

Being grown-up is bloody nice, so far.

* * *

Cheese and I go together or parallel for a long time in the Air Force. On arrival in the Transvaal we are given a fried egg sandwich apiece, and directed to a bungalow with twenty two beds in it. Most are occupied, we see, so we choose a couple with naked mattresses and sit down thereupon, according to the wisdom imparted us by the Rommel fighters in the train, to see what somebody will tell us to do. I have my bekfluitjie with me, so I take her out and I'm giving a New Orleans version of that stirring Welsh hymn: O where is my New Love, O where is my True Love?, when the door of this bungalow flies open and Greenballs and Loony Bin burst in, exclaiming Christ! What are you doing here? I am not Christ, says Cheese, though I am here to wage war against Adolf Hitler, who is the Anti-Christ.

No, man, when we got here last week Barkle and Torpid had been waiting a fortnight for enough blokes to arrive to make an aircrew course, and now you're here! Well now we're here you can start, says Cheese. Indeed, B and T do come in shortly, and we sit the old six of us, wondering at the coincidences and inevitabilities of life.

Barkle and Torpid have been mustered as air gunners in the aptitude tests, and Greenballs and Loony Bin as navigators. Cheese and I are summoned presently. A pack of psychologists sets to work on us doing wide-awake things on paper, and steering things by instrument, while sounds of horrible battles are going on, plus distracting lights and everything to slow up a reflex or make us angry. Then an end-to-end medical, dandruff to toenails, much of it in a decompression chamber. I am good at this, having got used to life without oxygen. Finally a doctor asks How does your sternum come to be collapsed like this? A horse called Mary stood on me when I was asleep. She walks about with her eyes shut. Blimey, says the doc, for he is an RAF soutie, and a city man too, otherwise I wouldn't give him such a piece of crap, blimey, he says, are you sure it was a horse? Come to think of it, no, I say. He he he! says the doc, you'll do.

Well, for what the Allied Air Forces have in mind I'm sure I will do. What they have in mind is that we should all fly to Japan and open bomb bays and bowels of B29s and spill out long, lean, love-ly, twenty-two-thousand-pound, high-explosive blockbusters and level sixty cities when we have finished doing this same levelling to sixty German cities on behalf of Bomber Harris of the Royal Air Force and sundry kooks of the US Army Air Corps who have had difficulty with potty training in infancy, and problems with their mothers at puberty.

Oh my God, what a relief! Don't forget to wash your hands

afterwards.

I make it into pilot training. Cheese has no problem. He is a pilot's pilot, you can tell that at a glance. He even looks like an aircraft when he's lying down, like a Martin Marauder, sleek, stubby and compact. We all sit back in the bungalow and laugh about this. Hey, says Greenballs, you know we've got here a complete Marauder crew, except we're one gunner short and one navigator too many; I think I'm going to apply for re-mustering as gunner and we'll see if we can fiddle things so we all end up in the same tactical squadron and the same kite. You can see he's an old hand of two weeks; already he talks of aircraft as Kites.

But we didn't do that. What we did was get turned into soldiers. On a firing range we shot soldiers' weapons, and on a parade ground we did army things to the yells and obscenities of a Flight Sergeant called Herry Oesh. We went on route marches across the veld and sang Where was the Engine Driver when the Boiler Burst?, which is of course Colonel Bogey, which is of course The River Kwai, which tells us

> Hitler has only got one ball;
> Goering has two, but very small;
> Himmler has something simmler,
> But Doctor Goballs has noballs at all.

We go on Church Parade. Members of the Jewish Community Church one pace forward, hollers Herry, riiiight turn, quiiiick march! The Rabbi and the Seventh Day Adventists can take it or leave it: Sunday is the day for prayer. I suppose they'd have taken it if it had been Thursday. Better than zilch.

Okay.

Christians, leeeeft turn, quiiiick... Greenballs takes a pace forward. What you want Herry? asks Herry Oesh. That's how he got the name Herry. He calls everybody Herry. Flight Sergeant, says Greenballs, I'm an atheist. The rest of the Blaue Kapelle take one pace forward, as also does a fellow called Benjie Segal. Ja, we're atheists too, we announce. Herry Oesh steps up to Greenballs and looks up in amongst the ginger hairs which grow from his nostrils, for he is a shortish man, whilst Greenballs is an exceeding tall macropod. He grinds his teeth something horrid, and extends and flexes his fingers a few times, like he'd get them on somebody's throat if military law allowed it. He stands up on his toes like a bantam which is about to crow, so his right-hand-side eyeball is practically touching all these luminous hairs which sprout from

Greenballs' shnoz.

Herry, he says, this pore blerry reverend come seventeen mile from Pretoria, and he not going to stand in a emty church cos yous blerry heathens want to play Crown and Anchor on Sunday!

The Catholics don't listen to this reverend, he explains with many a present participle, and we can not present participle listen either, that's up to us. Christians, leeeeft turn, quiiiick march!

The chapel was just another prefab, with a wooden cross nailed to the roof, painted white. I suppose it was made by the same military carpenter who made that item for the Q-stores stockpile: Crosses, Grave, Wooden, White, Troops, for the use of. It gave the place a serious aura, generally thought desirable in a church, I suppose, though I must say I preferred the informal farmyard atmosphere of Bishop Wisdom's cathedral.

So we're off to hear the Word, a mixed bunch; RAF lads in blue battle dress and snappy side-caps with a sky-blue flash, SAAF lads in khaki overalls and sun helmets with shady brims, Souties, Skape, Catholics, Protestants and conscripted apostates, and we all file into the chapel where the Rev Counter or Something is playing some sorry Lutheran tune on a portable harmonium like those used in Indian music. We all take off our headgear and sit on benches and get ready to listen or not listen, as the present participle case may be.

All except Benjie Segal, that is, who sits down with this bloody great helmet on his head to do his not listening.

So after a bit the Rev Counter puts down his harmonium and comes forward to give us a bit of Christian advice as an older man and, he hopes, a brother. What I want to talk to you about today is Sex. Now Sex is a matter which must be treated with Reverence and Respect, he says in his gentle fraternal voice, closely followed by the voice of Herry Oesh, a rasping whisper, Take your fucken hat off! Don't you know you in the House of the Lord? *Cunt!*

Thus the coarse nature of our early military career.

* * *

We fretted to be up and away, man, or rather away and up, for were we not aircrew, and were we not selected for this because we were not plodders but quick individuals, with quick reflexes, who could make quick personal decisions? We cared not a fig how to tell whether we had contracted the pox or the clap, nor how to construct a field latrine, nor indeed how a court martial might be constituted, in case we turned deserter or coward and might be shot by an officer of rank not less than General. Nor, indeed, did we give a rap for saluting people and getting our hair mostly cut off.

Patience, patience.

But it isn't only the poor bloody reverend that comes the seventeen miles to us from Pretoria. The Choral Society of that city also comes to us, to sustain our patience and our morale in the Recreation Hall. Amongst other entertainers, that is, of course.

A few of the South African kêrels have relatives around Pretoria, and this being a Friday evening they're off to a snatch of family life, lucky fish, and a few souties have gone a-whoring; other than that the main population of the camp is here in the smoke-laden atmosphere of the converted aircraft hangar.

Die Blaue Kapelle goes off each of us to purchase at the Naffy a stick of biltong or droë wors, a quart bottle of beer and a pint army mugful of pink raspberry ice cream for sixpence from the WAAF girl called Framboosdoos, with the nice tits which all lust after but precious few get to touch, and thus equipped settle down early on another backless bench, near the stage.

Not too strangely, rank sort of disappears after dark on festive occasions like these. The evening has to start with music, naturally, and here we have an RAF Flight Lieutenant, in army terms a captain, with his cap and tunic off, which means he has shed his rank according to military mysteries, and a couple of RAF aircraftmen, i e those at the bottom of the pile, known as erks with virtually no rank at all, even with their hats and tunics on, and he's at the piano and they are on double bass and trumpet.

They start the evening with Serenade in Blue, pretty schmaltzy Anglo-Saxon blues by my reckoning, but then the spirit of the thing is what matters, and the spirit is good. A bit suave, I mean, where blues should be rough, but good for the morale, as intended, and it is played with great polish, the greatest, the best. They don't sing, but we know the words:

When they play the serenade in blue
And darling I am in another world with you...

Next up is another Pom number, with the same Flight Lieutenant at the upright piano with a jug of beer on top, and a soft-shoe duet singing and dancing in the manner of Flanagan and Allen: Underneath the Arches, music of the London dispossessed of the depression, and the arches are those of the railway overpasses at Clapham Junction and the like:

Sleeping when it's raining,
And sleeping when it's fine,
Trains rolling by and by;
Pavement is my pillow
Everywhere I lay,
Underneath the Arches
I dream my dreams awahay.

A South African number next; the Adjutant, staff rank but without his red-band titfer and his tunic, steps up on to the stage and
asks What's this? The adjutant is gay. Hell, they tell me the navy is
the place for homos. Half the heroes of the Battle of Britain had
Problems, as they were seen to be in those distant days.

Anyway, the adjutant has this sort of fairy-type lisp, and he
stands up there with this aura of bewilderment he carries about
with him, and he says What's this? PHEEEEeeeeeewww (missile
sound) wwww PTUH! (like pulling a cork) Thxxx (raspberry
sound) xxxxx! Mehehheheheh! and he has everybody but totally
flummoxed for sure.

It is a golfball hitting a sheep, says the adjutant. With that kind
of apologetic expression he habitually wears on his face.

Not much balance in the matter of talent and presentation thus
far, but everybody likes the Adj and we give him a good loud howl
of mirth and a few cheers.

It's clear the big number will be the choristers from Pretoria,
though, and here they all sit to one side in their long white gowns,
and a few crippled-looking blokes in suits too, civilian suits which
rivet the attention a bit in this hangar full of uniforms. Sure
enough one of them gets up and bows to us from the stage and
clasps his fingers like half a swastika before his sternum and opens
his mouth wide like he's at the dentist and writhes his lips about;

Oeuahhhh nueao John nueao John nueao John nueaouh
he sings, and hell, we all want to laugh, but in the main we don't,
except a couple who pretend the golfball/sheep thing is still tick-
ling, because we all feel sort of embarrassed for this chap, he's
making such a clot of himself. A few from the audience find they
have to go outside because it's against concert etiquette to cough,
but as they come back from the cough he's into verse two:

Oeuahhh mahdahm ien youare feaice is beauateh
On youare lieps rrred rrroses grrruaow
Fi fie fum (I don't know the words) and foo fum fiddley
Mahdahm ahnswahr Yeauhs ourr Nueao

Oeuahhhhh nueao John nueao John nueao John nueaouh

The Adj is also Master of Ceremonies, and he reckons that so many lads and lasses are having trouble with their breathing and bladders that it's time for a ten-minute smoke break. He seizes the right moment as the last notes of song fade away, and signals to the sergeant gunnery instructor operating the lights, who shuts down the floods and spots and turns up the hangar lights as the Adj stands up and holds aloft a cigarette.

Well you can't laugh after the event, really, but we all go out and smile and smoke whilst doing a bospis against the barbed-wire fence while the WAAF lasses go and unload their beer on another of those secret parts of the planet that women find to pee on when there are a hundred of them and one toilet.

The Adj and the gunnery instructor have got all tastefully arranged when we troop back into the hangar. The entire choir of thirty or so is on the darkened stage in their white satin and pearls, and the few military reject men in their suits too, all doing their bit in this war, and as we all get seated the gunner up at the back of the hall gently slides open the rheostat of the lighting circuit, and the lights come up dramatically and reveal these smiling souls to us down below.

Nymphs and Shepherds come away, [they sing]
Come away, come away,
Nymphs and Shepherds come away,
Come come come come away.

And hell, man, there's still so much suppressed mirth in the minds and the hearts and the ears of these big-city souties and the boere-seuns en dogters that things look likely to get out of hand.

I mean everybody knows what a nymph is, and what is this band of nymphomaniacs doing with the bloody shepherds, or vice versa, anyway?

With dancing, sings the choir,
With dahahahahahahahahahahahahahancing...

Like this is a Handel Oratorio, and Unto Us a Son is Born.

And a little Limey called Eels here next to me has got beyond the joy of laughter. His hands are clamped over his ears, and head, hands, ears the lot are clamped between his knees, and he's muttering with the last breath given him upon this earth by his Maker; Please, please, God, they're killing me!

The Adj times it dead right, and as the last notes of nymphos and sheep farmers fade he gives some signal to the air gunner and all the lights come up and everybody claps and cheers and yells by way of release. Appointed ushers usher the choir off the stage midst the appreciative roar, before they have a chance for another bit of rural surrealism.

Patience, patience.

* * *

Between us and Zwartkops Air Station is but a single farm; we are right in the circuit area, in fact our parade ground is in line with one of the runways a mile or two distant. As we go about this ponderous military business the kites are overhead, with their undercarriage and flaps down, and the throttles pretty wide as they come grumbling in to land. In a way this is when they're at their best; potent, nicely balanced extensions of the human eye and brain and hand. Their bellies are battered by desert stones in Libyan and Egyptian takeoffs, for that is where they come from, many of them. The olive drab paint is hammered off their noses and engine cowlings by the small grit and sand flying off the unpaved runways along their flight the length of Africa. Back from the engine cowlings the nacelles are streaked with smoke stains and seeping oil. These aircraft are not pretty, as a tank is not pretty. These are working war-machines, and yet, and yet, and yet there is the elegance of anything that has to live in a fluid as dainty, unpredictable and violent as air, and there's a finesse in the handling of them, and the building of them, that's clear to the knowing and loving eye, however grubby the exteriors may be.

These, my ou maat, are not tanks.

And one Friday morning, in the middle of the Friday Morning Total Parade, with every living being in the camp present, including two desperate dogs which are knotted beneath the flagpole and have had a fire-bucket of water poured over them to no avail; every personal individual body, I say, all showered and shaved, the personal boots all shiny like anything, the personal rifles with barrels all glittery, and everything totally total while we wait in silence for some staff oom with all his red and gold and barathea to come and inspect all this personal stuff whilst everyone stands to attention, except the dogs, and the loudspeakers wheeze out a waltz called Spring in Killarney, which all present know as Somebody Shat on the Doorstep. In the middle of all this, I say, we hear an urgent pulsing roar, as of a quartet of two-thou-horsepower Rolls-Royce Merlins at full throttle, and every personal eye, even the four of the desperate dogs, turns to where this wild unsynchronised snarling sound is coming from.

It is coming from over the farm next door, where all these eyes perceive a Finger Four of Hawker Hurricanes; that is a Rotte, to give the formation its Luftwaffe name, since they devised it. These Hurricanes are at operational low-flying altitude, which is zero feet, and they're chopping the tops off the mealies with their props in a great plume of chaff as they come thundering toward us at maximum power, and by the time they are over us they are in an operational steep turn, which is vertical, and they would have taken Herry Oesh's present participle head off had he been just a pace or two farther north, for the altitude of the earth-side wing is five feet. We feel the slipstream turbulence and the wingtip vortices whoosh up dust from the parade ground, and they disappear in steep perspective leaving in our nostrils the pungent smell of burnt hundred-octane aviation fuel.

They are from Eleven Operational Training Unit at Waterkloof, and these fighter jockeys are so intent on their flak evasion exercise, they don't even notice they're in the circuit area of Zwartkops, and that's not only forbidden, it's bloody dangerous.

Herry Oesh is unperturbed. He has had enough of the real thing with real Messerschmitt 109s Up North. He happens to be opposite me during this hubbub. He struts over and takes the rifle from my hands and looks down the spout. You happen to know a man called Adolf Hitler? he asks in a very relaxed conversational sort of slightly smiling friendly way, A shortish man, about so high, with a little moustache and a bad haircut? Yes, Flight, I say. Ah, I thought you just might, he says. I thought maybe he is a friend of yours, maybe you on his side in this war, hay? still smiling. Well, not actually, Flight, I say. He rolls his eyes hideously, and grinds his teeth. You got a fucken big spider in this barrel, Herry, he says, take this fucken thing away and clean it, man! Yes Flight, I say.

Since then, I have seen more bizarre things happen than a world war get lost because some recruit hasn't cleaned the barrel of his WWI Lee-Enfield.

* * *

Well okay, okay, we did have some aircrew skills too at the end of six months, in addition to the bullshit and mirth: we knew dead-reckoning navigation, radio, aerodynamics, engine theory and weapons; that sort of stuff. Aircraft recognition. Gunsights and bombsights. But we itched to go and use it all.

Back of the camp was a simple grass landing strip, and a small unattended hangar, quite isolated, with a brass padlock on its sliding doors; not the sort of place with ground crew and all that, rather, I should say, the sort for which one would go and fetch a key somewhere if one wanted safe parking out of the wind and away from fiddling hands. Nothing is disconcerting like doing all one's pre-takeoff checks correctly and confidently getting airborne and then finding some inquisitive gloomper has been fiddling with your aircraft and it's not actually airworthy.

Well one lunch-time when we're full of soup and sausages and tea, and we're just off to the bungalow to get the old feet up for half an hour or so, and maybe a quick ziz with a bit of luck, we hear a chirpy sort of small-size growl in the spring sky and, looking up, we see this nippy yellow Tiger Moth flitting over us on the downwind leg of a teeny circuit, in that particularly sprightly way that Tigers have. They look as if they're lighter than air; painted with anti-gravity paint perhaps. This one does a highly professional fighter approach, tight tight with no corners, side-slips off all altitude at the last moment and lands out of sight behind the bungalows.

Cheese pulls my sleeve and says Come, let's go and have a look. How the hell have a look, I ask, have you not noticed a dirty great fence around this camp, and do you not know that if you climb through this fence you will face a court martial and have your kneecaps shot off in accordance to Military Law, and be demoted to the rank of Acting Unpaid Lavatory Cleaner in the Army? True, true, too terribly true, he says, come!

So we nip through the fence and trudge across the airfield to where an RAF bloke is standing next to the Tiger on a little concrete apron in front of this hangar. As we come up to him we see from the stripes on his epaulettes that he's a Group Captain, and he's pretty bloody adult too, at least twenty-five. Cheese was always a bouncy little sod, so he ups to this Group Captain, which is big rank, man, he ups to him and throws him a really deft salute like this is actually the King or something. 'Noon, he answers, smiling, tossing his Hairless Leather Flying Wig into the cockpit, hauling out a crumpled cap and straightening it sort of with his fingers and placing it upon his non-regulation haircut. He salutes too, in an uninspired sort of way.

We straightway know his whole history, such are the legends and mystiques of close-knit communities like air forces, especially in times of pressure, like these. Even we, the newcomers, know how to read it all. The top button of his tunic is undone; he is a fighter pilot. He wears a medal ribbon of slanted white stripes on blue, with a small rosette; it is a DFC and bar; he has won the DFC twice. He wears a small brass caterpillar on the edge of his lapel; he has had to use an Irvin Air Chute, he has had to bale out of something, at least once. Then there's the crumpled cap, crumpled from being stuffed fast into any old corner of a cramped cockpit, most times in a hurry. There's only one place he can come from, the Battle of Britain, and he's now been given an easy job for a breather.

Can we help you, sir? asks Cheese. Matter of fact, you can, he says, I thought there would be somebody here to help me get this aeroplane into the hangar. To call it an aeroplane you must know you have status and many many hours of flying, you come from history, otherwise it's an aircraft or a kite. I had a bad experience with one of my Tigers recently, he explains, some farm kids got through the fence and were looking at them and, when one of my lads tried to take off in this aeroplane later on, both starboard wings collapsed, upper and lower, and we found these little buggers had loosened off all the trailing-edge turnbuckles. He bloody near bought it.

Not a way to go, sir, says Cheese. How many Tigers do you have, sir? Twenty-two, says the G C, I'm the O C of Number Six Air School at Potchefstroom. A brief silence, because of status and rank. But if Cheese hasn't got aplomb, he's got nothing. With a bit of luck we might be with you soon, sir, he says. You couldn't be luckier, he replies, I've got the best flying school in the country. We exchange friendly grins. But here, help me get her inside.

We slide open the hangar doors and push her in, backwards. She needs little pushing. She is so bouncy and light it seems she finds it hard to be on the ground at all. Would you like a swing later on, sir? I ask. Yes, I suppose I would, he says, there's no ground staff around. Can you be here at five-thirty, he asks?

He has come to arrange about people like us to go to places like his, soon. He finds flying nicer than driving from Potch. Where is the main gate? he asks. Oh, a mile and a half at least round to the left there, says Cheese. Better just come through the fence with us here, sir, he says. You know you can't just climb through this fence like that, hey? he answers, I mean, it's an Offence! True, true, too terribly true, Sir, says Cheese. We pull open

WUW — E

the barbed wire strands for him, and he climbs through.

He hands us the keys to the padlock. Okay, five-thirty, he says. He doesn't tell us not to fiddle with her turnbuckles, he doesn't nag us not to talk about the unauthorised prop-swinging, which regulations don't allow. He doesn't tell us anything, because he knows how to make a pilot, and we're all airmen together. He knows we are going to get in there and run our hands over his aeroplane as we might over his woman, given half a chance.

That, indeed, is what we do. We're through the fence at five, and we have the hangar open, and we wheel her out easily, just the two of us, easily, and we lift her tail from the ground easily, just one of us, she's so nicely balanced. The parachute is still in the rear bucket seat, so we take turns sitting on it at the controls, looking back at the elevators as we gingerly move them up and down, then left and right at the reciprocal movement of the ailerons, then trying both together, with the rudder. Easy. Put a bit of air under this baby and we'll show you some flying. We open the engine cowling and gape at the hundred-and-thirty-horse Gipsey Major; four lovely big fat long-stroke low-rev inline cylinders, they drive the prop directly, no great weight of reduction gearbox here.

Sweet, sweet, a sweet 1929 aeroplane, sweet as a Garratt loco is sweet, or a nicely-tuned pushbike.

At five-thirty exactly he is there, but not through the fence this time; he arrives in a staff car via the Main Gate. He waits for the driver to clear off so he doesn't see me turning the prop, and drags out from the corner of the hangar a pair of chocks, which he places before the wheels of the Tiger. I'll tell you what to do, he says, and explains a starting procedure which is straight out of The Great War.

The switches for the double magneto circuits are outside the cockpits, so the prop-swinger can actually see whether they're on or off, and never take the pilot's word for it. If this motor fires while somebody's handling the prop it will dice him up plenty small.

Switches off, throttle wide, I call, and give a thumbs-down. Switches off, and I see his hand switch them off, throttle wide, he calls, and gives a thumbs-down as extra check. I grab the prop at one of the tips and turn it a couple of times through compression to clear the cylinders. Throttle closed, I yell, and Throttle closed he yells back. I turn her once through compression to suck in a quick gargle of fuel. Throttle set, I call. Throttle set. I give thumbs-up and shout *Contact!* I see him push the switches up, he gives thumbs-up and shouts *Contact!* I get carefully balanced, reach forward and take a blade-tip and mightily heave through compression as I step back. *Blog! Blogroarrrrrrrr!*, first spark, man, the Gypsey comes to full life, and the G C guns her for a few seconds to make sure she's properly alight.

He lets her idle till the temperature gauge says its okay, then he opens the throttle wide, to test for revs and voltage drop, with the stick hard back in his belly to keep her tail on the ground. He lets her idle again, and waves both hands in front of his face for Chocks Away. Cheese and I pull away the chocks and dump them back in the hangar and roll the doors shut and lock them. I hold my cap down in the prop wash and give the G C the key. Nicely tuned engine, sir! I yell. Of course! he shouts, winking, they all are! Come and try them!

Since the windsock tells him he's pointing straight upwind he opens wide, there and then, and the tail lifts after a pace or two, for this lady doesn't like any part of her body to touch the ground for a single unnecessary moment. A cheery waving arm from the cockpit and he's disappearing into the sunset. Well all right it's only 5 45 and the sun is still up there, but he's up there too, and he's disappearing into it. He looks a bloody sight better than Reagan disappearing into a horizon-level sunset shining through the bandy hind legs of a horse. Never mind Reagan; I realise that if this is to be Number One at my flying school I'll like him a hell of a lot more than the Number One at my last school. This is the Very Model of a Modern Battle of Britain Group Captain.

* * *

Well the gunners went gunnering and the navigators went navigating and the Blaue Kapelle bade each other adieu, go with God, and fare thee well, but not goodbye, for we knew we would coincide along the line somewhere, since Japan had to be civilised fairly soon now that we were so near finishing the civilising process of Germany. If we were all somewhere around in the aircrew pool we could by application on grounds of compassion or culture whatever get together in the same Lancaster or Superlancaster and go together to Japan and in ardent missionary spirit bring them into Western Culture by a better Christian route than the beastly Oriental thing they had tried.

There was one navigation school, and one gunnery school, so those members of the Kapelle would be okay, each would have an old pal along for company, but pilot training needed a lot of air-craft, so there were a few pilot training places, and Cheese and I might be split up, which would be a pity. Only two were available at the moment though: Witbank and Potchefstroom, so our chances were good. Well, we feared they might divvy us up alpha-betically, the middle letter being M, and that would have separat-ed us, but they did it out of a hat, whatever, and we ended up at the same place: Potch.

When we arrived at Potch at ten at night we each received a fried egg sandwich and directions to read the notice board.

I had been allocated to an instructor called Wold, who was so extraordinarily plump as to make a marked difference to the han-dling characteristics of an aircraft, and of temperament so satur-nine as to make one wonder why he hadn't volunteered for one-man submarines, while Cheese went to a fellow called Aitch, who was distinguished as being the only person in the history of avia-tion to have used a parachute whilst falling upwards.

He had been hacked by a Macchi 202 Folgore at high altitude over Abyssinia in 1940, rolled his fiercely burning Hurricane over and dropped out, straight into the cauldron of a vast, anvilled cumulo-nimbus cloud. It was really a case of Out of the Frying Pan into the Refrigerator, since he had more than twenty thousand feet of lightning-loaded sleet and stuff to fall through, violent as the biggest load of blockbusters ever, only cold, cold, cold.

Now if you bale out and open your parachute at thirty thou-sand feet, you're going to suffocate, pretty well, also freeze before you get to oxygen level. So the trick is to drop below ten thou, but even then there's a problem, because these are not steerable sport parachutes, and you're going to drift wherever the wind may take you, for a long time, which is often undesirable in times of war, and if you're near the sea you may end up in it; so the cleverest thing is to delay the opening as long as possible. This needs a bit of nerve, I suppose, but once you've reached your terminal veloc-ity of a hundred and twenty or so, it doesn't really matter how long you stay there, so you might as well take the shortest route down and open at a couple of thousand feet.

That's what Aitch decided to do. A good pilot, he knew his met, and that the cloud base would be two thou, thereabouts. It would take three minutes of falling. After twenty minutes, though, rough-ly speaking, he started to wonder if by some metaphysical process he'd fallen right through the earth and might emerge into the brilliant sunshine of the beach at Waikiki, or whether on the other hand he might have been sucked out of present reality by some sort of Bermuda Triangle time warp. The slipstream was slatting and flapping his flying suit about his body, and he clapped his oxygen mask to his nose to stop the frostbite. At this point he noticed a lot of hailstones all about him; the big ones were slowly moving down, the small ones slowly moving up, and he realised that though his terminal velocity was a hundred and twenty, he was caught in one of those vertical blasts that cunims have, which can move at two hundred knots. He, and the hailstones, were not going down, they were all going up together, overall, at eighty knots. Some more, some less.

Whatever the consequences, he had now to open his chute. Still with great presence of mind he waited until the hail thinned out a bit, otherwise it would have ripped the fabric to shreds, then reached over with his right hand, grabbed the D-ring, gave a last quick think, pulled the ring, I'm in the hands of the gods, and after a great jolt and a couple of minutes was spat out into the anvil of the cumulonimbus at twenty-five thousand feet, not much short of the altitude he'd started at. Gasping and frozen, he pulled down the forward shrouds of the chute to spill out air, and if possible to move him away from the cloud, which otherwise could well suck him in again just above the ground, and through the whole cycle again.

Well, all's well that ends well, and I wouldn't be telling this story if it hadn't ended well. Lieutenant Aitch had a frostbitten half-nose as a trophy, and there he was, all ready for Cheese.

So we're all issued with parachutes and helmets. We go on parade and the Group Captain comes to look at us; you can hardly call it an inspection. When he gets to Cheese and me he says Oh it's you two is it?, with no expression on his face, and moves on. Everybody wonders what the bloody hell sinister thing we have done to be thus known.

The very next day we are flying. I wrap the parachute harness about my body, and settle my balls in the loop that comes between the legs so they won't get squashed if I use the chute, and buckle the straps into the quick-release lock. I put the square-sided goggles on, over the helmet, and already I look like Sailor Malan. You can always tell a Tiger pilot by the little sunburnt triangle on his forehead, from the gap between helmet and goggles and sitting in an open cockpit. I shall soon have one of those.

Bertie Wold shows me how to get in and strap up and plug in the intercom, which is really just a length of hose pipe with a rubber funnel at one end and earpieces at the other, then climbs aboard himself. The Tiger sinks on its dainty undercarriage, and probably in its heart too, it seems. He flops into his seat, the whole kite goes *Woof* like an old divan, and the wings creak. What if they break?

Like new books, aircraft have a very nostalgic smell. It isn't actually a nice smell, as of food or sex or flowers; it is of high-octane fuel and cellulose paint and smelly flying boots and brake fluid. Tigers don't smell of brake fluid, though, for they have no brakes, nor flaps nor anything at all that requires any hydraulic system. They and butterflies have no need of such. There is no way to run off the end of the runway except by taxying there. Tigers smell mainly of aviation fuel, and after a bit you get to smell of it too, for every time you roll it over, even if your upside-down time is brief, a certain amount of fuel escapes from the tank between the upper wings, and since you're hanging out of the cockpit in your straps, dead astern of the tank, you get a certain amount of this about your head. Women of Tiger pilots complained of the petrochemical smell of their moustaches.

Not that we're flying inverted yet. Lieutenant Wold taxis out to the runway, weaving left and right so we can see past the nose, the Tiger being a taildragger. She waddles from side to side over the uneven grass, as a vulture waddles on the ground with its wings extended for balance, hating every moment of it. He stops crosswind and has a quick check for incoming kites, then he's down the runway at full throttle, the tail quickly comes up, the flying wires take the weight of the aircraft and after a couple of gadoomps on the wheels we're doing it. We're flying!

He takes us off to a nice quiet piece of sky, and I'm still staring around at the wonder of it all, of actually *doing* it, when he says to me Okay, you've got her. I've got her, I say, for I have been told this is procedure, yet surely he can't mean that I am now in control of this aircraft? But he *does*, and he hasn't even told me how everything works, he just assumes I know it all already, which in fact I do, and in the last brief moment of my remaining life I realise that there's not one of us on this course that doesn't know it all, otherwise we wouldn't be here, and in that case I'd better do something fairly soon; but when I start doing something I realise that we were both better off when I was doing nothing.

I am trying to balance a dinner-plate on my thumb. As I try to

132

check the wild rolling of the Tiger, and maybe getting it right just a little bit, she starts to pitch, so I leave the rolling and get to work on the pitching when she starts to yaw. Bertie Wold is a man with a manner of great weariness with the foolishness of this life and world. His eyebrows slope upwards in the middle, and he has a wrinkled brow. When he speaks, his every utterance begins with a sigh. His sentences are short, and he gives one the impression that in the main he would rather not be speaking at all. He speaks to me in that mode now, as I wrestle with the mechanical and intellectual aspects of flying, which somewhere inside I know is not the natural behaviour of man, as Mr Household's mother had told him.

Try not to overcorrect in the roll, he says, whilst I am trying to keep the nose on the horizon. No, he says after a bit, now you are getting the nose too high, and if you do that at your present airspeed you will spin in. Therefore, open your throttle. But I don't. I push it the wrong way and the Tiger gives the same sort of sigh as Bertie Wold, and with a great shudder drops a wing and falls straight toward the earth, spinning like a leaf. Bertie Wold emits an even greater sigh over the hosepipe intercom. Now you must understand, he says, if the aeroplane is in an attitude like that... He also talks of kites as aeroplanes, because... but I wish he would stop talking of aeroplanes or anygoddamthing else just now and take this aircraft off my hands, and save our lives. But ewe gerus, at his ease, in the middle of explaining the aerodynamics of it all he says Okay, I've got her, and there and then, after two more turns of the ten-turn spin, she's right as rain and steady as a rock. Well, all right, a vulture.

He says Look at your altimeter. I do that; we still have two thousand feet of air under us. We'll just climb a bit, he says. Whilst climbing he says nothing. I mean, this is not a chatty man. But I know he has just given me the first and maybe most important lesson in flying: short of something really bloody stupid like collision or setting yourself on fire, you can do almost anything in the air, as long as you have altitude. Your enemy in the air is the earth.

Earth, Air, Fire and Water. The four elements. When in the air, beware the other three.

Lieutenant Aitch has a completely rational approach; no intuitive stuff, no artistic demonstration, no melodrama. He takes Cheese logically along each axis of control, explaining the aerodynamics, and as soon as he can sort of fly, at all, lets him do his practising during circuits and landings. He shows him fire drill and how to do a forced landing, and after eight flights, at eight hours flat, the minimum allowable time, he sends him solo. When I come into the hangar after my flying I see Cheese there looking nonchalant, and I say to him 'Lo Cheese, how'd it go, man? Oh all right, he says, like a cucumber, all cool, I went solo. What! I am filled with anxiety and envy, but I smile a huge hypocrytical smile and grasp his hand in a manly sort of way and give it a good wring and clap him on the back. Ja, now I've got to get Aitch a cake, he says, condescendingly, It's traditional. Shortarse upstart, as if I didn't know that.

Will I ever go solo? In my eight hours I've done only two hours of circuits and bumps and no emergency stuff at all. Will I ever do it? I'm not at all sure I'm really cut out for this.

Take off and fly south, says Bertie Wold. I do. I've got her, he says, I'm going to show you forced landing and fire procedures. He chooses a field without antheaps and shows me how to lose height weaving at the leeward end of the field, instead of flying a circuit, where I might get caught short and have to land downwind. You do it, he says. I do it twice, without actually landing, of course, but pulling away at twenty feet or so. Okay, take me home, says Bertie Wold.

On the way home he says to me: Oh yes, fire procedures. If the aeroplane catches fire, bale out. There's a longish sort of silence and after a bit I say What about sideslipping to take the flames away from the cockpit...? but he interrupts me. This aeroplane, he says, is what is known as a braaivleis aeroplane. What you have here is a lot of wood, cloth and nice combustible lacquer. There's also some petrol to keep it going. This aeroplane, he says, all of it, will burn to a cinder in one minute flat. Any sign of fire, you understand, any fucking sign at all, and you undo those straps and roll this thing over and drop out!

Another silence. Well, *do* you understand?

Yes sir. Fire procedures are the simplest thing so far.

We get back to Potch and I land the Tiger. It is a beaut landing; I clear the fence nice and low and within a couple of hundred yards we're at a standstill. Taxi back to the fence here, on the left, says Bertie. At the fence I stop and Bertie Wold says to me You drive this aeroplane like a shit-cart. I'm getting out. Which he does. He hauls his parachute from the kite, dumps it on the grass, plants his plump bum upon it and lights a fag. I sit there in the

Tiger and look at him. He waves me away impatiently, telling me Voetsak with his soundless lips. Which I do.

I had thought the Tiger was sprightly with Bertie aboard, but this now was incredible. I could lift her tail almost at taxying speed. She still doesn't like waddling over the grass, but we're soon at the downwind end of the field, and I stop crosswind there and scan the final leg of the circuit for aircraft on approach. I turn her into the wind and open the throttle wide. In a few seconds the tail is up and she's nipping on tiptoe over the tufts of grass and my ears are filled with the loud hollow drumming of it, for she's as resonant as a guitar with her wooden sound-box construction. At about half the normal take-off run the drumming abruptly stops and it's really happening, I'm flying alone. I nudge the stick back at forty-five knots and without the great freight of flesh aboard she springs so wildly into the air that I have to push her down again and hold her just off the grass until she's doing seventy, then I pull back again and easily, elegantly, she sails up to a thousand feet as if she has just risen from the hand of Bellum.

I turn across and downwind. I wobble the wings and for the first time get a strange feeling that they are my fingers stuck out in the air there, and there are nerves running from the wingtips to my head. The air in the air feels different from the air on the ground, more sort of brittle as it hisses and tears at my helmet. I look at the empty front cockpit and get a sudden shock at realising what I'm doing. What if I should suddenly become faint? What if my arms should suddenly become numb? What then, hey? But I don't faint, and my arms don't go numb, and before the truth of it all has sunk in I'm turning into final approach and way down there I see Bertie still on his fat bum on the parachute, and it's all happened so fast that he hasn't finished the fag yet.

I bring her neatly over the fence with the throttle closed. I hold her off at about three feet and she sinks so daintily to the ground that I feel the grass brushing her tyres before the wheels touch it. We do a perfect three-point landing, no bounce, nothing, because she's totally stalled at touchdown, and we roll just a few paces before stopping and turning back to fetch Bertie. Well I wonder what he'll say about *that* one? I chortle.

I pull up next to him, he dumps his parachute into its bucket seat and heaves his bulbous buttocks into the cockpit. He speaks to me over the hosepipe intercom. I'll have biltong, he says, I don't eat cake.

135

chapter eight

I have noticed that many fat women are graceful dancers. I have noticed also that many have very dainty hands, and dainty gestures to match, so that in the days when one danced *with* someone, face to face, so that one was aware of body language, it was very often the best fun to dance with a nice plump lass who was elegant about it, and had expressive gestures.

If I say Bertie Wold was like this, I do not mean I went dancing with the sonofabitch. He was like this in flying, which I must say I hadn't noticed so far because any flying which prevented my being a smoking crater in the ground was good flying and okay with me.

The day after my first solo, however, he announced his intention to demonstrate that flying is an art, and if you do it mechanically, well, you would do better to go and mow the lawn. Go and practise staying alive for an hour, he said, and when you're back we'll do some aerobatics. For an hour I stayed alive and built up a bit of confidence for what I knew was coming.

I suppose you've been building up a bit of confidence for what you know is coming, he said while he buckled himself in and I taxied out for takeoff. Bad mistake. You are not a chauffeur in this machine which is going to do deadly things to you. This machine is going to follow you around in the air as your arse follows your head when you are swimming. This aeroplane is you; when you roll over, it rolls over, when you climb, it climbs, and when you decide to put your feet on the ground again, that's when it lands. Those wings are your feathers.

Aha! So this was the feeling I'd had on my first solo. I would never have guessed Bertie Wold could talk so much.

We climb to four thousand feet in silence. With the nose up, it's easy not to notice the ground, and to get that strange feeling of being suspended in aspic. There is no sense of movement at all, for there's no landscape rushing past a window, just the mechanical din of the Gypsey's urgent roaring and its physical vibration through the airframe and the buffeting of the slipstream over the fabric wings and its thumping about one's goggled face.

Bertie says Look around for other aeroplanes. I turn left and right and look up and down. There's a hell of a lot of Tigers in this piece of atmosphere and we don't need a collision. Stick forward, says Bertie, and bring her with you, go on, stuff her nose down till you've got a hundred and forty. I find it hard. Go on, do it, he says, don't fight her. Dive and bring her with you. I do it. Right, he says, when I've done it, I've got her but keep your hand on the stick. Now we pull hard back and open full throttle, and if you look up you will see the horizon, and as it comes down check your wings are level with it and whump! that's your slipstream you've just flown through which means you have done a good loop.

What? Me? I didn't do anything! Okay, you do it, says Bertie. Oh shit! Me? But whatthehell Archie, whatthehell, and I stuff her nose down, or rather my nose down with hers, and haul her up with the throttle wide open and I really don't know where the bloody hell I am until that strange flat thing appears from behind my head which on second thought I remember is the earth, and I also remember to level my wings against her, for she is my mother, and whump I actually fly through my own slipstream, and I have actually done a good loop; not only a loop, but a good loop. After ten hours' flying I have done aerobatics!

I suppose you think it's a bloody marvel that you've done a loop after ten hours' flying, said Bertie. How the hell did he always know what I was thinking, no, what I was feeling?

We're supposed to be doing navigation, said Bertie, but you might as well do it as a pilot rather than a shit-cart driver. We'll fit the aerobatics in between, he said. So as we went through the programme of formation flying and nav and stuff Bertie squeezed in half-hours of aerobatics, and in fact I got in extra besides, for along the legs of a solo two-hour navigation exercise I would do a series of barrel rolls and slow rolls, trying to get as polished as Bertie, but I never did. He could fly a slow slow roll along a horizontal piece of imaginary string without losing a single foot of altitude, when the wings were vertical he would keep her nose up with the rudder and throttle, using the side of the fuselage for lift, as one does, but so uncannily that he could have kept her at right angles for ever.

If you're flying a MiG 29 you will have more thrust than the mass of the MiG, and you can stand on your tail for as long as you choose. If you are in a Pitts Special you can't quite do that, but if you hang on to your vertical attitude too long you will have zero airspeed and slam back on your elevators and fall over into a vertically downward position, forward or backward. If you do such a thing in a Tiger Moth your whole tail assembly will break off and you will be dead.

In a Tiger Moth there are no expressionist falling and tumbling aerobatics, only classical aerobatics, in which the aircraft is always flying. Bertie Wold would fly a vertical stall turn, not safely tilted forward a bit, so if he missed turning her over with the rudder she would just flop into a forward stall; he would judge his airspeed to about walking speed, then swing the kite over in its own length.

This monstrous fat man, as fat as butter, was a figure skater. He never slipped.

So Cheese is now jealous of me, in an unexpressed sort of way, because I'm ahead of him in aerobatics. But eventually he gets in his hours, and being a bantam cockerel he now knows all about it, and tells me how to do it. One morning we're off to the hangars together, and he's down for solo aerobatics and I'm down for nav with Bertie, and I watch Cheese get into his kite and start her up and the usual pre-flight stuff, and taxi out for take-off while I wait for Bertie. But Bertie doesn't come for the nav and sends a message for me to go and practise my aerobatics.

Yissis, a real scramble! I fling my chute into the Tiger and myself after it; somebody gives me a swing and the pre-flight checks be damned, I do those as I'm buckling on the chute, and I do that while I'm taxying out with my tail in the air. A quick glance for landing aircraft, and I'm off after Cheese with throttle wide open, and I keep her at full throttle to five thousand feet, and there I spy Cheese below over wall-to-wall cumulus, closely packed, almost stratus, getting safely away from the Potch circuit area for his aerobatics.

From six thou I do a Hun-in-the-sun Fokker D VII type pounce on him, and a great wide barrel roll with him in the middle, but not too close; you think you know all about it with thirty hours'

138

flying in your log book, but watch it mate! Cheese rolls over and disappears through a gap in the cloud, and I continue rolling and go through the same gap. As I come out underneath I see him going up through another gap, and I follow. He ducks round a cloud to his left, then to his right, and he's in and out and round-about the cumuli for five minutes or so, but he can't shake me off. Then he goes into a steep climbing turn, and I know what he's going to do next, and he does it: he increases the bank of his turn till he's inverted and goes straight down and at 150 pulls up into a series of tight tight loops, but he can't lose me. He must now either duck back into the cloud or roll off the top of one of his loops. As he starts to roll I roll too. He goes into an operational steep turn, an oppie steepie, banked almost vertically, and now he's had it, because Bertie has taught me well how to hang in there at the absolute aerodynamic limit; he tightens the radius until the Tiger can't stand it any more and flicks out of the turn with its starboard wings stalled and falls away inverted. I close the throttle and roll the other way and fly after him. He sees a great cave in the cumuli and nips in, and so do I. He starts another steepie and we're busy squeezing each other into a narrower and narrower turn in this huge luminous bowl, this vast opalescent fishtank, when the mouth closes up, leaving us totally disorientated. While he still knows which way is up Cheese rolls over and dives straight down and out of the cloud.

I decide to test the theory that you can fly level by the seat of your pants, without horizon and without looking at blind flying instruments, and bore my way through the cloud getting more and more confused until I see that the aircraft is diving and pull back the stick to lift her nose, but what I don't know is that I'm upside down, so that I now come screaming vertically from the bottom of the cloud, and there is Cheese a safe thousand feet below so I don't fall on him, and waiting for me, because he knows what's going to happen.

We fly home in formation, Cheese leading, and along the way he comes down to a few hundred feet and we fly round and round a farmhouse where a girl with red hair waves her arms, and a pair of dogs run round and round the house barking at us.

***

The temperamental highveld summer hurried along, the high-veld skies wondrous as ever with their idyllic mornings, thermals at midday and brutal black mid-afternoon hailstorms. We revelled in our youth and our skills, proud of our friendship and the mounting number of flying hours we were accumulating. We seldom flew with instructors now, and thus often in each other's company, and on two occasions, long-distance nav with a refuelling stop along the way. We flew as pilot and navigator, and so got in a good hour or so of aerobatics together, with our pencil, sharpener, rubber and protractor all tied down with bits of string, so they wouldn't fall out in a slow roll.

We were such a crackerjack team, said Cheese over the hosepipe, just a few years ago we'd have broken the Croydon-to-Cape Town record, which stood at six days.

So intent were we on all this that one morning when we found it necessary to wear jerseys under our overalls we realised for the first time that the great storms were gone till next year, that the pellucid air of a highveld autumn was now filled horizon to horizon with small brilliant fairweather cumuli, the white light coming off them so brittle and sharp that we had to use pink-tinted blind flying goggles when above them. We also realised that our days of sport flying were now over. We were moving on to service training, war training, and the use of weapons.

Alas, the hat parted us. I was off to Central Flying School at Nigel, and Cheese to Seventeen Air School at Witpoortjie. Nothing to be done about it, but then again it was okay, because before the year was out we would both be in aircrew pool and take it from there. And anyway, during our time at Potch we had taken to eating at the Metro Cafe in Joburg, on Saturday evenings off, a thing called a Mixed Grill, which mercifully seems to have disappeared from menus of this country in recent years. We would continue to go there on weekend passes; the chances of coinciding were pretty good.

I arrived at CFS at 10 p m after a chilly train journey from Potch with eleven others, and a bloody cold ride in a troop carrier with another dozen from Witbank. The Pupil Pilots' Mess was vacant and dark but for two blokes playing snooker at a table illuminated by big five-hundred-watt lamps. Glen Miller was playing Falling Leaves, the nostalgic, lonely music filling the hall, silent but for the music and the clicking of the snooker balls. It was an Edward Hopper painting. We were each of us given a fried-egg sandwich and directed to our quarters.

* * *

I share a room with a couple of Welsh lads, Sid and Ed. In the morning we draw full operational flying gear, because this is not fairweather club flying, this is bombing and fighter evasion techniques, advanced navigation, beam landings in zero visibility, that sort of thing. Our night flying is not circuits and bumps; it is long-range nav to distant cities, our hypothetical targets. We get heated flying suits and much disciplined radio training. In fact everything in this place is much disciplined. I welcome it, for it may just keep me getting old. It is not the arbitrary discipline of a macho sub-standard rugby master.

Sid is my co-pupil; we train in pairs. We fly a very trim little twin-engined aircraft made by Airspeed, all wood, but not the wood-and-rag construction of the Tiger; it has a stressed plywood skin over a spruce airframe. We sit side by side in the cockpit, and it's all Perspex, plenty of light. The engines are Armstrong-Siddeley Cheetah Tens, nice gutsy-looking radials with a really feline snarl to them. The fin is pointy and elegant; all round a neat number; also a bit combustible, perhaps, being of wood, but neat, man, neat. She is called an Oxford.

It is clear what we are being readied for. Early days we get a lot of daylight nav and many hours of instrument flying in a simulator. There's a lot of emergency stuff: single-engined flying, fire drill again, forced landings and the like. The big one, though, is long-range night flying. I am allocated to an RAF Flight Lieutenant called O'Dowd.

There is nothing he doesn't know about strategic night bombing, for he comes from the bomber streams raiding the Ruhr. Well, not only the Ruhr, to be exact, and for that matter not raiding either, for what they have been busy doing is pounding the urban population of Germany into extinction, no more, no less, the Yanks by day and they by night. Anglo-Saxons are violent and very vengeful people, O'D opines, though they don't much care to hear it said. Clearly he has given it some thought, perhaps on those long, lacerated, anxious flights home, for he points out the similarity between the thinking of Bomber Harris and that of Hermann Goering. If the English bomb one German city, the Luftwaffe will eradicate ten of theirs, said the Reichsmarschall. Bad mistake to give Coventry and London the Rotterdam treatment, though. Harris and chums had sat down and ticked off twenty German cities for Ausradierung.

But our techniques are better, says O'D as we drone our way over the Transvaal; we are able to generate fire-storms with our massed heavies. The whole city starts to ignite spontaneously, from radiant heat, even if you drop no more incendiaries. Even the tarmac roads ignite, and the wind roaring along them at a hundred and fifty knots takes everything along with it to the centre of the furnace: vehicles, cats, puppy dogs, trees, old newspapers, old people, young people, babies, everything. In the bunkers, the shelters, fugitives suffocate to death because this furnace has consumed all available oxygen. At the centre the temperature is that of a brick kiln. You can fire ceramics in there.

Our first fire-storm was Darmstadt, says O'D. We didn't know it would turn into anything like that, a cumulative ignition of the whole city, an entire wipe-out half an hour after the incendiary bombing had stopped. Who could calculate or predict it would be such an inferno? What's the matter, hey? Are you okay, then?

Where did you say?

Darmstadt. Are you all right?

No, I'm not; I know somebody there.

Oh shit! A silence, a long silence, as he writhes.

Never to worry, I say, it's okay. No but, I mean, who was it, hey? he can't drop it. I would like to say Mr Glissop, and I wish I had, and indeed I wish it were, but you don't talk futile rubbish to your mates at times like these. A gentle, sexy woman, I say.

Oh *shit!* he says. I mean for fuck *sake!*

No, come on man, I say – I'm supposed to be calling him Sir, but the urgency of the moment doesn't allow that futile rubbish either – come on man, we don't even know she's dead, and if she is, it doesn't mean you set out personally in some bloody Lanc to murder her personally, does it?

No but *shit!* he says, come *on*, you know?

I take care not to tell him I know that's why the picture postcards stopped arriving.

When I say there's nothing he doesn't know about it, I don't mean just the techniques of saturation bombing; he also knows about the psychological bit. He is also a survivor of the Nuremberg raid, when ninety-eight Lancasters were burned in one night.

There was no doctor on board a Lanc. There was no turning back against the stream of a thousand if the Fliegerabwehr-kanonen, the flak, had laced her with shrapnel and your body was holed and ripped. If you were lucky enough not to be the Arse-end Charlie inaccessible back there in your four-gun turret, your mates would tie and bandage and strap you up somehow and shoot you full of morphine, but beyond that you were on your own. And if a black Kammhuber Line Messerschmitt 110 night fighter with two 37-mm cannon mounted obliquely forward in the rear cockpit were to sneak up beneath your Lanc and blast the starboard fuel tank which was known to be still full, well then, if the aircraft were not cartwheeling and plunging with a missing wing in a vast ragged sphere of flame, and if she didn't collide with others of the thousand, and if your mates had time for it, they might clip a 'chute on to your gunner's harness and chuck you out into the blackness, and with just another wee bit of good luck you just might not get chopped up by one of four thousand props, nor land in the middle of the firestorm which you yourself had started, where even the tarmac of the streets was ablaze and the temperature was as the inside of a brick kiln.

But never mind that sombre stuff, man! O'Dowd has a delightful Irish sense of humour, and I piss myself laughing at his Irish jokes, which have the same daft twist to them as Yiddisher jokes and Indian jokes in Natal. He explains to me whilst making our way to a daylight bombing range how the Irish got the reputation for being absurd: it was an Irish Lord in the eighteenth century who exclaimed during a debate in the House, And is it a fowl of the air that you think I am then, that I can be in two places at the same time?

He is a delightful fellow by anybody's measure, going about the hangars and briefing room with his cap down over his eyes in the manner of an Irish Guardsman at Buck House. On these cold winter mornings he does an Irish navvy's tap-dance with this ancient endless woolly scarf about his neck and his hands in his pockets and whistling a jig. Occasionally he removes his hands from in there and clasps his fingers over his heart and sings in the manner of an Irish tenor in an Irish pub a sentimental South African song he has composed, called Linger a Little Longer in My Donga, which sounds a little bit like Danny Boy, only worse.

So one evening of early winter we're off to Bloemfontein as our target city on my first night raid, and I've just had a nice supper, but leaving out the soup and coffee because peeing in an Oxbox is awkward since you have to open the door to do it, and you can't get your knob out with a parachute harness about you so you're scared of falling out; and whereas I have heard of people doing a crap through the camera hatch by sealing off the hole with the backside, although I don't believe this unlikely thing, it is clearly impossible to pee through there because of the high-pressure area underneath which will blow it all straight back in your eyes. One can, of course, take along an empty beer bottle with a suitable bung, but you've still got to get the parachute off to do the pee, and stand up somehow, or kneel, in order to get the old man out from under all those clothes, and he's only about three inches long when not in action, while the clothing is four inches thick. So it's easier just to leave out the soup and coffee. I have got my whack of soup in a thermos, however, for the way back.

So here I sit, all complacent and snug in the cockpit, the Cheetah Tens growling away contentedly as they warm up, and I'm going over my nav charts and things with the little adjustable green nav light shining on the chart clipped on its extending arm above my lap, and feeling smug and expectant of a really nice night's flying because I've got really skilled at this nav thing, man. I'm waiting for my instructor.

O'D climbs in and sits next to me, but doesn't do or say anything. After five minutes or so the Cheetahs are ready and I start feeling maybe I should do or say something, so I say Okay, we're off then, and he nods his head silently. Half an hour later he is still silent, and it seems to me he has the 'flu or something, so I ask him if he'd like us to turn back so he can report sick, but he just shakes his head. At this point I turn and have a good look at him. He is clutching his seat in his gloved fists, and staring at his lap, leaning forward. He is afraid to look out of the window.

It is a crystalline winter night, every star clear and brilliant, and I can tell where the Milky Way ends and the lights of Joburg begin only by the change of colour from white to yellow. The Universe, the air, the earth are one great slash of light, and I am new to it yet and enchanted, but O'D is immobilised by the sheer horror of it, and can't lift his head. After a bit he gets a grip on himself and says Look, you know what to do here, I'm only along as supervisor. Just ignore me. I've got a bit of a problem. Quite a big bit, I think to myself, you're flak-happy. There's such a blaze of light in the centre of Joburg it does in fact look as if it's on fire.

Randall Jarrell was a Bl7 ball-turret gunner. He had it thus:

> In bombers named for girls we burned
> The cities we had learned about in school
> Till our lives went out; our bodies lay among
> The people we had killed and never seen.

So I do ignore O'D, and I realise that there must be many people covering for him, and since he's not the sort of bloody fool who would allow his problem to endanger anybody, I decide to cover for him also. After a bit he gets up and moves back in the aircraft, where there are no windows. I notice that he has taken his 'chute with him. When I look round later I see him sitting near the door, wearing the parachute. Baling out is the main thing in his mind. It seems he almost can't wait for it.

* * *

Cheese brought along his co-pupil to the Metro Café, a nice English lad with blonde hair and an insatiable appetite for meat, which was just as well, considering what was about to happen in his life, namely The Mixed Grill. Just to look at this thing caused the arteries to occlude and the heart to labour. It comprised a rump steak of some acreage, whereupon were laid randomly a pork sausage, a mutton chop, a length of boerewors, bacon, liver, a fried egg, a fried tomato, and the lot accompanied by a mound of chips, also fried; no single part was grilled at all. All was fried, and not in oil, mark you, but dripping. We each had one, with tomato sauce and mustard and bread, the lot laid down on a good bed of beer and topped off with rum-and-raisin ice-cream.

Cheese's mate was Will. They were also flying Oxboxes, of course, but their instructor was a tactical bomber man, fast twin-engined aircraft rather than the big four-engined strategic Lancs. We were so busy comparing and arguing, we forgot the Alice Faye flick. We slept at the Soldiers' Club and the next day found it was Cheese's birthday, he was nineteen; we had a party at the Zoo Lake Tea Room with a lot of cake and raucous laughter.

We told Will about the Blaue Kapelle, and how it would be an idea to keep it going and maybe after the war to buy a cheap surplus Tiger. I told Cheese about the motto I'd found: on a wall in one of the maintenance hangars at CFS was a crest of acanthus leaves and things about the index finger of a clenched fist, pointing heavenward, spray painted in aircraft duco, with a curly ribbon underneath bearing the words *Nil Carborundum Illegitimae* which, interpreted, mean I Won't be Ground Down by Any Bastard. This would be the crest of the Kapelle.

We went to look at animals in the zoo. But always, always the talk was of flying, and never anything but flying. We could as well have been looking at the goldfish as the polar bear. We had become, or been made, totally obsessive about flying. They had done a good psycho job on us; those blokes who were taken off flying, for some reason, would some of them become suicidal, I mean it.

Over the months we met, I suppose, every second weekend, on average, and always at the Metro. Sometimes Cheese couldn't come and Will or Sid and I would knock about together and drink beer and talk flying. There were always some of us there at six. I was still nice and close to Cheese, and we would soon be in the same squadron somewhere or other.

* * *

At about this time a very eerie thing happened to me.

The Transvaal Highveld is bitterly cold on winter nights; it lies about six thousand feet above sea level. One doesn't get much snow there, because it is a summer rainfall area, but the night temperature often drops well below zero, and it can't be beat for frost.

One icy morning I go to use the Oxbox and find she has been used for night flying, and not been hangared for the five or six hours before my using her, which makes sense. I struggle aboard with woollens, leathers, my nifty white silk evening scarf and a parachute, all these wrapped and strapped about me, and flop into the seat, only to find that she hasn't yet been refuelled. Well, I see the fuel truck at work back there and reckon my turn will come, and I might as well stay put as heave myself out and in the kite again.

I stick my hands under my armpits and look over the white iced airfield and flat frozen veld beyond, frigid, forbidding, grim, and over the top of the wing and the engine cowling next to me, thick, thick with frost in the dead still silence of the pale grey winter morning. It is a Caspar David Friedrich painting, lifeless, loveless, bleak. I see it with that awesome awareness of youth, still with that acute sense of the reality of the moment and the place, which seems to be lost with age.

Feet thumping up the wing break the silence. A voice calls Won't be long, fella! and a face appears suddenly at the window next to mine, pink and puffing a plume of condensation from her lips. It is one of the refuelling crew, in a huge khaki greatcoat and blue woollen gloves. She plonks her nice soft bottom down on the engine fairing, wipes her nose all red and eyes all watery from the cold on a great big hanky, and starts to sing

Der Vogelfänger bin Ich ja, stets lustig, heisa hopsasa!

146

She is more or less against the sun, so I can't see her face, but I am enjoying the sight and sound of all else: the soft warmth of her thighs in the coarse army coat against the deep cold white frost on the fairing and along the wing. She has a small tear in a leg of her overalls, and I can see she hasn't taken off her pink pyjamas. I wish I could reach out my hand and touch all this pinkness of it, and feel the rough and smooth of it, and the cold and warm of it, and even the colours of it in some way. I am so engrossed in these realities that another reality doesn't strike me for quite a bit...

No, surely, it can't be, but it is. No, but it *can't* be, but it *is!* It is the voice that gets to me first. It is the same voice, and I don't mean a similar voice. I look at the motions of the hands as she sings the great white puffs of Mozart from her happy mouth, and they are the hands I remember. But then the face! This girl has the same carriage of the head, upright; the eyes sensuous as they glance down at me, and the faint smile with its irregular teeth, and the whole Gustav Klimt gesture and texture and colour...

At an impulse I think What the hell anyway and I say the name: Marthe?

She stops singing and looks at me sort of skeef, quizzically, and asks Why do you call me that? It makes me sound like a Jerry. Oh well, good try, I think, and I say Sorry, I thought I knew you; what is your name anyway, mine's Jock.

Martha, she says. There's a really stunned silence now, because for Chrissake, it *is* her. She looks at me as if I'm daft, but still smiling and friendly, and quite enjoying the puzzlement she senses. Do you have another name? she asks, chuckles. Ja, Lundie, I say, and you? Don't say Guldenpfennig, I think, it will be too much, but she doesn't.

Pengold. She says her name is Pengold, and it really pitch-poles me, man, it turns me totally turtle, because I *know* this is the same woman, the first sexual woman I ever saw, the first flower ever amongst the dreary field of cacti that were the femalekind of my early years.

How the bloody hell did she get here? Last time I saw her she was sixty. Did she creep through some wormhole in the fabric of time? Or what? I suppose I must have gone red or white or something, for she sees my perplexity and gives me a great big hearty reassuring unrefined smile, showing her teeth right back, like a dog, as of course she would do.

I break the silence and my confusion with small talk. How can you be the birdcatcher when you yourself are the bird sitting warbling here on the wing of my unrefuelled aircraft, and who taught you to sing songs like that anyway? Her mother was the singer, she says, in Cornwall, and taught her the love of Mozart. I'd rather her mother had been in Pretoria or Darmstadt, I think; it might help explain this impossible piece of parthenogenesis.

And what reason do you have to be so cheerful on such a bloody miserably cold morning? I ask. Our dialogue sounds increasingly like a piece of recitative. The reason for my cheerfulness, she says, and she could have been singing it, is that I am in love and sexually replete. Ah, I inquire, still in recitative mode – it should be in Italian, with cries of Ha, scelerato! – this being Monday, well, Tuesday morn, am I to understand that you have had a successful week-end? Ah, yes, kind Sir, she says, the extent of this sex was such that we are stunned with it. This is not very ladylike language, I observe. This was not a very ladylike week-end, she replies.

The object of her affection and lust, she tells me, may well be the best man ever born, well, up to now anyway, and she doesn't expect another such to be born in the foreseeable future. He is a flying man eh? what else?, certainly the best flying man ever born, presently an instructor at 'Poortjie, and but recently awarded a second DFC in addition to the DSO, the Distinguished Service Order, which he'd got after the first, for what I must agree, when she tells me of it, is about the most distinguished piece of flying I have heard of, well, up to now anyway.

He was with Twelve Squadron, stationed at Udine in northern Italy, near the Jugoslav border, and doing his second tour of operations, the first having been on Douglas Bostons, nice tough potent-looking twins and a pilot's pal, and the second now on Martin B26 Marauders, fast and slick, and elegant to boot, but fearsome to all who had dealings with her, friend or foe. You'll know what sort of aircraft this was when I tell you it had no nickname, as a Mosquito had a diminutive Mossie, a Wellington was a Wimpy after the Popeye character, and a Walrus was a Shagbat because of all its rags and wires, that sort of thing. Her enormous wingloading and the stub wings sometimes got her called a flying tart, a whore, because she had no visible means of support, but that was no term of affection. You had to adjust your personal flying habits to accommodate this next-generation bloody bitch; but, man, she was a lady to have around in a gutter brawl.

He had more than two thousand flying hours, had Martha's man, not a hell of a lot if contrasted to the fifteen thousand and more of today's airline pilots shlepping great cargoes of human livestock round and round the world, interminably, but a great number of hours indeed in knife-edge operational flying. His name was Roos, a Rose, what a name, I ask you with tears in my mince pies, for a man like that. But Johan was okay, his first name.

The main role of the squadron was attacking the retreating Wehrmacht in Italy and the Balkans. To this end they were out one morning over the Golfo di Venezia, the northern end of the Adriatic, along with an American squadron in B 25 Mitchells and some useful fighter cover from a gaggle of P 51 Mustangs at thirty thousand feet. Ah, were Life but as predictable as that! From absolutely the wrong place, below, came a Schwärm of yellow-nosed Focke-Wulf Hunderd Neunzig Ds, taking out four aircraft and lacerating six in two minutes, which is as long as it takes to use up all the ammunition carried on a fighter, if you work at it, and very scarce for the Luftwaffe too, I may add, at this stage of the war.

Well they worked at it, and the Mustangs up there didn't even know they'd been and gone and left a visiting card, and why indeed waste time slugging it out in some macho contest with a cowboy in a kite named and decorated after some dumb chick in a Milwaukee high school, when we can quickly pull down a few of these numberless birds from the bottomless Ami economy, and cripple a few, and get our arses and valuable aircraft home, and waste no valuable rounds doing it?

Johan's concern, though, was not such statistics and the fate of his squadron; they were more immediate. The way the 190 had sliced him he had half a rudder, half an electrical system and no hydraulics, along with many structural pieces blown away by the cannon shells and, most urgently, a burning starboard engine.

Dropping away, he made due west for Comacchio and an American field. The Marauder was a wreck, finished. Looking at the mangled scrap-metal about them they could see no logical way this carcass could actually be airborne, but as I say, this wiry lady was good company in a scrap; and anyway such logic, also, was scarcely their concern at the moment. The only concern was to get to the coast, just get to the coast, the coast, and get out, bale out, leap the hell out of this alloy coffin once we hit the coast. Just please, dear God, compassionate and all-forgiving God, give us the coast!

He had shut down the burning motor, feathered the prop, switched off fuel and ignition and triggered the built-in extinguisher and praise the Lord for one mercy: the fire was out, and he was flying now on his port engine only.

They made it! There were the breakers of the Italian shore. He got the crew ready; 'chutes on, they were at the hatches. He checked them as they went; that was his job, he was the captain. Tail gunner, ja, Go!; dorsal gunner, ja, Go!; navigator, ja, Go!; nose gunner, no. No response. Johan left the kite to the co-pilot and got out of his seat and looked down there: he had got ready for baling out but was now unconscious in his perspex turret, one foot more or less blown off by a cannon shell and a great hole in the nose of the aircraft.

Get out, he tells the second-dickie. There's a sort of formal fumble: No but let me help, sort of stuff. Get out, I'm the captain; and he goes.

Having no hydraulics, this aircraft has no wheels: there's no way to extend the undercarriage from retraction, and lock it down, except manually with an emergency crank, but there's nobody on board to do that. For the same hydraulic reason there are no flaps. Being quick and heavy, even when empty, with this huge wingloading, as I say, 80 pounds per square foot, the only way to keep her airborne is to fly fast and never less than 120 knots; without flaps that's her stalling speed, her landing speed. But the really interesting bit is that with half his electrical system gone he can't open the bomb bay either, and there's a full load aboard.

He calls the Yanks at Comacchio and they clear away everything movable in twenty minutes, aircraft, vehicles, and especially themselves from the control tower, because that will get plenty blast when this baby goes up, even if it's half a mile away. The fire trucks and meat wagons are parked in a sandbagged redoubt, there for the purpose, with engines running.

He comes straight in from the coast, no circuit, no formalities, and never mind upwind or downwind or sidewind. Five minutes away he dumps all his fuel barring a gallon or two and that in the carbs, for there's going to be no going round again for a second shot at a nice smooth landing. He starts the dead engine again, which straight away starts burning, but will give him steering at touchdown in the absence of sufficient rudder at low speed. He comes over the boundary at just a few feet, and on the grass next to the runway, so as to give a long, long feel, a sort of tickle of the ground with his belly, then catches just the right moment and shuts her down and lowers her on to the earth, using the throttles differentially, only for steering, as I say, because he has no rudder. He can do this because the wing is high-mounted and the props clear the ground more or less, maybe with the tips bent back. He must keep her running dead straight as she gouges out a great ditch in a spray of grass and dirt; once she swings she will break up and blow up.

The most delicate part of all this ghastly careering machinery is the perspex nose turret with the unconscious gunner in it. Tip this kite up, and he's dead. Come to think of it, tip it up and we're all dead. I mean both.

Both engines stop, fuelless, just as the Marauder grates to a halt at the end of its quarter-mile furrow. The starboard is really blazing now. Johan grabs the short hatchet-cum-crowbar from its catch in the kite and scrambles out and starts smashing away perspex from the nose, but the gunner is jammed in there in such a way that he would have to smash metal too, so he leaves that to the fire crew who are emerging flat out from their redoubt in the distance, and whips off his flying scarf instead and starts binding up the ankle stump, tight, tight. The gunner looks dead anyway.

Well he wasn't dead, and he didn't die, though he had but a teaspoonful of blood left in him. In fact, nobody died. In fact, they even put out the fire and removed the bomb load. The only part salvaged from the Marauder was the port engine. The rest they just threw away.

The 12 Squadron Stores Officer, Udine, dispatched to his opposite number at the American Base, Comacchio, the appropriate requisition forms, in triplicate, to be signed and returned to him, please, for twelve 500-lb HE bombs and one 2,000 h.p. Pratt and Whitney R-2800 Double Wasp radial engine, so that these items could be removed from his stock inventory. It was efficiency, in the final analysis, that won the war.

* * *

Martha Pengold had come to South Africa as a fifteen-year-old in 1940 when the Luftwaffe was working on London and the kids were evacuated to the ends of the earth. Well, the Empire. Having her friends here, and liking the climate, when she left school and was old enough to join up, she decided to do it here, and stay for the war years. When she met Johan Roos, though, she decided to stay forever.

His two tours of ops were the maximum, according to the statistical probabilities of death and good luck, and he had been put to more easeful occupation, to grass, as they say, and close to his home and his parents, too, in Joburg. He was in the position of the Potch G.C., only luckier, because he was doing the actual flying training, which he believed in doing well, not just to win the war, but because flying is a thing which ... well, it must be done with skill and polish and, dare one say it, a sort of beauty. Luckily, his mind was not fried, like O'D's, though as she talked about the DFC I wondered why.

He and Martha being close to Joburg and his home, then, they met often, and never had to go to hotels for their weekends; as she tells me this she notices I am looking at her in some unusual way, and she suddenly stops and says What's it, then? I'm jealous, I say. Cheeky bugger! she says, you can't have him, he's mine! Of him, stupid. Well you can't have me either, I'm his!

She lays another vast canine smile on me, and wrinkles up her nose, and says Here, have a fag. She hauls a rumpled 20-pack from amongst her greatcoat and things and pulls out a butt for me; it is warm with her body-heat, and somehow it seems to me that this body-heat is different from other ordinary everyday heat, the heat of the stove and the sun and the Solar System. It smells faintly of cosmetics, too. It is a sort of intimate female heat. Hell, woman! I say, you're not going to sit here and smoke on this flammable heap of tinder, are you? And the fuel caps open too!

You forget, she answers, patting my arm through the window, that I am a petrol-monkey, and know all about fire, and I assure you, lad, you and your nice yellow aircraft will be just fine while we have this smoke. And in any case, she says, casting her eye critically over the kite, if it's as combustible as you claim, wouldn't you rather it just combusted here on the deck where you can walk away and have a nice cuppa, rather than have to jump out later up there?, thrusting a finger at the sky. Garn, shuddup! I say, for like all aircrew I am quite deeply superstitious, though I try not to be.

But she couldn't smoke her fag anyway, because the fuel tender came trundling up; and I'm not crazy about cigarettes, because they do stink; so all ended well. The big aluminium funnels, no sparks, with their chamois filters are quickly in the mouths of the tanks and the singing of Martha has an accompaniment of swirling, gurgling petrol sloshing its way into my nice yellow kite.

Sie schlief an meiner Seite ein, ich wiegte wie ein Kind sie ein.
She sleeps by my side, and I cradle her in my arms, like a child.

I was soon away on my nav or whatever it was, I can't remember.

We would come across each other in the busy time ahead, but never meet socially, of course, for when she wasn't pumping petrol she was off to the arms of her man. We would wave across the tarmac, she always with both arms extended in her great big army coat, and vigorously, with one of the dog smiles, so wide you could see her teeth from a couple of hundred yards. She passed me once on the fuel tender, and I gave her one of her own sort of double-arm waves, and blew her a few kisses. Go find your own bloody woman! she yelled. Cheerful, easy. But clearly there would be no chance for another conversation; friendship would have to wait till after the war, probably.

All the time I had available for going out and having fun was with Cheese, because we didn't get a great deal of it, and new friendships were likely to be a bit transitory anyway. We were very near the end of the course now; only about three weeks to getting our wings, and very busy and bustling indeed, mainly with night bombing, using the latest Norden bomb sight and navigating entirely by instrument. The target was distant, and illuminated very dimly with small coloured lights, arranged in a code way out there in the remote otherwise blacked-out bundu, and there mainly to make sure nothing went horribly wrong and some poor bloody farmer got a load of practice bombs dumped on his cowshed.

One Friday midday during this high-pressure programme I am in the middle of a nice bit of dreamy REM sleep, the deepest, with my eyeballs all wobbling about, when the Italian POW cook from the mess knocks at the door and puts down a slip of paper next to my bed. I struggle up from the depths; Thanks Luigi, what's it man? Your sister, he says, telefono. Oh shit, what's this now, what family kak at a time when I'm so busy? I have a premonition of disaster in Maritzburg, and I'm ready to phone home.

But it is not disaster. My kid sister is in Joburg for her school holiday, seventeen and eager to be out at night and drink real booze in a night club and dance all night, especially with a couple of airmen, the dream of every schoolgirl. She is staying with her old pal Cookie who is also from Maritzburg but now lives in Joburg; they both know Cheese, and they think it would be jolly for four old friends to hit the town. I am a bit exhausted from hitting other, hypothetical, towns, and tonight I've got to go and hit another one, and I didn't actually mean to see Cheese this weekend, nor he me, I'm sure, for what we both of us need is a good normal kip, at night, and a nice late snuggle in bed on Sunday morning with a bit of that special late breakfast that Luigi makes all off his own bat when he knows we've been night bombing, God bless his soul, and whose side is he on in this war anyway?

But she's a dear lass, my sus Betty, and Cookie too, so on Saturday I struggle up from the depths again, at about midday, and take a cold shower and more or less wake up and get across to Dunnottar station and catch the train to Joeys. I call at Cookie's place and we all hug each other and laugh a while and drink tea, and I tell them this horrid lie about how I did try to phone Cheese but couldn't get through and left a message for him to be at the Metro, when in fact I had thought well why should both of us forfeit a good Sunday kip-in? If Cheese feels like a night out he will be at the Metro anyway, and why should I lay a whole sentimental obligation on him?

So we're away to the Metro Cafe, and neither Cheese nor Will is there, as, to be truthful, I expected they wouldn't be. But never to worry, I tell my sus, we will go and see the Bing Crosby flick with Ingrid Bergman as a Catholic nun and himself as a priest, and many a schmaltz song and many a tear because, you know, their lives are darem tough without carnal love. We will then go and eat at eleven at a really swish place I know of, instead of the Metro and its farm food, and drink real booze and not get home till the early hours, and you don't really need a night club to stay up late; what for?

We are a happy trio, myself all stunned with night flying and sleeplessness, and these two nice girls, and as we march arm-in-arm down the Joburg street I think to myself, like, maybe what is happening to me is maturity.

But as we make our way to Bing and the tragical Nun we come across a figure staring disconsolately into the window of the Anglo-Swiss Confectionery and Patisserie, and I wonder why any figure staring at a sight of such delight should be disconsolate, and as I wonder this I recognise the disconsolate figure as being the figure of Benjie Segal, the Well-known Atheist, and I say to him

Benjie, man, hoe gaan dit, jong? this is my sister Betty and this is Me Ole Chum Cookie. He raises a wan smile and looks back at the cakes.

Why do you gaze thus disconsolately at the cakes? I ask. I need wider horizons than those provided by the Central Flying School and its bombing programme, he explains, and the only other horizon I have available is that of my Uncle Basil of Lower Houghton, for whom I am now about to buy one of the cakes here before us. Other than that I can bed down at the Soldiers' Club and disconsolately roam the streets until I become sleepy. Anything to make a break from the Norden Bombsight.

Benjie, I say, why do you need a bed at all? Why do you not come with myself and these two delightful women and dance away the night in the Four Hundred Nox Box, and in the morning we will take a tram to the Zoo Lake Café and eat there an atheist breakfast of bacon and eggs and catch a kip in the sun on the grass and kiss these beauteous girls farewell bye and bye and get a good ziz on Sunday night and bomb the Free State on Monday? His eyes light up at this proposition, for experience has not come easily to him in his prescribed life. He is a very handsome young man, and he doesn't know what's coming to him.

So we're away to eat Crayfish Mayonnaise, already a bit naughty for Benjie, and get to know each other, and make our way to the Four Hundred at about ten. Betty and Cookie and Benjie find it real sinister because of the low-wattage illumination, and maybe expect Ingrid Bergman to enter in a different role, with Humphrey Bogart maybe.

Well, the atmosphere is sort of decadent, to be sure, but the music good, as it often is in these places: melodious, sentimental, carefully harmonised and very intimate, in the early hours, because, for God's sake, so many people need to be close to *somebody* at times like these, when the general nature of things is separation, loneliness and pretty cynical betrayal.

Though I prefer straight dop myself, we drink Ginger Squares, disgusting mixtures of ginger brandy and ginger ale, fashionable amongst fast women at the time; and the girls think this is really the life they've heard of beyond matric, and though Benjie doesn't really mind all that much staying up all night learning how to blow Japanese women moertoe, he finds it really sinful and atheist and delicious to sit and be in love with two shikses at the same time, and all three of them drinking uncertified booze in this questionable place.

About one o'clockish I'm just great, and I love all my family and friends and we share many an anecdote and reminiscence and hold hands and dance in between. My retinae are nicely adjusted as I notice a group of young Air Force women come in and settle into one of the alcoves. One of them is Martha Pengold, but she can't see me because her eyes are so dysfunctional in the dark. I enjoy the process of watching her vision come right, so when it eventually does I'm already smiling and ready with the two-arm salute, only small, because there's not all that much room in here. She gives it back to me, and I can see in the dusk one of the luminous smiles.

I give it half an hour or so and say to my party Scuse me folks, do you mind if I go and chat up an old buddy there? These are formal days, and one has obligations to one's party. But we're all old chums and present comrades-in-arms, and Benjie certainly doesn't mind having all this new-found crumpet to himself, so they all wave me away with cries of dismissal and get down to the next round of ginger squares. I haul over to Martha and she reaches out a hand to me with her big grin and says Come, sit here next to me, and we have our tunics unbuttoned and ties loosened in a most unmilitary fashion as we sit there and drink, thank Christ, some real whisky, and get to the first bit of personal friendship between us away from the pressures and duties of military timetables.

I can't hear much of what she's talking about, though, because of the chat of her party and the closeness of the musicians, they're only an arm's reach away. After a bit she says Come, let's go over to the bar there, which we do, and there's nobody else there but the barman, so we order from him, more Haig, and she unfolds to me the most recent plans for her life.

The RAF, she tells me, is training women pilots to ferry Liberator bombers across the Atlantic to Britain from the US, via Greenland. Since she is British, and has the necessary educational qualifications, and done the medical and aptitude tests, she has applied for transfer from the SAAF to the RAF, and has been told of her acceptance, pending the results.

Liberators. Oh lovely, what an aircraft! Not a pretty machine, but sort of the Yankee equivalent of the Lanc, hey? You lucky devil! Yes, she says, and what's more I think I have the makings of a good pilot, don't you think? I surely do, I say. But Libs, oh what a marvel of flying! You make me jealous. Then I remember the last time the matter of jealousy arose, and I say to her with a wry smile By the way, what about that very special ultimate man you had back there, eh?

He's dead, she says.

Paralysis. I am paralysed.

What on earth can I say?

But I don't have to say anything, do I?

She can see my confusion, and after a bit she takes my hand and says Never mind, as if *she's* got to put *me* at ease. We sit and hold hands there for how long? I don't know, and then she tries to tell me what happened, and I realise she hasn't tried this before, because she's a bit jumbled, and she's spilling it all out, as they say.

Tango Control, the Witpoortjie tower, had it all on the radio. It was during the Norden bombsight training: they had plenty of altitude when the starboard engine failed. Johan had called Tango, and found there was no emergency field within range and available. At three a m the emergency flarepath crew at Rusdal had packed up and left, a little prematurely perhaps, since this, the last flight, was OK and on its way home. No problem.

But there was a problem. The port engine was not putting out enough power to maintain altitude, and by a bit of simple arithmetic he was able to calculate that they wouldn't make it back home to 'Poortjie. What, logically, to do? Answer, easy: bale out. But his pupil could not bale out. He was frozen. Neither military discipline nor threat of rank could make him budge.

Johan's pupil wants to go to Rusdal and drop a flare and land by the light of this flare, Martha tells me, but Johan says it can't be done and it's never been done, and if this idiot tries it he will die for sure because the flare will not only illuminate just a tiny area round about, it will also dazzle him so that he can't see any part of the earth at all. But the pupil turns for Rusdal. Johan gives him an order to get up and go to the hatch and open it and step out, but the pupil cannot, because he is frozen to his seat, which his irrational primaeval instinct tells him is fixed and safe, while the black, cold emptiness out there is an unknown place where animals die.

So what do they do? Do the two of them sit there and grapple for possession of the controls?

Ordering, cajoling, pleading, arguing, Johan threatens to assault this fellow and wrestle him out of the aircraft. They hear it all on the radio. How the hell do you have a fist-fight in a fuselage that size? He threatens to take the emergency fire hatchet-cum-crow-bar from its catch in the kite and stun the pupil with it and chuck him out.

At this point the Officer in Command, Night Flying, comes on the radio and orders Johan to bale out, and he in his turn compounds the bloody idiocy that's going on by refusing to obey a disciplined order and refusing to abandon a living being in a doomed aircraft. The cajoling continues. Ignition and fuel to the dead engine are shut off, but this prop has a fixed pitch, and can't be feathered, so it's windmilling away out there and causing a lot of drag, which is one of the reasons they can't maintain altitude.

You don't want to leave baling out much below two thousand feet, but at one thousand, critical in extreme, Johan realises he has to go, and tells them on the radio he's going, and maybe actually hearing these fateful words will make the pupil snap out of his trance and pull finger and come along.

No chance! As Johan moves away the windmilling prop generates enough friction to ignite something and the whole engine bursts in a blistering ball of fire, and the wing and the fuel tank with it, and the Oxbox starts to fling about on her way earthwards with such violence that it's impossible to make one's way purposefully to a door, a hatch, or anything else. Luckily they hit the ground before they get burned.

During the narration I put my hand out a couple of times to hush her, to stop the distress of putting the horror to words, but she waves it away impatiently. They would not let her see his corpse, so her animal mind could not know he was dead, somehow, and making him dead with her words is what she is doing now.

Then she suddenly stops and puts her fingers to her mouth. Oh my God! she gasps, I shouldn't have made those jokes with you about your kite burning up! She looks at me with eyes wide and mouth agape and her breathing stopped at a gasp, and I know that the same old superstition is at work in there, trying to establish a system of guilt between the two events: her jest and Johan's death.

Now why do you have to do that to yourself? I ask, but she can't just drop it, just like that, because of the demands of logic. I lose eye contact with her for a silent minute or so as she hangs and shakes her head, but it's not hard to read her body language, and it tells me she's going over and over the circumstances and the responsibilities, obsessively, again and again, because somebody must be responsible, surely, for such an outrageous waste of life and love. There must have been a mistake *some*where, and *some*body must be responsible for this unnatural thing.

Of course her rational mind takes over soon enough. No silly fiemies. Yes, she says, that's stupid, isn't it? But it does occur to me it's just as well she wasn't stationed at Witpoortjie, as she by random and equal probability could have been, and on the refuelling crew there too, where she might well have been the one who put the high-octane petrol into his nice yellow combustible aircraft, and made the joke with him about its rather combusting on the deck down here, and going to have a nice cuppa char.

But no fuss, man. We drink more Haig in silence, holding hands. Here, give me your pen, she suddenly says, and give me your home address. She writes it down on her cigarette packet; I don't yet have an address in England, she says, but I'll write to you and after the war you can come and visit me and I'll be nice and fat, with my hair in curlers and kids all over and a nice old husband in braces.

I feel sure she will have those things; she is not a woman to give up because her man has died. Men die all the time. But she was probably right when she said another one like Johan would not be born in the foreseeable future. Not for her, anyway.

She grins at me and shakes my hand side to side as if to say Come on, snap out of it fella! Come, let's dance a bit, she says, then you must go back to your party. We move in amongst the couples on the dim dance floor and put our arms about each other as a gruff saxophone goes about its after-midnight business. You don't use a great deal of energy in this type of dancing, for the music is slow, and very sad, for all its being so tuneful. The words are dreadful kitsch, really, if you think just a wee bit seriously about them, but true, true, true in days like these, and what this saxophone is gruffing about is I Don't Mind Being Lonely.

In the dimness I see she is gently smiling as she sings along, but then suddenly, unexpectedly, she lets go my left hand and gets both arms around me, and pulls herself tight against me as I get my arms about her, and I realise whatever smiles her face may be wearing, her body is weeping, in small catches of the breath; small, barely perceptible catches, as she sings.

She is haemorrhaging internally. She is bleeding grief. The soul is seeping out of her as she stands here crushed against me, she is

159

dying. The smile will dutifully remain, and these breasts will feed the babies of the man with the braces, but Gustav Klimt is gone, forever, and when she again sings Mozart there will be other arias. She will never be a bird again.

She has sung her song.

After a bit the survival mechanisms start to work, though. Illogical, irrational, but they work. As we go to finish the Haig, and That's It, she turns to me and says I'm so *angry* with him! If he were here I'd *hit* him, I really would! Bloody fool, see what he's done to us! Really, I can't stand a man who's a bloody fool! Why couldn't he just go to the bloody hatch and *step out?* That's all he had to do, and leave that stupid bastard to fry, if that's what he wanted.

Hell I'm so bloody cross with him, really I am, she says, if he were here I'd *hit* him!, and she bangs her fist on my shoulder a few times as if to get at him that way.

Well, she never did write to me. Maybe it was too painful when the scar tissue was forming. Maybe she lost the cigarette packet. As she left the night club with her party she turned and gave the two-hand wave and the dog smile, and that was it. We never met again. The music in my head as she went was not the lonesome sax music, but the lonely, remote, desolate notes of the solo flute passage in the Brahms Symphony. What on earth would make me think of something like that in a night club, of all places? But when I think of her now, that's the music in my head.

* * *

I was a bit subdued during the atheist breakfast, but then all were, for different reasons: Betty and Cookie had never before been up all night, and Benjie had found multiple heathen love more exhausting than the Norden bomb sight, so it didn't show. But lolling half-asleep on the train back to Dunnottar I found myself thinking Man, if this is the process of maturity that I'm going through, well thanks all the same, but on the whole I think I can get along without it. I'd rather be five, any day.

Well you can't go back to being five again, just like that, because it suits you, and anyway, as my ma and her sisters had always observed, Life Goes On, My Dear. It did indeed go on, and very busily too, because the training went on right to the day before the Wings Parade, and then there were all the small and not-so-small personal things to fix up: meet Cheese at the Metro and book a place at the Four Hundred for him and Will and

Benjie and me and maybe Sid, and that makes ten, with partners, and get Betty booked on the train for Cheese, if he hasn't already done it. Don't forget to have the barathea uniform dry-cleaned. What else? Ummm, well, many things. And then we were so sleepy all the time, on top of it all.

What a sense of fulfilment, though, of triumph, even. This was the first bit of status I'd had in the world, and I'd gone out there and got it for myself. And what a thing to have status in! What a thing aviation was, and where it was going to be after this war could not be imagined, and I was in it, and right there at the centre where the thing was happening, that aviation was about; I was flying. I was in complete possession of my adult life after only eighteen months. I was nineteen years old and had a curly Air Force moustache six inches across when stretched out. I wasn't handsome, like Benjie, but I had presence, and girls would sometimes whistle at me in the street. Excelsior! Ever onwards, ever upwards!

I think they wanted to give us a break, towards the end, or perhaps they didn't want us to look like a bunch of bloody spooks on the wings parade, with local dignitaries coming from the undignified local platteland towns as a reward for their tolerance of our night-time din in the air. We could see everything getting laid on: twelve Oxboxes doing a few quick fly-past rehearsals, the Native Corps brass band moving in and doing a few quick oom-pah rehearsals, and a new bunch of that unfortunate sub-species called sprogs, beginners, taking up residence for when we were gone; pimples all over and no moustaches.

So the last week of the course was daylight stuff, and mostly in a simulator, which in those days was called a Link Trainer, no electronic screens and all that modern virtual reality apparatus; just an electric Frog remotely tracing our instrument flying on a chart on a table, but deadly enough in its technology, deadly enough to wipe out Hamburg and Cologne and Schweinfurt and Dresden, and, of course, Hiroshima and Nagasaki eventually.

I go to meet Cheese on the Saturday before Wings; his Parade is the same day as mine, of course, since we're running parallel. I have a whole list of busy things to do, and so will he have, and we must see where we coincide and make our arrangements together.

The train pulls in at Park Station with its Pierneef murals, and that strange stink of Joburg hits me, for even in those days it used

161

to smell, before the word Pollution had been invented, and make my way to the Metro with that strange sense of expectation in me that Joburg always engenders for its own neurotic reasons.

Well, Cheese can't make it, but there is Will, and that's okay; Howsit, Will, man! Call up the grills, I'm starving. Maybe we should get a couple of beers first, though, hey?

Yes, he says, let's do that, and we're off to the boozer.

Cheese couldn't make it, eh?

No, he's dead.

Paralysis.

I sit down on the seat at the bus stop there. How did it happen? I ask. And as Will starts to tell me I put up my hand to hush him, because I know, oh Holy Jesus Christ I *know*, this is the man who killed Martha Pengold's Johan.

We haul in at the nearest bar, one of those sordid all-male places where according to South African Law an all-male must sit and look at his all-male reflection in a wall-sized mirror behind an array of brandy bottles and cheap sherry. This is the last time I will ever be in a place like this, because as of next week I will be an Officer of the King, and my drinks will have to be brought to me in a lounge, and on a tray.

Bring me a bottle of Haig, I say.

You can't buy unopened bottles of liquor here, you must go to a bottle store.

Well for fuck sake open it, man!

You can't buy a whole bottle in advance, and you are not allowed to pour your own liquor, it's against the law.

Well open the bloody thing and keep pouring it out and we'll pay you in arrears!

You can't do that, you have to pay for each drink as I pour it out.

I take out the contents of my pockets, and so does Will; pound notes, ten bob notes, half-crowns, tickeys the lot, and slam them on the bar; for fuck sake take what you need here and pour out this fucking booze, man!

So Will and I sit and get pissed without a hell of a lot of conversation, and after a bit my survival apparatus comes into action, and rage builds up in me, and I say Will, man, if this bloody little bastard were here I would *hit* him, as true as God I would! See what he's *done* to everybody! What the bloody hell was *wrong* with him? Why couldn't he just *make* his stupid brain tell his stu-

162

pid bloody body just to get up and walk to the bloody hatch and just *step out*? Shit, if there's anything I can't stand it's a *stupid bastard*! What *right* does he have to do this to us? As true as God, if he were here I would *hit* him!

So gaan dit mos.

* * *

The frigid wind whipped and tore at our trouser legs on the parade ground, and many a dignified military flying man made an undignified grab for his flying military hat in the middle of a dignified military salute as the thing got airborne, gold braid the lot. Eyes ran and noses trickled, but there's no procedure in the military book of formalities for blowing the formal nose on parade, nor sneezing the formalised sneeze.

One by one we got wings stuck to our uniformed breasts with temporary Q-stores issue safety pins as the low-fly-past Oxboxes flailed crabwise overhead in the disobliging sidewind. Ground turbulence above the hangars was such that they needn't have pretended to be flying in formation, the way they were poep-scared of colliding.

Dads hadn't reached retirement yet, I should think not, they were just moving into middle age, and they couldn't take time off from the office even if they weren't away to war, but on the spectators' stand all the mums and sisters and assorted sweethearts sat in duffel coats, those wise ones from the highveld plateau, while the dumb ones from sea level sat huddled in borrowed hotel blankets, and irreverently wished their sons and brothers and lovers had joined the Royal Navy instead, so all this might be happening in the incubator environment of some sea-level base.

The brass band of the Union Defence Force Native Corps steps off to a command from the Drum Major in his own curious dialect: Aaaara centaur! he cries, EEeek ots! They blast off there and then with a stirring Sousa march. The drumming is tribal African. The brass makes shebeen saxophone jazz. He flings his mace in the air as drum majors do. The howling north-easterly catches it. The trumpeters have to duck as it lands amongst them. What should he do? Run back and retrieve it? Such loss of face, but he can't turn the band around without the mace; that's what drum majors use for their signals, that's its purpose. He takes off his big white helmet with its big silver spikey thing on top, and uses that instead, and turns the band around without missing a note and picks up the mace on his way downwind with the uttermost equanimity, as if he intended all this.

* * *

Other ranks aren't allowed to have women in their habitat, nat-urally, but officers are allowed to have lady guests in their mess, so we're all off to stand packed in there like cattle in a kraal, and eat slim sandwiches with cups of tea, and smile less from congratula-tion than relief at being out of the wind. The little tables all over the lawn, where the slim sandwiches and tea were supposed to stand, have all had their cloths ripped off, which are now stuck to the barbed wire of the camp boundary fence.

We haven't been notified of our commissions yet, of course, nor have we pips or stripes on our epaulettes, but we take the blue bands and flashes off our SAAF and RAF caps, and that makes us sort-of officers, and kosher to be in this mess. My eldest and youngest sisters and Cookie are here as my guests. Betty was booked to go with Mama Kreis to Witpoortjie, but she's along with Lola now to my wings parade instead. You are not supposed to embrace and hug women in an officers' mess, only a discreet peck on the cheek is permissible with family ladies, but Betty takes my arm and comes in close and stays close. She doesn't feel like tea and sandwiches.

Our week's passing-out leave starts here and now, and I'm away to my billet to fetch my packed bag. I can see she'd like to get away from this place.

It's a fair step to the Pupil Pilots' quarters, and I'm hunched up in my tunic with my head down and my hands in my pockets, because I'm still in my parade uniform and my greatcoat is hang-ing in my room. I feel something a bit ticklish on my cheek and I look up to realise I'm in a flurry of snow, and there's a white patch here and there where some of it has settled out of the wind. Strange stuff. Always strange stuff to the people of Africa. I haven't seen it since our Drakensberg days, four long years ago. I turn up my collar and trudge on.

I couldn't have heard a footfall in that gale, so I'm surprised when a voice behind me calls Jock! and I turn around and there catching up is O'D. He can call me Jock now, and I can call him just O'D. He's also got his hands in his pockets, but he always has them there anyway: I've often wondered why he doesn't just buy a pair of ordinary non-flying gloves. He's wearing that Lancaster scarf of his again, about a mile long, the colour of an old camel and as ragged too. I'm sure he sleeps in the bloody thing. We walk our brisk way to the Pupes' Mess with heads down and nothing to say, and as before, I think after some minutes maybe I should say something, but as I open my mouth to speak he reaches out his arm and in a most unmilitary fashion puts it about my shoulders and pulls me close to him, and says Never mind, I know.

Some paces further, still with his head down and arm about me, he gives a hug and says again: I know! I know!

* * *

O'D is not allowed to be in other ranks' quarters, according to military bullshit. He waits secretly in my room there while I go to find Luigi and say goodbye. Everyone's away on a weekend pass because of the Wings Parade, and the mess is empty and as cold as it was when first I saw it a year ago. Luigi is on duty, though, in case some bloke hasn't taken off for Joeys and now wants food. I find him in the kitchen preparing for himself a fried-egg sandwich.

I observe that he is learning a taste for South African cuisine, and he likes that sarcasm and grins and hums something Italian. He walks with me to the door of the mess with his mouth full from this double-egg beaut, and shakes my hand. Glenn Miller is playing Falling Leaves again, the clear, simple, sentimental sound filling the empty snooker hall. There is nobody here at all, except Luigi, and the big five hundred watt lamps are off. He is playing it for himself.

It is Luigi's favourite.

First published 1998 in southern Africa by David Philip Publishers (Pty) Ltd,
208 Werdmuller Centre, Newry Street, Claremont 7700, South Africa

ISBN 0-86486-355

© Harold Strachan 1998

Printed by Natal Witness,
244 Longmarket Street, Pietermaritzburg, South Africa